# TEARS IN A BOTTLE

# TEARS IN A BOTTLE

A NOVEL

# SYLVIA BAMBOLA

Multnomah® Publishers *Sisters, Oregon*

TEARS IN A BOTTLE
© 2001 by Sylvia Bambola
published by Multnomah Publishers, Inc.

International Standard Book Number: 1-59052-570-1
Previously 1-57673-802-7

Cover design by Uttley DouPonce DesignWorks

Cover images by Tony Stone Images and The Image Bank

Scripture quotations are from:
*The Holy Bible,* New International Version © 1973, 1984 by
International Bible Society, used by permission of Zondervan
Publishing House
*Holy Bible,* New Living Translation (NLT) © 1996. Used by permission
of Tyndale House Publishers, Inc. All rights reserved.

*Multnomah* is a trademark of Multnomah Publishers, Inc.,
and is registered in the U.S. Patent and Trademark Office.
The colophon is a trademark of Multnomah Publishers, Inc.
Printed in the United States of America

For information:
Multnomah Publishers, Inc.•Post Office Box 1720•Sisters, Oregon
97759

Library of Congress Cataloging-in-Publication Data
Bambola, Sylvia.
Tears in a bottle : a novel / by Sylvia Bambola.
p. cm.
ISBN 1-59052-570-1
ISBN 1-57673-802-7 (pbk.)
1. Abortion services—Fiction. 2. Pro-life movement—Fiction. 3.
Abortion—Fiction. I. Title.
PS3552.A47326 T4 2001    813'.6—dc21    2001002176

05 06 07 08 09 — 10 9 8 7 6 5 4 3

*To every precious soul who weeps in secret.*

# ACKNOWLEDGMENTS

To Vincent, my husband and best friend for over thirty-four years. Thank you for your patience, for being my sounding board throughout this trying year of discovery and sadness as I digested material so shocking it often gave me nightmares. And thank you for all those wonderful meals you cooked so I could meet my deadline. I praise God for you and rejoice that even after this life we will continue to be together for all eternity.

To Lorraine Gariboldi, president of the Life Center of Long Island. When I hear your sweet voice and the way you speak about ladies damaged by abortion, I can envision Jesus and His tender love for the hurting. Thank you for taking the time to share the inner workings of your center and for helping me to understand how devastating abortion is. Thank you for patiently fielding my numerous phone calls and for your willingness to answer all my questions, no matter how busy you were. And thank you for the wealth of information you provided through your pamphlets and books.

A big thank-you to Lawrence and Joanna Cervellino, who head up the Long Island Coalition for Life, for going out of their way to get me the information I needed on Planned Parenthood and for their willingness to spend as much time as it took so that I could understand some of what was going on. Your vast knowledge and kindness humble me.

Andrew Daub, director of Youth Outreach for American

Life League (ALL), was incredibly generous with the volume of material he sent me and his willingness to go the extra mile. Thank you, Andrew.

Mark Crutcher of Life Dynamics Incorporated has authored the well-documented book *Lime Five*. That plus his monthly *Life Talk* video magazine was without doubt one of the most valuable resources I had. *Life Talk* kept me current with all that is happening in the abortion industry as well as kept me focused during those times when I just didn't want to write about abortion anymore. It was Mark Crutcher and Life Dynamics that uncovered and helped expose the selling-of-baby-parts scandal. I send my heartfelt thanks and greetings and say, "Keep up the good work. You're making a difference."

Thank you to Domenick Roberti, PetLand manager in Islandia, who gave me a crash course on tropical fish. And grateful thanks to the kind and helpful Suffolk County police officer of the Fourth Precinct, who wished to be kept anonymous, but who provided insight into the workings of a police station.

And finally, I want to thank my kind and gentle editor, Rod Morris, as well as the many other wonderful people who make up the Multnomah family and who have made this book possible.

While the story and characters in this novel are fictitious, the facts concerning abortion and abortion clinics are very real. The abortion industry in America today is not an effectively regulated industry and is protected on almost every front. A prime example of this is the government agency Centers for Disease Control (CDC). Heading the Abortion Surveillance Branch of the CDC at different times were Dr. Willard Cates and Dr. David Grimes. Both have been practicing abortionists. The Abortion Surveillance Branch has since been abolished, but the new head of the CDC's abortion statistics is Lisa Koonin, who was on the Editorial Advisory Committee of a magazine published by the Alan Guttmacher Institute—the research arm of Planned Parenthood—and has been a presenter at the National Abortion Federation conference. Her department's 1996 study on the safety of abortion was based on information supplied by the abortion industry itself, then was massaged and passed along as a government statistic. This type of practice has permeated our nation for years and amounts to a performance akin to the proverbial fox watching over the chicken coop. With such practices, is it any wonder that the American people are being deceived and, generally speaking, have a false picture of what abortion is and what the industry is all about?

My prayer is that we will come to know the truth and that the truth will set us free.

*You keep track of all my sorrows.*
*You have collected all my tears in your bottle.*
*You have recorded each one in your book.*

PSALM 56:8, NLT

# 1

THOR EMERSON SAT BEHIND the oversized mahogany desk, fingering his Mont Blanc. He was all alone. Eleanor had gone home hours ago, so there would be no interruptions. The only noise in the office was a barely discernible hum coming from his fifty-five-gallon fish tank. But that was not an intrusion. It was more of a pacifier, though it didn't comfort today.

He finally uncapped his pen and scribbled several numbers on a three-by-five card. Then he hurriedly crossed them out. Just what was this going to cost him? No use in guessing. He'd find out soon enough. He finally picked up the phone and dialed. By the third ring he was cursing. *Isn't this guy ever home?* He pictured Newly boozing with one of the young girls from the clinic. At least when he played, Thor did it with women old enough to know what they were getting themselves into. He just had to get rid of this guy.

It surprised Thor when a hello finally slurred across the

other end of the line. For a moment, Thor was at a loss for words.

"Hello?" came the voice again, more insistently this time, but the slur was unmistakable.

"Dr. Newly, glad I caught you at home."

Sardonic laughter rippled over the wire. "My loss, your gain."

"What?"

"I wouldn't have been here if I'd gotten lucky. After you scrape 'em and tape 'em, you'd think they'd trust you. But the silly child wouldn't buy the line. I just couldn't convince her that I loved her for her mind."

"A girl from the clinic?"

"Where else can you find such easy pickings? I mean, they don't have any virtue to defend, now do they?"

"That's how doctors lose licenses." Thor pulled the phone away from his ear and waited until the raucous laughter on the other end subsided. "Look, what you do on your off hours is your business, but when your actions begin to affect the clinic, then it becomes mine."

"Has Flo been tattling again?"

"She's conscientious. She cares about the girls and she's concerned about how you handle them and about some of your slipshod practices." Again Thor had to pull the phone away as Newly began singing at the top of his lungs.

"Good night ladies, good night gentlemen, good night everyone—"

"This isn't the first time I've had to call you on this matter. I've got two pending litigations thanks to you. I can't—"

"...we're sorry to see you go!"

"I can't afford you anymore, so I've come up with a retirement fund, so to speak. Say fifty thousand to carry you until you find something else."

Newly laughed, but not so loudly this time. "There's nothing else. I've been drummed out of four states. Can't go back there."

"Seventy-five thousand."

"I didn't know you thought so highly of me. Thanks, but no thanks. I like it at Brockston."

"One hundred thousand, and that's my last offer."

"You don't get it. I have no place else to go."

"No, *you* don't get it—you're fired, Newly. So if I were you, I'd take the money and run."

Newly started laughing, almost howling over the phone. "This is rich, just beautiful. If you insist, I'd be happy to take it, but I'm not leaving."

"You have no choice."

"I do if I have fire insurance."

"What are you talking about?"

"Fire insurance—the thing that keeps you from getting fired. Like a list of State Health Department violations and a list of companies that purchase all sorts of interesting body parts from you. Think of what the press could do with that."

"I don't like being threatened."

"So we're even. I don't like being fired."

"Maybe if you behaved more like a doctor and less like a derelict—"

"Colorful, very colorful. But save it and let's just call it a draw. You're stuck with me and I'm stuck with you. Let's make the best of it, agreed?"

SYLVIA BAMBOLA

Thor slammed the receiver down and cursed loudly. Flo had warned him not to hire Newly. She had told him about Newly's track record. But sometimes in this business you had to take what was available. *Now what?*

Becky Taylor tried to fly past her father when she heard the car beep. "See you."

"Not so fast, young lady! Where're you going?"

"Dad, I'm late. The guys are waiting." Becky cringed. Wrong word.

"What *guys?*"

"Paula, Katie, the crowd."

Jim Taylor turned in his chair to peek out the window at Paula Manning's red Nissan. "They aren't guys, Becky."

She let out an exasperated sigh, and her father turned from the window and looked at her.

"Becky Taylor, what's that purple all over your lips!"

Becky planted her hands on her hips. She had been planting her hands on her hips like that since she was two years old. As she did, her little cotton top rode up and exposed her navel. She quickly dropped her arms.

"If you think you're going out half dressed, think again. I'll not have a daughter of mine prancing around the neighborhood with her...with her belly sticking out!"

The teen's hands were back on her hips. "My belly's not sticking out."

"Upstairs and change. And wipe that goo off your face!"

"Mom." The car honked again. "Mom!"

Nancy Taylor came from the kitchen drying her hands on a towel.

"Mom, what's wrong with this outfit? Daddy's never happy unless I look like a geek."

Becky watched her mother's eyes seek out her father's. "Go change," her mother said softly.

"Mo-om!"

"Go change!"

Becky gave her mother a hurt look, then stomped upstairs, but not too loudly. When she got to her room, she tore off her top, threw it on the floor, and ransacked her drawers. She took out the green tank she had previously borrowed from Paula and pulled it over her head, then went to the mirror.

"Hi Raggedy," she said, pushing her doll aside to find her comb. "Boy are you lucky you don't have parents to boss you around all the time."

The doll slumped over and Becky readjusted it so it sat upright against the corner of the mirror. The doll was old and worn, with a tear above one eye. Still, it was the only doll she hadn't either thrown away or given to the Children's Hospital in town. Paula said it was because Becky was still a child at heart. Becky giggled. What would Paula think now, if she heard Becky talking to it?

She heard the car honk again and quickly combed her hair. At once, Becky's eyes went to her mouth. They always did. She wished her lips weren't so big, so clownlike. Sometimes she'd look at herself and think of a circus. Her mother said she was pretty, but mothers couldn't be trusted. They always said dumb things like that, as though it was their job or something. She once heard Mary Lou Potter's mom tell Mary Lou she had the prettiest face of all the girls in her class. *Mary Lou Potter?* The girl had to be at least a hundred pounds overweight. Just proved her point. Mothers lie. So why did Becky believe Skip when he told her she was pretty? Because Skip wasn't her mom, and guys don't lie about a girl's looks…unless…. But that was another matter.

From the top of the stairs, Becky could see the back of her father's chair. She thought of bolting down the steps and straight out the door, but stopped herself when she heard her mother's voice. "She's seventeen," Becky heard her mother say. "You need to give her some slack."

Becky heard the snap of her father's *Gazette*. "She's pretty like you, Nance, and pretty's not an asset. Becky'll find that out. Flowers attract bees and bees are only interested in gathering pollen for their own use."

Becky backed away from the stairs and pressed herself against the wall.

"No matter how hard you try, you're not going to be able to stop her from growing up. You have to start letting go. She's *seventeen.*"

"You were only eighteen, remember?"

"We're talking about Becky."

"You want your daughter going out looking like a trollop?"

"She wants to fit in. All the kids dress like that."

"Like hookers?"

Becky bit into her lip.

"Oh for heaven's sake, Jim."

"I don't think we should be reminding heaven, do you? An apple doesn't fall far from the tree, Nance."

"Becky's not me."

"No. Becky's going to college."

Becky remained pressed against the wall for several minutes after the conversation ended. Only when she heard the noise of pots and pans banging in the kitchen did she slink down the stairs and out the door.

"I thought you'd never come!" Paula Manning twisted around as Becky pushed a pile of books from the leather backseat onto the floor and slipped in. Becky saw Paula's eyebrows raise when she recognized the wrinkled green tank top. "What took so long?"

"My dad."

"Boy, am I glad my dad's not a pain," Kate Lawrence said.

"Fasten your seat belts, girls!" Paula put the car in reverse and screeched out of the driveway and into the street.

"Did you have to do that?" Becky said, watching her father press against the window. "My dad's just looking for an excuse to tell me I can't go out with you anymore...ever since...boy were you stupid!"

Paula turned up the radio, and the loud rock music made the car vibrate. "My dad didn't make a big thing out of it. Why should yours?"

"Could you turn that down?" Becky said, and watched Paula grudgingly comply.

"I still can't believe you and Denny did it in the school parking lot," Kate said. "I must admit that took guts."

"Yeah, I think I surprised even Denny."

"It was just plain stupid," Becky said. "Why do you think you're having so much trouble getting into college?"

"Because I have a 1.85 grade point average," Paula said.

"Exactly, and when your average is so low, colleges look even harder at everything else: your club participation, your extracurricular activities—"

Both Paula and Kate laughed.

"Now with that suspension on your record, well…you really messed up."

"So kind of you, Miss Prim-and-Proper, to share that with us," Paula said. "Of course you don't see me uptight. In fact, the only one uptight about this whole thing is you. Now why do you suppose that is?"

"You should just do it, Becky, and get it over with," Kate said. "I mean, Skip's a great guy. He's good looking, popular, a basketball star. What more do you want? And believe me, if you don't wise up you're not going to keep him interested long. There are plenty of girls waiting to take your place."

"Right. And who's been complaining about Skip's inattention, lately?" Paula said. "You want him to start writing those love notes again, don't you? And walk you to your classes like he used to?"

"You have to do it sooner or later. I mean, you can't stay a virgin forever," Kate said.

"Why don't you two try minding your own business?" Becky chewed her lip.

"Listen to me, girl," Paula said, "You better make that boy happy or else."

"You're sickening, both of you. That's all you ever talk about, guys and sex. Hello! There's a big world out there. Other things to think about. Why don't you girls grow up?"

"Grow up?" Paul turned her attention from the road to look at her friend. "Grow up? Look who's talking. You want to be a virgin forever?"

Kate poked Paula's arm. "Look at the road when you're driving."

Paula made a face, then turned around. "I think you and Mary Lou Potter are the only virgins left in our class."

"I don't think so!"

Kate laughed. "Well practically, and you don't want to be beaten out by a room divider do you?"

"Stop calling Mary Lou that."

"Okay, okay," Kate said. "But listen to Paula. She's giving you good advice."


Thor stopped by the small foyer table and dropped his keys into a large crystal dish, then scanned the pile of mail. Bills. Was there no end to them? He could hear the TV blasting in the theater room and at once noticed his headache was worse.

"Teresa, lower that TV, will you?" Thor shouted, already on his way up to the bedroom. To his surprise, he saw his pretty, dark-haired wife suddenly appear out of the kitchen. The startled look on her face told him she had not heard him come in.

"You're home!"

"Yeah, just got in. I'd appreciate it if you'd lower that TV. I don't know why you like everything so loud. It's making my head split." Thor noticed how shapely his wife looked in her silk loungewear. When he saw the bag of fruit in her hand, he frowned. "Going to see Eric?"

Teresa nodded. "I miss him. It's been over a month."

"Don't try to justify it."

"Why do you make it sound so wrong every time I want to go visit my son…our son?"

"No, you had it right the first time, Teresa. You think Eric is only yours, that only you care about him."

"You want to come? You haven't been to Oxlee in ages."

"You know that's impossible. Who'll run my clinics?"

"That's what I thought." Teresa patted the fruit with one hand. "Wish I could eat heavier during the drive, but it makes me so sleepy."

"You coddle him, you know that."

Teresa sighed and hugged the bag to her chest. "You can't stick a little boy in boarding school and just leave him there. It gets so…so lonely."

"For you or him?"

"He's still a little boy. He needs—"

"He needs to grow up. In a few years he'll be a teenager, and he's been boarding since he was what…seven? You'd think he'd be used to it by now. Maybe if you didn't go visit him every month he'd get a chance to acclimate." Thor saw the familiar tears well up in his wife's eyes.

"I'm lonely, Thor. My son's a hundred miles away…you won't let me work. What have I got—"

"I'm not killing myself six days a week so that my wife can go out and work! Look at this house, just look at it, Teresa! Plenty of women would commit murder to have a house like this. I've given you everything you could possibly want, and then some. Crying out loud! You're just like all the other ungrateful women I see every day. What do you want from me?"

Teresa wiped the tears with the back of her hand. "You, Thor. I want you. But you're never home."

"Oh, now it's my fault that you're not happy. Is that it? I slave day and night and it's still not enough."

"*Things* aren't enough. There's a difference."

"You can't have it both ways. I just don't have the time to give you everything."

Teresa smiled sadly. "You have time for the others though, don't you, Thor? Time for all those other nameless, pretty *business* associates."

"Are you going to start that again?"

"I didn't start this, Thor. You did. With your lipstick-smeared shirts, with bills for perfume and jewelry I've never seen, with late-night phone calls from women like Julie What's-her-name—and she's told me plenty, Thor. She's really given me an earful. Shall I go on?"

"Suit yourself. But I don't plan on listening. I'm tired. I'm going upstairs to change, then I'm going for a swim."

"That's right. Your ten laps. Must not forget to do your ten laps." Teresa blotted her eyes with her hand. "Is that where you were tonight, Thor? With another woman?"

Thor stopped in his tracks and looked down the stair-case at his wife. "No, I was working."

"I love you, Thor. I still love you, even after…after everything. But I don't think I can go on like this much longer. You've changed. Your work has changed you. I know your heart has been broken. I do know, Thor. You've broken your own heart with the things you've done. And you've broken mine, and you keep breaking it, and I keep letting you. But I can't take much more. Maybe I'm foolish to worry about you, all things considered. But I do worry. I do. How will you manage when I'm gone…when I'm gone and you're all *alone?*"

Thor smiled down at his wife and blew a kiss. "If I don't see you before you leave in the morning, be careful on Hunter Mountain, especially around the lake area. You know how I hate you traveling that stretch by yourself. Maybe when they open the new interstate, the drive will be easier. But just be careful, okay?"

Teresa nodded, not returning the smile, then walked sadly toward the kitchen.

As soon as the car pulled into the parking lot of Brockston's Convenience Store, Becky could see that Skip was ticked. She watched him stride to the car with those long legs of his, stiff and wary like a soldier marching into combat. In the background, Becky could see two of Skip's friends watching, snickering.

"Sorry." Becky leaped out of the car and threw her arms around Skip, then gave him a big kiss, the kind she reserved for more private moments. She hoped it would make him look good in front of his friends.

At once she could feel his body relax. And when they finally parted, she could see his eyes, soft and misty, looking at her the way they used to.

"What took you?"

"My dad."

"I still don't know why we have to sneak out like this. Why don't your parents like me?"

"They don't even know you, and because it's easier."

"It makes me feel like a jerk. Like I'm not good enough or something."

"Look, it's not about you, okay? It's my dad. He still thinks I'm a little girl. He's not ready for all this. Believe me, fifteen minutes of being grilled by him and you'd understand why I'm taking the shortcut."

"Well, okay, but it still makes me feel like some kind of creep. Are we going to have to sneak out on prom night too?"

"Are you taking me?"

"Who else?"

Becky shrugged and tried to look nonchalant, tried to keep the joy she felt from leaping out of her and making her jump up and down like an idiot.

Skip pulled out a paper from his jeans pocket and glanced back at his friends. "Ah...do you think you'd like to go to the Teen Health Conference with me?"

"What's that?"

"You didn't get the flyer?"

Becky shrugged. "Maybe. I don't remember."

Skip looked back again at his friends then at the paper in his hands. "Ah...I think it might be good for us...I mean..."

"What are they doing?" Becky nodded toward the two boys lurking in the shadow of Brockston's. "Why are they acting like idiots and why are they here? I thought it was going to be just you and me."

Skip looked over at the red Nissan. Paula and Kate were still sitting inside, watching them. "I could ask the same question."

Becky put her hands on her hips. "All right, Skip. What's the deal? What's going on?"

"Nothing. I mean…we just thought that this conference might do you some good. That's all."

"We? As in your idiot friends back there?"

"Yes, and as in *your* dumb friends over here."

Beck yanked the paper from Skip's hands. "What's this conference all about?"

Skip moved closer and put his arm around her. "It's great, really great. I went last year. It's like a field trip, put out by Planned Parenthood. You get out of school for the day and the conference is over by 1:30. It's at a really nice hotel, and you get breakfast and lunch."

"And?"

"And…and all you have to do is sit through a few lectures."

"About sex education and condom use? I've already learned about that stuff in health."

"Well, maybe you need to hear it again. Maybe you're not comfortable with it all and need to be reassured."

Becky glared at her friends and then at the two tall shadows against the building. "Was this a group decision?"

"Ah…well, we're just trying to help, Becky, that's all. You seem so uptight about it, we all thought that maybe in a nice environment, over a little lunch, you'd, you know… see things differently."

"Is that what you *all* thought?" Becky fought back the tears and her anger. "It gives me such a nice warm feeling knowing that all of you sat around discussing this. Discussing me, like I was some kind of mental case."

Skip drew her closer. "It wasn't like that at all. It's just that we think you need a little help…to get through this. I mean, you're a senior and we've been going out three months, and you still freeze like a glacier. A little help to get you through this, that's all you need. You'll see."


Becky tiptoed into her room, then closed the door before turning on the light. She didn't know why she bothered. She was sure her father was up anyway. He never fell asleep until she came home.

She pulled off her clothes, threw them in a pile on the floor, and put on her pajamas. As she brushed her long, silky black hair, she studied her face. The only good feature she could see was her complexion. Paula once told Becky her skin was "to die for."

That was one consolation anyway. Still, it didn't make up for those lips of hers. She tossed the brush onto the cluttered dresser and glanced at her Raggedy Ann.

"Boy, do you have the life, just sitting on my dresser all day and nobody telling you to grow up."

With a sigh, she pulled her diary from the middle

drawer. She opened it, found her pen, then threw herself on the bed and began to write.

*Dear Diary,*

*I saw Skip tonight. I don't think he's going to dump me after all. Not yet, at least. And just when I was getting used to the idea. I never thought being in love could be so terrible. It's like playing chicken with a bus, seeing if it will run you over or if you'll jump out of the way, instead. I figure either way you lose, not the bus. So why do people play?*

*Skip thinks I have a problem with sex. So do all my friends…and his. I never thought I did. Now I'm not so sure. I let him do things tonight that I never let him do before, but not the real thing, not the thing that really mattered to him. I wanted to. I want to do everything I can to please him, to make him happy. But I'm not ready for all of it. At least I think that's the reason. I don't know anymore. I'm so confused. I'm going to college next year. Shouldn't I be over this silly notion that virginity means something? There can only be one 'first time.' Should that be with Skip? Will we last? Does it even matter? It seems like I'm getting stupider with age. Why can't I make sense of this? Or is it supposed to make sense? The whole virginity thing is getting old, anyway. I'm tired of it. It doesn't mean anything. So why can't I throw it away like some useless outgrown toy? Maybe for the same reason I can't throw Raggedy away. Maybe I'm afraid to grow up, like Paula and Kate say. I don't know. But why is it so wrong to be a virgin? I think everyone's*

*right. I really am afraid to grow up. I just wish I wasn't
so confused.*

# 2

TERESA EMERSON WALKED INTO the dingy little office and smelled mothballs. She smiled at the large perspiring man behind the desk and noticed that the smell became stronger the closer she got to him. It was almost overwhelming by the time she reached the cheap pine desk. She took the empty chair. The man wore a wrinkled brown wool suit and wheezed whenever he inhaled. She could deal with the mothball odor and was actually getting used to it by degrees, but the wheezing made her nervous. She found herself breathing harder as though trying to aid him in his.

She opened her purse and pulled out a swollen envelope full of large bills. She held the envelope in the air for a moment, then placed it on the desk in front of her.

"Before I give this to you, I'd like to see what you have."

The man in the brown suit chuckled good-naturedly. "Can't say I blame you. I'd want to see the goods, too, before I forked over that kind of cash." He pulled out a black folder from a side drawer and slid it toward her. "Like I told you on the phone, he's an easy study. Very casual about what he does. Not worried about covering his tracks. You'll like the pictures. A good lawyer can do a lot with these. I must admit that not all my jobs are this easy. I almost feel bad taking your money—I mean, the job was that easy."

Teresa opened the folder and took out an inch-high stack of banded black-and-white photos. She removed the rubber band, thumbed through them quickly, then put them back. She didn't have the stomach to view them any closer. She picked up her envelope and handed it to the man. "I was told you're the best. I was not misled."

The man started to laugh then stopped because of the wheezing. "You'll have no trouble now, not with these. I suppose this concludes our business. I mean the deal was for six months, and you have everything you need."

"If you look in the envelope, you'll see that I've given you an advance for another six months."

The man scratched his head. "Okay, lady, it's your money. If you want to throw it away that's fine by me. But you've got the guy cold. I've just given you an insurance policy and all you have to do is fill in the amount."

Teresa smiled sadly. "In some cases, one can't have too much insurance."


"Kirt, you've got to do something! You're the best friend we've got in the Assembly. If you don't help, who will?"

"Cool your jets, Maggie. I didn't say I wasn't going to help. But you sure can pick winners, can't you?"

"You afraid of him?"

There was silence at the other end of the phone, then a heavy sigh. "You know some people say he's connected, has a lot of muscle power."

"Since when do you pay attention to rumors?"

"You pick up a lot here at the capital. More times than not, the rumors turn out to have merit."

Maggie pulled a paper from beneath the blotter. Words, cut from a newspaper, were pasted on a single sheet of inexpensive typing paper. She had read them a hundred times and was about to read them again, to Kirt, but stopped herself.

"Those people don't play nice, Maggie, and that means when we go after him we have to do it right and we have to do it smart. It might be wise to tread a little softer, for now, anyway. Your people have been pretty rough on him."

"First off, Kirt, they're not *my* people. They're people following their own consciences. And second, they're not about to tread any softer. They'll go right on picketing his abortion clinics until this madness stops."

"Maggie, have you forgotten? Abortion is legal."

"Is it legal for a doctor to perform an abortion while intoxicated? Is it legal for a doctor to carve his initials into the stomach of a patient? Is it legal for a doctor to rape the young girls that come to him for help?"

"Slow down, now. That's a mouthful of accusations you're hurling at Dr. Emerson, and somehow I just can't see him doing any of them."

"No, *he's* not. But some of his staff at Solutions are."

"Any proof?"

"Stop sounding like a lawyer."

"I am a lawyer."

Maggie fingered the sheet of typing paper, then slid it back in its hiding place with the other one she had received the week before. This had to be the work of a kook. *There can't be any connection between these notes and Dr. Emerson.*

"Maggie? I asked you if you had any proof?"

"A room full of them, Kirt. Broken, hurt, damaged. I see them every day. I have to look into their eyes, watch them fight the tears, the self-hatred. It will take years before these girls are whole again."

"Will any of them testify?"

"Come on, you know better than that."

"So what can I do?"

"Make the State Health Department do regular inspections. They're supposed to anyway, but don't. If it were anything other than an abortion clinic, the Health Department would be all over them. When are they going to stop protecting this industry?"

"Suppose I could get the Health Department to do an inspection? What's that going to do?"

Maggie squinted at the nameplate on her desk: Maggie Singer, CSW, CASAC, Community Life Center. Some days she wished she had gotten into something else, like retail, where your heart wasn't always breaking into tiny little pieces. But God had placed her here. She was glad that at least one of them knew what He was doing.

"Maggie? You there?"

"Yes." She took a deep breath. "*Somebody* has to be."

"That's not fair. You said yourself I'm the best friend

you've got. But I don't see it every day, and that gives me some objectivity. Emotions don't cut it here at the state capital. I need hard facts. Give me something I can work with."

Maggie pressed the phone to her ear and rose from her desk. "That's why I love you, Kirt. You're so logical, so clinical."

"I wish you meant that, I mean *really* meant that."

"You know I never say anything I don't mean."

"Well, the Bible uses several different words for love. Which one did you mean exactly?"

"You want the facts, okay—Solutions is notorious for improperly maintaining their surgical equipment, being understaffed, performing abortions too quickly. You do an abortion every five to six minutes, where's the time to monitor patients, pre- or post-op? Where's the time to prepare the room for the next patient? And Solutions has no equipment to monitor patients undergoing general anesthesia. None!" She paced around her office, her small, 100-pound frame poised for battle.

"Sit down, Maggie, and take a load off," Kirt said. "Give me a chance to roll this around in my mind and figure out how best to pressure the Health Department into doing some spontaneous inspections."

"Then you'll help?"

"Cut it out, Maggie. You knew I would."

"I had hoped...well, okay, I *knew*. But thank you, Kirt, and God bless you. And that love word—it was *agape*."

"Yeah, that's what I was afraid of."

❦

Becky watched her mother pile dirty dinner dishes into the sink. She pulled a rumpled paper from her jeans and took a deep breath. "Could you sign this?"

Her mother wiped the counter, then pulled a plastic drainage rack from beneath the sink.

"Mom!" Becky shoved the rumpled paper and a blue pen into her mother's hands.

"What's this?"

"Permission for a field trip."

"'Substance Abuse, Healthy Relationships, Communications, Stress Management.' Sounds like stuff you've already had in health class."

"Yeah…" Becky watched her mother frown.

"'The Responsible Choices—knowing when to have sex. Interactive workshops between boys and girls.'"

"It's supposed to be really good. My health teacher raved about it." She watched her mother turn the paper over.

"Why doesn't it give more information? How am I supposed to know what this is all about?"

"The principal got on the loudspeaker this morning to remind everyone about the seminar. *He* thinks it's great."

"I don't know…one of the neighbors was telling me about these Planned Parenthood sex seminars and—"

"Who? Not that religious weirdo? Mom! You know what Daddy says about her."

Nancy shrugged. "Okay, let me ask your father and see what he thinks."

Becky let out an exasperated sigh. "Do you have to?" She followed her mother into the living room.

Her father was slumped to one side, reading the evening paper. He looked so worn, so tired. She tried to grab her mother's arm and stop her from disturbing him, but it was too late.

"You want something, Nance?"

Becky backed into the kitchen and leaned against the door frame.

"You look tired. You really need a vacation. It's been so long, Jim."

"Can't do it. The shop's too busy." The newspaper crinkled as he turned the page.

"So why is it that Nick always manages a vacation every year? He and Cynthia just got back from a week in Jamaica."

"You don't understand the business. There are reasons."

"Equal partners should get equal benefits. But all you get is to work harder."

"Don't start, Nance."

"I worry about you, Jim. I'm not trying to nag. You need a break, a rest."

From where she stood, Becky could see her father's face. A look of love flickered briefly through the cloud of fatigue, then all was exhaustion again. "Thank you, but don't worry about me, honey," her father said.

"Can't we even discuss it?"

He stretched the *Gazette* across his upper body. "Nothing to discuss. When the time's right I'll take you on a nice long vacation. But now's not the time."

Her mother turned and walked toward the kitchen. There was a frown on her face. Then she stopped and looked at the paper in her hand. For a moment Becky thought her mother was going to backtrack. Instead, she gave Becky a weak smile, walked to the kitchen table, and signed it.

The large glass aquarium bubbled noiselessly against the left wall of Thor's office, filling him with serenity. He watched his pair of Clown Triggerfish swim in and out of the ceramic sunken ship. Clowns didn't breed in captivity, but that hadn't discouraged Thor. He was sure the recent artificial insemination of the female would produce results.

In addition, Thor had hired a specialist to come twice a week to check water temperature and pH and to clean the tank when necessary. The specialist also brought the Clowns live fish for food and stocked up the freezer compartment of the small office refrigerator with frozen clams and shrimp.

Thor thought of Hugh Brockston. What would a man like Hugh think of an heir who squandered so much money on pet fish? Would he be proud? Thor laughed. Who else did his great-great-great-great-grandfather Hugh have to be proud of? All the other Brockstons had killed themselves off with excess. And even he didn't have the name, only the bloodline.

He thought about his successes: the only Brockston who had made anything of himself in six generations—

thanks to his mother. *Poor Mother.* Not exactly the line of medicine she had envisioned for him. But she was the one who had pulled him from his dream of being a business-man into the world of medicine. She said it would provide a good living. She had been right about that. It had pro-vided a very good living. Taking inflation into account, Thor was sure he had made as big a fortune as his Grandpa Hugh. The trick was keeping it. The trick was not losing everything to Louie.

Yes, strange how fate had corrected his course and put him back on track. Proved he was right all along, that he was meant to be a businessman. His six facilities were pulling in more money than a colleague's string of eight. That's because he knew how to maximize. Put the money in the little extras that paid off big in the end—waiting rooms with piped-in music, pretty pastel walls, large framed watercolor pictures, artificial plants. It made his facilities a cut above so he could charge cut-above prices: $400 for a first trimester abortion instead of $350.

He also had two technicians who knew how to wrap and freeze placentas for shipment. His cosmetic accounts paid well for the placentas, and used them in collagen preparations. But the real money was in fetal tissue harvest-ing. And so was the future. Everyone was doing research, and researchers needed to be supplied. Before his eyes, Thor had seen the worthless by-products of his business turn into gold.

He didn't do abortions anymore. He didn't have to.

Thor glanced at his Rolex and smiled, then headed back toward his desk. Carl Langley would be calling any minute to finalize the biggest contract that had ever come his way. That's where his mother had missed it. "The future lies in medicine. People are always going to get sick," she had said. *No, the future lies in procreation. People are always going to procreate.* That's what made the world go round. So why shouldn't he cash in on it and do a little good besides?

He was still smiling when the phone rang. He picked it up and was greeted by a gruff voice.

"Hello, Thor, I have good news." Excitement permeated Carl Langley's voice. "Our client has raised the price 10 percent across the board. So you win on that one. But they won't budge on the other issue. They insist on *fresh* only, collection no more than ten minutes after abortion. Seems prudent for you to instruct your doctors to encourage girls to go to fuller term, then do a D&X, a partial birth, for better specimens. Maybe let them know there was going to be a benefit, a good, with the research and all. More money for you in the D&X anyway. Better all around. But hey, I don't need to tell you your business." The president and owner of Second Chance Foundation paused and cleared his throat. "Only thing is, if you can't deliver the quantities required, I'll have to go elsewhere. You need to understand that. And once I pull a contract, it may be a long time before another one like it comes around again."

"I hear you, Carl. No need to threaten."

"I wasn't threatening, just stating a fact. I believe in being honest and aboveboard. You know, in today's business there's not much integrity left."

"I know that, Carl. And I appreciate your candor."

"I figure with your six clinics you can handle this. And it's a big one, Thor. Really big. And there's a sweetener at the end of it. A bonus if you meet demand with good specimens."

"I love a challenge. You might as well write that check now and put it aside."

Carl laughed. "A man after my own heart. Course it might be prudent to share some of that bonus with a few friends at the capital, just to keep the right attitudes alive. We don't want any of them getting rambunctious about banning partial-birth abortions. But hey, I don't need to tell you your business."

"No Carl, I'm on top of things."

"Oh, did I mention, I'm sending you a few technicians. They'll be collecting the samples. You fax them a printout the night before of all the abortions you plan on doing the next day, give them the age of the fetus, planned procedure, the usual info packet, and they'll decide what clinics will best satisfy their purchase orders."

"Is that necessary, using your techs? I have some good ones, ones I trained myself and—"

"No, gotta be this way, so you can bill me for site space. Gotta keep it on the up-and-up."

"No way to get around it?"

"None."

"Then I guess my people will be working with yours."

"Right. And that's about it…oh…I heard you were having trouble with a bunch of picketers at your Brockston clinic. Causing you to lose business, I understand…or is that just a rumor?"

Thor forced a laugh. "An exaggeration, Carl. Just an

exaggeration. A few right-wingers spreading their intolerance. Nothing to worry about."

"I hear you. But just remember if business drops and you can't—"

"I said it's nothing to worry about." There was an edge in Thor's voice.

"Well, if you say so. I guess that about covers it…oh, yeah…just one more thing. If an order comes in that requires a special procedure to insure that the specimen remains intact, would you…that is…would your staff be receptive to changing their procedure to one more favorable for collection? We would, of course, tell you beforehand which procedure we'd like changed, depending upon age and size of the specimen."

"My staff will be at your disposal. I'll instruct them to check with your technicians each morning."

"Fine. Now I'm sure I've covered everything, unless, of course, you have any questions or anything to add."

"Only that I think we'll work well together."

"Then we have a deal?"

"We have a deal."


Thor had hung up with Carl and was just about to leave his office suite when the phone rang again. His secretary answered it, then waved her arm for him to stop.

"You'll want to take this one," she said, cupping the receiver in her hand. "It's Mr. Louie—"

Thor nodded and backtracked to his office, then closed the door.

"Hello, Louie." Thor forced his voice to sound cheerful.

"You sound well…jubilant even. Perhaps after our conversation your spirits will be elevated to an even higher stratosphere. I believe it's a day for celebration, Thor, but you tell me."

Thor shifted his weight from one foot to the other. "Are you going to turn this into a novel? I'm on my way out."

"That's the trouble with you college types. You've never learned how to savor the moment. You're too busy rushing to who knows where. Oftentimes, you make me grateful that I'm a self-made man. But I suspect I've told you this before."

"Yes, Louie, many times."

"Well, out of respect for you and your time, I'll come to the point. I have a proposition of some weight, involving a company that I and others have invested heavily in."

"What others?"

"Now Thor, you know I don't discuss my business partners with anyone. They're of the ilk that—how shall I say it?—that prefer anonymity. We've been friends long enough for you to understand that."

"Yes, but as a businessman, you should respect my interest and concern."

"Concern?" Thor heard soft laughter. "There's no need for such trepidation. Do you think I'd lead you down an erroneous path? Believe me, Thor, your success is in the forefront of my mind. How else will I ever collect all that money you owe me?"

Thor forced his laughter to join with Louie's. "Let's hear what you've got, and if it sounds good, maybe we can work a deal."

"A company called Galaxy Cosmetics Inc. is developing an entirely new product line called Dorianna Gray…by the way, how do you like the name?"

"Ah…fine…sounds fine."

"The name was my suggestion. Rather clever if you think about it. You know, Dorian Gray, the ageless man; Dorianna Gray, the ageless woman."

"Right. Good choice." Thor rolled his eyes.

"There's a fortune to be made in cosmetics. Broads are always trying to make themselves more beautiful, always looking for that fountain of youth. And we're going to be Ponce de Leon to them. Only this time, we'll not go sailing off to some obscure island looking for that fountain. We're going to manufacture it. I'm telling you, Thor, this is a money-maker. Broads will pay anything to make their wrinkles vanish. And we're talking top of the line, the *crème de la crème*. We're talking five hundred dollars and up for a four-ounce jar."

Thor grunted. He wondered if women paying five hundred dollars for a jar of collagen cream would appreciate being called "broads."

"This line will be cutting edge, you understand. A great volume of money is being invested, money from *big* players."

Thor walked around his desk and sat down. "How do I fit into all this?"

"As I previous stated, this is cutting edge. The geniuses in the lab coats will be doing a preponderance of research. This is not business as usual, Thor. A whole new approach will be taken. What I need from you, what you will do, is supply the specimens of various…body parts. I have already pledged your cooperation and I have given my assurances that you can handle the great volume that will be needed for success."

Thor felt his face flush with anger. "I've just completed a deal with a wholesaler for much of my stuff. I've also got several other smaller accounts. I'll do what I can, Louie, but I can't promise I'll be able to meet demand. I wish you had spoken to me before—"

"You have not grasped the true picture, Thor," Louie said, his voice cold as a glacier. "As a part-owner of sorts in your clinics, I have made the commitment for you. Dorianna Gray *will* be your top priority. The leftovers can go to your other accounts. I don't believe I can state it any more succinctly."

How had he gotten into this mess? How had he ever allowed someone like Louie to gain this much control over him?

"Well, Thor, what's your answer? Can you…will you do it?"

Again, Thor forced a laugh. "Was there ever any doubt? Of course, Louie. Anything Dorianna Gray needs, I'll provide."

"You will make it your number one account, your number one priority?"

"Of course."

"Marvelous."

Thor could almost hear Louie smile, could almost see those barracudalike teeth.

"And naturally, you'll be well paid. Your specimens will

command top dollar, that I can guarantee you without hesi-
tation. I dare say that in no time you'll be able to clear up
all those IOUs. And if you perform well, which I have no
doubt you will, then I'll even consider slicing off something
extra from your balance due. Call it a bonus."

Thor wiped his free hand on his pants and closed his
eyes.

"I dare say you could use a bonus."

"Yes, thank you, Louie."


Dr. Thor Emerson was seated behind his desk, still brooding over the conversation with Louie, when his wife
pushed open the office door. Her face was ashen and Thor
noticed her lip tremble slightly.

He forced a smile to hide his intense irritation at being
disturbed. "Teresa, what are you doing here? I thought you
were out with the girls or something."

"I need to talk to you." Teresa remained rigid in the
doorway and ignored his gesture to sit down. "I'll be as
brief as possible."

"Couldn't this wait until I got home?"

"No. I won't be there when you get home."

"Don't tell me you're going to see Eric again? Even for
you this is—"

"No."

"Then, what are you talking about?"

"I'm on my way to see a lawyer, Thor. It's settled. I've
decided. I just didn't want to do it over the phone. After
fourteen years...well, for the sake of the fourteen years."

Thor saw that the quiver in her lip had intensified. Slowly, he pushed himself away from the desk. "We've gone through this before. This is *not* the time, Teresa. You'll not have one of your tantrums in my office."

To Thor's surprise, Teresa broke a smile even though she was still visibly upset. "Fine. I've told you to your face. I've done what I set out to do." She turned to leave.

"Where are you going?"

"I've told you, or tried to tell you, that I'm leaving you."

Thor rose from his chair and quickly went to where Teresa stood, pulled her away from the door frame, then closed the heavy maple door. Squeezing her arm a little too tightly, he led her to the chair in front of his desk and practically shoved her in it. He studied her face for the first sign of tears. There weren't any.

"If this is about the other night, if this is about Julie, I've told you a hundred times she's just a business colleague, nothing more. I can't help what she tells you or how she feels about me. But she's nothing to me. Nothing. When will you get that through your—"

"It's not about her, it's not about *any* of them. It's about you and me. It's about love and trust and respect and—"

"I'm not in the mood to listen to you whine—"

"—and dignity. It's all lost. We've lost it. I want a life, a real life. I've tried to hang on. But I can't anymore. I won't anymore."

"Dignity? You want to talk dignity. What about that house I bought you, the one you've filled with expensive antiques? What about the summer place at the shore? What about being a doctor's wife? You—"

"A doctor's wife? You're not a doctor, you're an abortionist. You think I'm proud of that? You think anyone really likes an abortionist? Surely you don't believe that all those politicians are your friends? Oh, they may smile when you give them those fat contributions, but afterward, Thor, afterward they go and wash their hands. And about the house...I don't give a hoot about the house...or the antiques. I only care...about you. But it's not enough anymore. Not anymore. I've stayed this long because I saw how bad it was for you, how angry your work made you. I thought I could help but—"

"Wait a minute, just back up. Are you telling me you're ashamed of what I do, ashamed of *me?*"

"I wasn't at first. I thought you were helping these girls. That you were doing some good. I remember how soft-hearted you were. How the first time you did an abortion you came home and cried and threw up, then went to bed for two days. I should have realized then that this was not the line of work for you."

"But I am doing good. These girls come to me when they're in trouble. Someone has to help them. And it's me they come to for—"

"You've changed. It was gradual, but I've seen it coming for a long time. First the anger, then the hardness. Sometimes the way you talk, I think you hate your patients."

"How would you feel if the same girls kept coming in over and over again? They don't see what you scrape out of them, they don't *see*...and no gratitude, never any gratitude. I read it in their eyes, the fear, the anger, the sorrow, but never any gratitude, never any thanks. That's why I'm out of it. I'm a businessman now. Let the others scrape and suction, I've no stomach for it anymore."

"So, you do hate your patients. Then I was right. Maybe in some strange way, your work has made you hate me. Made you hate all women."

Thor laughed. "I don't hate women. I just hate the fact that every time they get themselves into trouble they expect some man to bail them out. Just like you, Teresa. Every time you're unhappy about something, you think I can fix it. Well, I can't. You think all you have to do is shed a few tears and I'll fall all over myself to make you happy again. Well, I'm not happy either. Did that ever occur to you?"

"When I cry it's for us…because of us. Because you're so distant and you keep pushing me out. I love you and want—"

"You think I want a crying, whining wife hanging around my neck all the time? Why do you think I had so many…*female* colleagues? I'm tired of baby-sitting you, Teresa. Talk about dignity! *You're* the embarrassment."

Teresa rose from the chair and adjusted her blue suit jacket. She looked stunning even with the frown on her face. Her lip was no longer quivering, and she stared into his eyes for an instant then looked away. "I don't want to hurt you, Thor. And we're both vulnerable right now and it's too easy to say mean things. So please believe me that what I'm going to say is not out of spite. Stop trying to compete with your Grandpa Hugh. You can't build what he did with abortion clinics. It's killing you, Thor. This whole business is killing you. It's killed our marriage and now it's killing you. I tried to hang in. I didn't want you to be all alone."

"What do you mean, all alone? You think I have no one else?"

"Other women, yes…but no one…no friends."

"You forget about Louie?"

"A man like Louie doesn't have any friends."

"You couldn't be more wrong, Teresa. They don't come better than Louie."

"I'm glad you think so. At least it won't hurt so much when he ends up owning everything. And the way you're going, he'll own it all." Teresa opened the door to leave but stopped when Thor called her name.

"You're wrong, you know."

"About what?"

"I am doing good. I help people. I provide a valuable service. Because of what I do, a cure for cancer may be found, or some new medicine discovered. I do a lot of good. A lot of good."

Teresa shook her head sadly. "Hang on to your name, Thor. Because being related to Hugh Brockston may be all that you're going to be left with."


Thor sat staring into his fish tank, not really paying attention to the black-and-yellow Clowns as they darted past the staghorn coral. All his life he had heard the whispers that he was just another Brockston who wouldn't amount to anything. Mother had not wanted him to follow the "family foolishness," the propensity to squander large amounts of money. He knew that's why she had talked him out of business and into medicine. No Brockston had ever gone into medicine.

But his less than brilliant performance in medical school landed him near the bottom of his class and with few options. Well, he had made the best of them. And he wasn't going to lose everything. The hemorrhaging would stop now. He was going to get rid of Newly…and Louie. If he could pull off the deals with Dorianna Gray and Second Chance Foundation, it would go a long way toward curing his financial ills. He'd finally have enough money to get out from under. Teresa would see how wrong she was. *Then let her try crawling back.* Who wanted her anyway? But as he dialed the phone, Thor could feel a dull ache well up inside where he had not felt anything in a very very long time.

"Louie? Yeah, hello again. Listen, I need another favor…put it on the tab…. No, I don't want to place a bet… No, nothing like that. What I want is for you to get one of your friends in the persuasion business, someone who's not going to get carried away… No, the letters didn't work… No, I don't want anything drastic. Get someone with a soft touch. I just want a friendly message sent. Nobody gets hurt…"

Becky and Skip held hands and talked in the back of the school bus, waiting for the other thirty kids to get off first. When the bus was nearly empty, they got up and went outside. Behind their bus was a string of other buses, like a giant yellow ribbon bending and winding along the curb. A dozen schools across the county had sent their interested high school students to converge in front of the shimmering glass hotel. Mammoth blue windowpanes, stretching ten stories high, made the hotel look like an ice mountain.

Becky smiled at Skip and snuggled closer to him as they walked through the blue-glass door. Ever since she told him she was going to the youth convention, he had been less uptight with her. Yesterday alone, he sent her two notes telling her how much he loved her. Coming here was a small price to pay for such devotion.

For too long she had been on the wrong path. It was like her body chemistry had been out of balance, her brain not thinking clearly. But she was thinking a lot straighter now. Not so confused, so childish. After all, she was going to college next year. She didn't want to go away like some silly goose, some country bumpkin who didn't know the score.

Two Planned Parenthood staff smiled and greeted them in the plush hotel lobby, then pointed to a thickly carpeted hallway. Two more Planned Parenthood staff ushered them into a room filled with rows of chairs. Each chair had a little desktop that collapsed to the side when not in use. All the desktops were snapped into place. Blue and pink folders, alternately placed, made the room look like a giant checkerboard. Another smiling staffer instructed the boys to choose a desk with a blue folder and the girls a pink one.

Becky headed for a row of chairs closer to the back, and

Skip obligingly followed. When they were settled, Becky opened her folder and began leafing through some of the brochures. Out of the corner of her eye, she watched Skip leaf through his. She noticed he had a booklet in his folder that she didn't, and grabbed it.

"Hey, how come I don't have one of these?" She quickly read the title. *The Problem with Puberty.*

Skip smiled and shrugged and tried to get it back, but Becky held it so he couldn't reach. Then she began leafing through the pages. She suddenly stopped when she saw a drawing of five people in a bathroom, all nude. A young man sat in the tub. Around him sat an old woman and young girl. Behind him stood another man and a woman. In front of the tub sat a dog. She could feel her face redden, even before she began reading the caption, "It is normal to have all kinds of fantasies while you are mastur..." She snapped the book shut and handed it back to Skip. Her cheeks burned and she wouldn't look at his face. They couldn't all be wrong: Skip, her parents, her friends, her teachers, her school, and now this organization that her principal spoke so highly of. They couldn't *all* be wrong.


Maggie sat on a metal folding chair, praying for wisdom as she looked into the faces around her. She had been meeting with this Project Rachael group every Wednesday afternoon for eleven weeks. Next week would be their last, and it would not be held here in the little Life Center kitchen but in St. Ann's Chapel, two blocks away.

She smiled at the ten women who sat around the table.

How different their faces were from when she first saw them. *I will repay you for the years the locusts have eaten…you will have plenty to eat, until you are full and you will praise the name of the Lord your God, who has worked wonders for you; never again will my people be shamed.* Maggie knew these women still had a long, difficult road to travel, but they had come so far. Yes, God had done a mighty work.

She was sure the ladies were all ready for next week when they would spiritually baptize their babies at St. Ann's, or rather Father Talbert would. The women were hungry for closure. They had all written their baby a letter, had acknowledged if it was a boy or girl, had named their child. The baptism would give them all a finality they craved.

Maggie cleared her throat, took a deep breath. "Okay ladies, any questions about next week, about what we're going to be doing there?"

A heavyset woman in her fifties raised her hand. "Tell us again about that little angel pin."

Maggie's smile grew. "Well, you and your husband or boyfriend will stand before Father Talbert and—"

"But if we don't have a husband, is that okay?" the woman asked.

"My new boyfriend wasn't the father of my aborted baby. Can I bring him?" asked another girl.

Maggie put up her hand. "Ladies, you can bring whoever you want to stand with you at the altar. And if you don't want to bring anyone, that's okay too. But as I was saying, you and your guest will stand before Father Talbert, and he'll lay hands on you and pray for you. And then he'll

---

spiritually baptize your baby."

"Go through that again, would you? The spiritual baptism, I mean," one of the ladies said.

"You'll speak out the name of your aborted child, then symbolically hand him over to Father Talbert, who will symbolically hand him over to Jesus."

"And that's when he'll give us the little gold angel?" the heavyset woman asked.

"Yes, he'll give you one pin for each child you have aborted."

"To remind us our child is now in the arms of Jesus and waits for us in heaven?" The heavy woman closed her eyes.

"Yes," Maggie said, and watched the woman smile.


Two teenage boys entered the Life Center, each carrying a large cardboard box.

"Delivery," one of them said, not looking up at the receptionist. His cap was pulled low over his face. "Where do you want them?"

The receptionist leaned over her desk to get a better look. "I don't believe we were expecting anything."

Strange noises were coming from the boxes.

"All I know, lady, is that we were told to deliver these to you and to open them so you could check out the contents."

"What is it? Who sent them?"

The two youths deposited their boxes against the opposite wall, and one of them pulled out a utility knife.

"Wait! Don't open it. I can't accept unauthorized merchandise." The receptionist appeared flustered and rose from her desk. "Just wait here while I get the director. Please don't do anything until she comes."

But even as the receptionist walked down the hall, the boy slit open the top of his box, then handed the knife to his companion who did the same to the other box. Then both boys ran out the front door.

By the time Maggie and the receptionist rounded the corner of the hallway, they could see a black mass swarming over and around the boxes. A few of the girls had left the group to stretch their legs or go to the ladies' room and were trailing behind. Maggie stopped suddenly and turned toward them. "Go back to the kitchen."

"We'll just be a minute," one of them said.

"Go back to the kitchen, now!" Maggie's face was tense, and the girls strained to see beyond her for the cause.

Then someone screamed, then someone else, and before long the hall was full of screams. Other women came out of the kitchen to see what was happening, and they added their screams to the chorus. Then they began pushing and shoving and running blindly, trying to get out of the path of the swarming mass headed their way.

Maggie tried to lead the women into the kitchen where they could close the door. But the rats were already crawling over their feet.


"So, what did you think of the conference?" Skip ran his fingers through Becky's hair and watched it fall and shimmer against the headrest.

"It was okay."

"Most of the day you look embarrassed."

"I wasn't embarrassed... Well, some of it was pretty raw, you must admit."

"Yeah. But I'm glad you came. I'm surprised your father let you, being the way he is, so strict and all."

"It was my mother, actually. And she must've thought it would be okay with Dad or she wouldn't have let me. She never goes against Dad, even when he gets weird."

"Didn't your dad ever talk to you about sex?"

"Once."

"What did he say?"

"He said, 'Be careful, just be careful.' I guess that's why Mom thinks he'd want me to learn about contraceptives and things."

"Makes sense. He's a guy. He knows the ropes. He just wants you to be sensible and not mess up your life. Every father worries about his daughter. I mean, it's the girl who gets pregnant. It's the girl who really has to be careful."

"Yeah..."

"Yeah, but?"

"If that's the case, why does he dislike Paula so much? Ever since that incident with Paula and Denny in her car, well, he's given me such a hard time and doesn't like me to go out with her. I always thought it was...well, because he didn't approve of girls doing that."

"Becky, no father wants his daughter to be like Paula."

"Why not? You just said he's a guy and guys know the ropes and they don't struggle with sex the way girls do."

"Yeah, but Paula's different. She's...well, she's fast. She'll do it with anybody. She's not *selective*. You have to think 'disease' nowadays. You have to think, 'Who has this person been with?'"

Becky pushed Skip's hand away and rolled down the car window. She hated the smell of the vanilla air freshener that hung from his rearview mirror. It gave her a headache, or had she come with it? It had been a horrible day. She hated the conference. People blowing up condoms, playing with wooden dolls. She had counted the minutes for it to be over. The whole thing didn't feel right. Nothing felt right. Maybe that's why she had agreed to come with Skip to Lover's Cove. Why she was sitting in his car enduring the disgusting smell of mock vanilla. Why she would let him finally have his way. Because she had to make it right. She had to get over this virginity thing. To get rid of it once and for all. Maybe then it would all make sense to her.

Skip gently put his arm around her shoulders. "What are you thinking?"

Becky inhaled the crisp night air and continued to stare into the darkness outside. She didn't turn around. She didn't want to see him, to see the eagerness, the hope she knew was etched on his face like a child beneath a Christmas tree. "I'm wondering if someday you'll say about me what you just said about Paula."

"Becky, that's impossible. You're nothing like Paula. Nothing at all. You're special and I love you. You're the only girl for me. I love you, Becky. I really do."


Maggie pulled into an empty parking space behind her apartment and sighed with relief. She felt she had lived through a nightmare. Even now she could visualize the mass of furry bodies swarming over everything. Maybe a hot shower and fresh clothes would help her forget.

When Maggie got out of the car, she noticed a black BMW pulling alongside the curb. She had to pass it on the way to her apartment, and when she did, the door flew open and a thin, very attractive woman jumped out. For a moment the woman just stood on the sidewalk barring Maggie's path. The stranger looked as if she was about to say something. But then she jumped back into her car and sped away.

Becky undressed slowly, dropping her clothes, like rose petals, along a path by her bed. She slipped into her pajamas, then pulled her diary from its hiding place. She wondered if she should write anything. *What if Mom found it?* But before Becky even came upon the proper page, she knew there was no way she could stop herself. Not tonight.

> *Dear Diary,*
>
> *Today I became a real woman. Funny thing is, I don't feel more grown up. I feel…betrayed. It was nothing like the movies make it out to be. It was awkward and embarrassing and…painful. It's not supposed to be like this, is it? Maybe it was my fault. Maybe it's me. I'm beginning to think there's something seriously wrong with me. I thought I loved Skip desperately, madly. But something wasn't right. I tried to fake it. I told Skip it was wonderful for me. I don't think he believed me. I could*

*tell by the caring way he spoke to me afterwards, telling me it would be better next time, that it usually gets better and better. But what he said didn't comfort me at all. The only words that kept ringing in my ears and that filled me with dread were "next time." Because suddenly I knew there was going to be a next time, and a next time, and a next time. As long as I keep going out with Skip, there could be a thousand "next times." Because now, how could I ever say "no" to him again?*

*So, Diary, you want to know how it feels to be a woman? It feels sad. It feels very very sad.*

# 3

THOR EMERSON THREW A few diced clams into the tank and watched his Clowns rush to the surface. This exercise didn't give him any pleasure today. It had been almost a week since Teresa left, actually had a van come and move out all her things.

But she only took what was hers, nothing of his, and nothing that could be construed as "theirs." Teresa was funny that way, had a strange sense of integrity. If the shoe were on the other foot, he'd have cleaned her out.

Yet strangely enough, it irritated him that she hadn't. Weren't all the things he had bought good enough? No, that wasn't it. He wasn't being fair. But he didn't want to be fair. Then again, he didn't know what he wanted. Was it Teresa? Did he want her back? Maybe…probably…yes. He never thought she'd go through with it. Never thought she had the guts to go it alone. Never thought the house would feel so…*empty*.

It was her expectations that ruined them. Her always expecting to be happy. Expecting him to be happy—as though happiness were the natural human condition instead of sorrow. Maybe if she'd spent time at one of his clinics she'd see for herself how miserable people were, how fortunate she was.

The intercom buzzed and his secretary's voice sputtered out of the box. "Flo Gardner on line one. Says it's urgent."

Thor walked over to his desk. "Eleanor, I thought I told you to hold my calls."

"I tried to tell her you couldn't be disturbed, but she started yelling something about an emergency. If I didn't tell you and there really was some trouble at the Brockston clinic, you'd be mad and then—"

"Put her through... Flo? What's the problem?"

"Dr. Newly."

Thor ran his fingers through his salt-and-pepper hair. "I've told you, you've got to try to get along, to make the best of it. Until I get a replacement, he stays."

"He can't stay, Thor. He simply can't. Sooner or later he's going to kill someone and you'll be paying lawyers for the rest of your life."

"What's he done now?"

"He's in there, drunk as a skunk, doing a procedure. Can hardly stand. These girls deserve better, Thor. They come to us for help and they expect a competent physician to work on them. The other day, I saw him molest one of the patients again. I've instructed the staff that one member of the team must be with him at all times. They are *never* to leave him alone in the room with anyone. But you know how it is, Thor. People get busy. Some of us are doing the job of two."

"Okay, Flo. Okay. Work with it. Just until I can come up with a solution. See if one of the techs can finish the procedure, then try to sober him up."

"A tech? You can't mean it, Thor."

"What's worse? A tech finishing the job or a drunk? I'll let you make that decision. No one knows the Brockston clinic like you."

"Stop trying to manipulate me."

"I'm not manipulating. I know how much you care about these girls. That's why you're the best OM I've got. I'm just trying to tell you that I know you'll make the right decision, so I'll leave it to you. And as far as Dr. Newly's concerned, just hang in there. I promise I'll speak to him."

"*Speak* to him? Thor, you've talked to him a dozen times already. The man's incorrigible. He's a menace. He's—"

"Flo, you know that with the new accounts we can't afford to get rid of anyone right now. We've got to work at maximum output or we could blow these contracts. You know how much good we can do, Flo? We're supplying some pretty important research teams. You know the cures they could find? The number of medical advances? I don't want to jeopardize that. Do you?"

"Well…" There was a long pause.

"Flo?"

"Okay, I'll try. But you better find a replacement for Newly soon, or so help me I'll quit!"

Thor laughed good-naturedly. "Now Flo, you know you don't mean that."

"Don't put me to the test."

Again Thor laughed, but this time it was dry, hollow. "Okay, okay, I *promise* I'll do something."

A brisk wind whipped through the open window of the car, and Maggie let it tangle her long red hair. She tilted her face, then closed her eyes. She felt the wind flutter her eyelashes and gently tickle her skin. It felt so good to be racing down the highway toward a destination that only God and Kirt knew. She breathed in the fragrant mountain air and glanced over at her friend behind the wheel. He almost made her feel carefree and young. Almost.

Maggie watched trees, packed like bristles in a brush, whiz by in a blur of green and brown. Here and there clusters of wildflowers grew along the roadway—a patchwork of blues, yellows, and reds. Everything shimmered and glowed and was wrapped in gold. Had there ever been a more beautiful spring? She didn't think so. Color everywhere, and smells of good rich earth—life bursting in all directions. The joy of resurrection. *The earth is the Lord's and the fullness thereof.*

So why didn't she feel that joy now? She rested her head against the seat back and let the weariness ooze from her. She hadn't realized how terribly tired she was. Was it because of the Life Center? No, that was God's burden. She could never carry it on her small shoulders. She loved her work, even though it often broke her heart, just like she knew it broke the heart of God. But it wasn't her work that was draining her. So why did she feel like a dried-up old woman? Because she was dried up—thirty-five and all dried up. But she had come to peace with that. Hadn't she? So why was it starting to bother her again? *After all these years?* She watched Kirt navigate a pothole and knew the answer. She hadn't counted on falling for someone like him.

"Don't you want to know where I'm taking you?" Kirt said with a smile.

"Nope."

"Trusting soul. I could be taking you to my office where a pile of dictation is waiting to be typed."

"Are you?"

"My secretary quit. Did I tell you? Said I worked her too hard. I'm really piled up now."

Maggie turned toward Kirt. "You should see the mess of paperwork on my desk. It's scary."

"I guess the rat incident really put you behind."

"Don't even mention that word! I have nightmares when I sleep. I see hundreds of them, crawling all over me."

Kirt laughed.

"It's not funny. The exterminator's been trying to clean them out for a week. Says the Center may have to stay closed for another five days. Now the Board of Health has gotten involved. They say they have to inspect the facility before it can reopen. I've tried to keep up, paperwork-wise, to hold my head above water. But it's hard. You know, I can still feel them crawling over my feet. In the office, I walk on tiptoe."

"So, this is a good break for you. Gives you a chance to learn how to walk again."

Maggie laughed. "Yes, I'm so glad you called. It's great you're in town now, when I can see you. If the Center hadn't been closed—"

"Why do you think I came?"

"To see your family? To check out how Fergason, Fergason, and Fergason is doing?"

Kirt shook his head.

The Chevy climbed upward, its nose pointing toward an emerald-colored mountain. Maggie could feel the car downshift to maintain the set speed of cruise control.

"I hope the rat incident won't discourage anyone from coming to the Center. Many of the ladies who just finished Project Rachael said they were planning to send a friend or family member."

"They'll come, Maggie, rats or no rats, because they have to. Because they hurt and they need to stop hurting."

"They really do hurt so badly, and it takes so long to recover. The pain's so deep only God's hand can touch it. I want so much to help them, to show them there's life after an abortion. But it's such a long, painful journey and takes so much patience."

"I know."

"What?" Maggie turned her full attention on Kirt.

"I know all about patience. I've been waiting for you, haven't I? Waiting for you to come to the end of your own journey."

Maggie's face reddened. "That was a long time ago. God has healed me."

"Has He?"

"Yes… What brought that on?"

"Look at us, Maggie. Really look at us. We're both alone, never married except to our jobs. And forty isn't that far away. Do you want to be this way forever? I don't. I love you. I've told you that before. And I want to marry you."

"I'm not ready for marriage."

"Why? Because you can't trust me? Because you don't believe I could love you just for you? That the other thing doesn't matter? That I don't care about that?"

"I've heard this before, from other women. Before the marriage, the man says he doesn't care that she can't have children, that they'll adopt. Then after the wedding, after the glow fades, the resentment settles in. It's not their fault. The men don't want to be resentful, but it happens when they realize they're never going to have that son or daughter they've always dreamed about. Then they begin thinking about that other man in their wife's life and the whole reason she can't have children in the first place. Kirt, I know you believe what you say, but you don't know how it is, and you just can't know how you'll really feel."

"And you're not willing to take a chance on me. Right?"

"You put things so harshly."

"Do you love me, Maggie?"

"I can't afford to."

The car had reached the summit and Kirt made a sharp right. Stately maple trees dotted the sides of the road, and between them were clusters of flowering azaleas—white, red, pink—all pointing the way to a large Tudor-style building overlooking a bluff. Maggie had only heard about this place. Her finances could never stretch to accommodate an outing here.

"The Eagles' Nest! Oh Kirt, I never dreamed…"

Kirt pulled the car into a spot not far from a maple that looked at least a hundred years old. Then he turned to face his companion.

"From the restaurant you'll be able to see the valley below. They say it's the best spot in the entire county. I think they're right. When I first saw it, it made me think of that Scripture in Isaiah: 'They that wait upon the Lord shall renew their strength, they shall mount up with wings as eagles.'" Maggie felt his hand gently cover hers. "But it takes courage to fly."

"Your mother did *what?*"

"She told your mom about Skip."

"I don't believe it!" Becky glared at Paula Manning. "Now I'm in for it. Thanks a lot!"

"How was she to know you hadn't told your parents?"

"Why couldn't *you* keep your mouth shut? Why did you have to tell her anything?" Becky shoved some books into her locker and slammed the door.

"She heard me talking to Kate about you and Skip, and then she asked me about it. What was I supposed to do, lie?"

"You've done it before."

"How was I supposed to know she'd bump into your mom at the food store? Besides, she likes Skip. I'm sure she didn't say anything bad about him."

"That's not the point," Becky said, walking down the hall so fast her friend had to jog to keep up. "Now they're going to ask me about him. And they're going to be really really mad! Especially my dad. He always overreacts to everything."

Becky felt Paula's hand on her arm pulling her to a stop. "Sooner or later you were going to have to face your dad. This isn't the dark ages. Girls and guys date. So what's the big deal?"

"My dad works very very hard. He's partners with a man he can't even stand."

"Yeah, so?"

"He's been doing all this for me. He's been saving for my college since I was two years old."

"Like I said, so what?"

Becky shook her head. "You don't understand anything, do you? I don't want to let him down."

"You're just afraid of him."

"No I'm not!"

"Yes you are. You're so afraid of him you'd rather sneak around than tell him the truth."

"I just don't want him to be disappointed...in me."

Becky wiggled into her jeans in the cramped backseat of the car. "I though we were going to have more time together tonight." There was a whine in her voice she hadn't noticed before.

"Sorry, hon, but I promised Tommy I'd go look at a car with him. The seller's only holding it one day and then Tommy's got to decide. He wants me to see it."

"What about his dad? Why can't he go check it out?"

"Not all dads are like yours, Becky. Some dads know *nothing* about cars. His dad's an accountant, for heaven's sake."

"Lately, you've been spending more time with Tommy than with me. Between basketball practice and—"

"C'mon, Becky, cut me some slack. I spend every spare minute with you. What do you want? Blood?"

Becky bit into her lip. She hated acting like this. So possessive, so desperate and pathetic. But she also hated Skip picking her up and having sex with her and then running off. Skip had been right about one thing. Sex had gotten better for her. Still…that nagging feeling persisted, that feeling of sadness, like every time they were together in an intimate way, she was losing part of herself, like she was being drained of something and didn't know how to get it back.

"I'm sorry," she found herself saying, her voice small, almost babyish.

Skip drew her to him and gave her a hug. "You know I'm crazy about you, Becky. I think of you all the time. And when I'm not with you, I feel sort of lonely…like I'm missing something. But I have to have a life too. I can't be with you every minute. Even if I wanted to. You can see that?"

Becky bit her lip again, trying not to cry. She'd just die if she started blubbering all over Skip's shoulder.

"But we've only been together two nights this week and both times…both times we just did it and then you had to go. How do you think that makes a girl feel?"

"It should make you feel good. I thought you liked it now. Didn't you tell me that? You weren't lying to me were you?"

Becky pushed him away, then opened the door of the Mazda to get out. "Don't be a jerk, and don't try to twist my words. You know perfectly well what I'm talking about. It makes me feel cheap. Like you're just using me."

"I've never forced you to do anything you didn't want to do, so don't go trying to give me a guilt trip. Okay? All I want to do is spend some time with Tommy. I did promise the guy. I mean, you're really getting *possessive.*"

Becky slammed the back door and got into the front. "Just take me back to Paula's."

Skip slid in beside her and started the engine. When it turned over, it sounded like a rocket taking off.

"Why don't you get that muffler fixed? The whole world knows we're here, for Pete's sake!"

Skip looked over at her and made a face. "So now you're tying to boss me around. Tommy said you'd do that, but I said no. No way! Not Becky. He said after a while, the girl thinks she owns you and gets mad every time you go anywhere or do anything without her. And then she starts trying to tell you what to do. But I didn't believe him. That's because I never believed you could be like that."


"What did you tell him?" Becky asked, pacing Paula's bedroom.

"I told him you had gone to the convenience store for soda."

"You think he believed you?"

"No."

"He *never* calls here. Mom must've told him about

Skip." Becky looked at her watch. "If I call now, he'll really know something's up. Nobody spends an hour buying soda. I'll just tell him I forgot to call back."

"You shouldn't have taken so long with Skip."

"I didn't take long." Becky watched Paula shove a textbook off her bed and plop down. "And keep Skip out of it!"

"You don't have to bite my head off just because you two had a fight."

"Who said we had a fight?"

"It won't be your last."

Becky could feel her face flush and hoped it wasn't as purple as the polish Paula was using to paint her nails.

"And pretty soon, when you're fighting all the time, that'll be the tip-off. That's when you'll know he's going to dump you, or maybe you'll dump him."

"You think I'm like you? That I go through guys like Kleenex? Skip and I aren't ever going to break up! Not *ever!*"

By the time Becky got home, she didn't want to talk to anyone. She still couldn't believe she had yelled so loud at Paula that even Mrs. Manning, who seldom bothered them, came running into the room frightened that someone was hurt. But how could Paula even think Skip would dump her?

She was irritated when she heard a knock on her bedroom door. She pulled open the door, almost savagely, and saw the worried face of her father.

"I want to talk to you."

Becky groaned and looked at her clock on the night-stand. The large green hands pointed to ten. She hadn't even started her homework.

Her father entered without an invitation and began pacing the room, not caring that he stepped on the tank tops and skirts and socks and jeans littering the floor.

"I know you weren't at Paula's tonight. And I know who you were with. Your mother and I know all about Skip Johnson."

Becky dropped to the bed as though she had been pushed, and sat limp at the edge.

"I'm really disappointed, Becky, disappointed and hurt that you couldn't come to your mother and me and tell us that you had a boyfriend. Disappointed and hurt that you felt a need to hide it."

Becky looked up at her father. She saw his gentle face streaked with worry and grief.

"Why did you lie to us?"

Becky opened her mouth, but nothing intelligent came out.

"Didn't you know that we would understand?"

"Well…I…"

"I can't have you lying to us."

Becky rose slowly. "You mean you don't mind that I have a boyfriend?"

"I knew sooner or later there'd be boys in your life. That's how it is. I just wish you'd told us."

"I'm sorry, Daddy. I know that was wrong. But Skip is so nice. I think you'll really like him. He's so nice and—"

"They're all nice, Becky. That's the sorry part of it."

"What do you mean?"

"I mean be careful, just be careful."

Several hours later, after Becky finished her homework, she crawled into bed with her diary. She wrote slowly, as though trying to separate her thoughts into logical segments that could be dissected and examined later.

*Dear Diary:*

*My parents know about Skip. And I'm not grounded or anything. I suppose I should be glad that everything is out in the open. But for some reason, I feel disappointed. Dad was really great about it. Said he understood. Said he expected it. Which makes me realize more than ever that guys know more about sex than girls do. The only thing he told me to do was to be careful, which he's said before, so I was right all along. Dads know the ropes and just want to protect their daughters from disease and pregnancy. They really understand the whole sex thing. I guess I should feel proud of my dad for being so modern and understanding. I guess I should be grateful he's not the old-fashioned buffoon I thought he was.*

*But I don't feel that way at all. Strange isn't it? I don't feel pride or gratitude or even relief. I feel…I feel sort of disappointed. I feel…well, I feel angry and almost like I don't like my dad very much right now. Silly isn't it? Oh, why am I so silly? I'm going to college soon. How can someone so confused be going to college? I have to get my head on straight. I always thought I was so mature. Especially when compared to Paula or Kate or anyone of the other guys. But now I'm not so sure. I wish my daddy had been mad or told me something else, or…I don't know what I wish.*

4

DR. THOR EMERSON WALKED in circles cursing into the handheld phone.

"You better believe I'm serious! You're fired! This is the second time in as many weeks that the temperature has dropped in the tank. I warned you last time. I told you the female is pregnant and the water must be a constant seventy-eight degrees."

He stopped pacing and looked into the bubbling tank. Ribbons of seaweed swayed like drunken sailors around the sunken ship. The pair of Clowns swam among them, seemingly unaware of any temperature problem.

"How far off is it?"

"Right now it's reading seventy-seven point six!"

"I swear, Dr. Emerson, I adjusted the heater before I left. That thermostat read seventy-eight degrees on the nose. Maybe it's broken."

Thor thought a moment. "If I change it and this happens again, you're out. Understand?"

"Yes…absolutely. Thank you, Dr. Emerson."

Thor saw the light flashing on the intercom. Without another word, he hung up, then punched the intercom button.

"What is it, Eleanor?"

"Flo Gardner on the phone, and she's very upset."

Thor groaned. *Now what?* "Okay, Eleanor, put her through… Flo? How's my favorite OM?"

"I'd be a lot better if *they* weren't here. They're all over, Thor, poking into everything. I told you this would happen. I told you that if you didn't get rid of—"

"*Who's* there, Flo? Just calm down and tell me what's going on."

"The State Health Department, that's who! They're going over the place with white gloves. Why didn't you tell me they were coming? You've always let me know ahead of time, so I could prepare."

"I didn't know." With an almost savage jerk of the wrist, Thor picked up his Mont Blanc and began writing *Newly* over and over down the page of his planner.

"We're really backed up today and haven't been, well… we haven't been exactly following the manual, if you know what I mean."

"Any feedback? Anyone say anything?"

"Plenty, and none of it good. What do they expect? We can only do so much. How do they expect us to help these girls when there's so many of them *and* to follow the book? They don't understand the strain this clinic is under. They want everything to be paint-by-number. There's only so much I can do with what I've got to work with. You know how Dr. Newly operates, no matter what I tell him about changing linens and giving us time to sterilize the instruments. I've told you about this, I've warned—"

"What exactly are they saying, Flo?" Thor began crossing out Newly's name, one by one.

"They said they're fining us and giving us a warning to come up to standard or cease all operating room procedures."

Thor cursed into the phone. *Why didn't the Health Department warn me about this?*

"Thor, did you hear what I said? They're fining us and warning we must—"

"I heard, Flo. Don't worry. I'll handle everything. You just keep a lid on things. Keep the customers from panicking and going elsewhere, and keep Dr. Newly under control."

"But what are we going to do? How are we going to cope with—"

"I said I'll handle it. You just get back to your job. I'm counting on you to keep things together until I can come up with a solution."

After he hung up, Thor walked over to his fish tank to recheck the temperature. Seventy-seven point six degrees. It had to be the thermostat because he had set it for eighty an hour ago and the temperature hadn't budged one degree. He moved the large Ficus away from the window and noticed the dust on the leaves. *I'll have to notify the cleaning woman about that.* Then he studied the sunlight that streamed through the window. Yes, that was better. The added sun would help warm the water. Tonight, he'd pick up that deluxe heater on the way home.

He began walking around the room. A massive mahogany desk was against the far wall. On the opposite wall was a leather couch and chair. The fish tank and Ficus stood against the window wall. The office was of considerable size, but the large furniture left floor space only in the center of the room. Thor paced on the plush carpeting, leaving a zigzag of footprints.

His office was located in the prestigious Rolston building in downtown Brockston. His command center, he called it, and from it he oversaw his six abortion clinics spread over a radius of a hundred miles. He was proud of what he had built. But lately, he hated the turn his life was taking. He looked at his prints on the carpet. He was like a dog chasing his tail—going nowhere. *And I had better change things fast.*


When Maggie looked up and saw the tall lean figure in the doorway, her heart leaped.

"Kirt! I hardly recognized you."

Kirt laughed and threw back his head. He was dressed in khakis and a pale yellow cardigan. He had never come here before dressed in anything but a suit. He appeared boyish, carefree. Maggie watched him brush back his windswept hair with one hand. In the other, he held a bouquet of red roses.

"I see by the waiting room that the rats didn't discourage anyone."

"Can you believe it? More than fifty women have come

through those doors in less than a week."

Kirt pulled out one rose from the bouquet and handed it to her. "Then I think you might need this."

Maggie buried her nose in the flower. "Thank you," she said, breathing deeply and enjoying the fragrance.

"The rest I'll put in a vase if you have one."

Maggie walked to one of the cabinets and pulled open the door. "What are you doing here?"

"I've decided to take a few days off."

"Didn't you just have a few days? It's a good thing you have daddy's law firm to fall back on, in case you get fired from this job."

Kirt laughed, then slipped beside her and began rummaging in the cabinet beneath the bookshelves. He pulled out a green-tinted glass vase and shoved the roses into it.

"These cabinets look a lot like mine. Maybe this weekend you can come over to my apartment and help me clean them out?"

Maggie laughed. "Don't hold your breath. Besides, you said you were going to hire someone to keep your apartment clean."

"It doesn't fit into my budget. An assemblyman's salary is pretty dismal."

"Well, if you'd stop taking me to places like the Eagles' Nest and stop buying me flowers, maybe you could afford a cleaning lady."

"Nope. This is more fun."

Maggie went to the watercooler, filled a paper cup, then poured it into the vase. She did this five times before the vase was filled. "At least when the session's over, you'll only have one apartment to support. And by then, your dad and brother will probably give you a nice raise because they'll be so happy to have you back."

"They won't be the only ones, I hope."

Maggie smiled and began arranging the flowers in the vase.

"Did the police ever catch the boys who delivered the rats?"

"No, and I don't think there's much chance of that happening," Maggie said. "No one saw anything. At least, no one's talking."

Kirt walked over to her desk and glanced down at an article cut from a newspaper. He read it quickly. "So, Canon Edwards is getting out of jail." He looked anxiously at Maggie. "Can you handle him?"

"I don't think he'll come around. But if he does, yes, I can handle him. I've done it before."

Kirt nodded. "They say you were the only one who could talk to him after his wife died."

Maggie's finger brushed against a thorn and she flinched. "Canon went crazy after Patsy's death. Maybe if he hadn't been the one to find her like that, maybe if someone else had gotten to her first. But he didn't let too many people into his circle after that."

"I heard that he wrote *liar* all over the house with her blood. Is that true?"

"They found him on the floor next to her, holding her in his arms, blood everywhere. He just held her...crying. Tooley said he'd never seen so much blood." Maggie shook her head. "It must've been awful. But it was only after the police took Patsy's body away that he began dipping his fingers into the puddles and writing everywhere."

"Why? Did he ever tell you?"

"He said they were all liars, the doctors and nurses at the clinic. That they had lied to Patsy...to him. They told them abortion was a simple procedure, nothing to worry about. Canon swears he'd never have encouraged Patsy to abort if he'd known. He blamed himself...still does. Even men can have post-abortion syndrome."

Kirt's eyebrows arched. "A lot of people say he's always been dangerous, that he's always had a screw loose."

Maggie shrugged. "Even in grade school he was different...odd...maybe a little unstable. I guess he's always marched to a different drummer."

"I just don't want him to hurt you—to hurt the clinic. I mean, everyone thinks he's a pro-lifer."

"Canon is driven by his personal demons, not by the pro-life movement."

"That may be true, but they lump us all together."

Maggie put her face close to the arrangement and inhaled. "Let me handle Canon." When she looked up, there was a twinkle in her eyes. "Thank you for the beautiful flowers." She began fussing with the vase again, knowing he was watching. She wondered if he was thinking about their last time together, after he had taken her home from the Eagles' Nest and she had kissed him for the very first time. Not a passionate kiss, but short and sweet, and with something like a promise or a hope in it. But when she looked up, she could see it was not kisses he was thinking about. She watched him finger the newspaper clipping.

"I've tried to tell you before, Maggie, that I think Thor Emerson is connected, that he has mob connections. Did you ever think that maybe he's the one responsible for the rats? I mean, you've been pretty hard on him, you and your picketers." He put up his hand to stop her from speaking. "I know they aren't *your* picketers, but in his mind you're all one and the same. You and the Life Center represent, at the very least, a thorn in the side, and at the most, an outright threat. I've done what you've asked. The Health Department will and probably already has inspected his clinics, starting with the one in Brockston. But Maggie, be aware that Emerson is not a man who can be pushed. He'll fight back. If he begins to think you're a menace, he could get rough. Maybe even do something crazy like send you boxes of rats."

Maggie began to laugh. "And I always thought you were so logical."

"What?"

"Does it sound rational that a wealthy abortionist would hire a mobster who then hires two teenage boys to deliver boxes of rats to us? We're just a small outfit, a *little* center. I'm more inclined to believe it was the angry boyfriend of a girl being counseled here. When you're dealing with abortion, there's all kinds of backlash."

"Maybe…but consider taking some—"

The phone rang. Maggie made a mock sigh of relief, like the phone had spared her his lecture, and picked it up.

"Maggie Singer?" It was a strange, muffled voice.

"Yes."

"Did you like my gift?"

"What gift?"

"Because if you did, I can send you more. I got an endless supply."

"Who is this?"

"What's wrong?" Kirt mouthed.

Maggie shook her head and waved him off. "Who is
this?" she repeated.

"I'm just a friend with some friendly advice. Don't make
trouble. It ain't healthy. You hear?"

"What kind of trouble? What are you talking about?"

"Look out your window."

Maggie moved toward the window and peeked out into
the side alley. She looked up and down, but saw no one.
Then she noticed a large cardboard box under her window.
The top was open and inside there appeared to be a pile of
black fur. She strained to see through the screen and studied the box for several seconds, then gasped. The box was
filled with rats, but this time they were all dead.

"The first time we was playing with you. This time we
ain't playing."

"Who is this? What do you want?"

The phone went dead, and Maggie, with trembling
hand, hung up. Kirt gently put his arms around her.

"Was this a threat, Maggie? Did someone threaten you?"

Maggie nodded, allowing him to hold her. "A strange
sounding man. He said he wasn't playing with me."

"What does he want? Did he say?"

"No."

"But you know, don't you Maggie?"

Maggie separated herself from Kirt. "Yes," she whispered,

then moved to her desk and pulled two papers from under the paperweight. She handed them to her friend, and his face became hard with anger. All manner of obscene words were pasted on the first paper and at the very bottom, one sentence: "Get out of town." The next page was filled with pictures of knives, guns, nooses, and words cut out to form two sentences: "You're not wanted here. Close your Center and leave."

"Why didn't you tell me about this?"

Maggie shrugged. "When I got the first one, I didn't think much about it. Like I told you, boyfriends can get bizarre sometimes when their girlfriends get talked out of an abortion. When I got the second one, I took it more seriously, but didn't really know what I should do."

"You should've told me, and then gone to the police."

"I thought of that. But I didn't want to worry you and didn't want bad publicity for the Center."

"And after the rats, Maggie, why didn't you go then?"

"I...I don't know. I was still thinking...hoping it was a teenage prank."

"Well, we're going to the police right now, both of us. We'll show them these letters and tell them about that box under your window. But we have one thing to do first." Kirt put both hands on her shoulders and began praying for protection and wisdom and guidance.


Skip pulled his black Mazda into a secluded spot, far from the other spots in Lover's Cove. It was "their spot." Skip had found it after Becky pleaded for more privacy. And it was perfect—a path big enough for only one car to squeeze through and surrounded by thick vegetation.

He turned to her and smiled. "Gosh, I wish we had the whole night together, like we used to. Things seem so hectic now, with basketball and term papers and all. Seems like we hardly ever have time to spend together anymore."

Becky nodded. He really was so sweet.

"You coming to the game?"

Becky nodded again.

"After the game, you want to go out with the guys? Hopefully it'll be a victory celebration. We've just got to win. Can't let this team beat us three years in a row. I think we have a real chance too. Their leading scorer is injured. And Tommy's hot, really hot. Yesterday at practice, he was swishing threes all over the court. He's the only one who—"

"We haven't gone out in ages. It would be nice."

Skip made a face. "You know how busy I've been, Becky. I've had to work really hard to pull up my grades, otherwise I can forget the basketball scholarship. And Tommy's had a lot of problems with his dad. Should I tell him he can't count on me when—"

"I'm not complaining, Skip. I just stated a fact."

"We're not going to fight about this again, are we?"

"Not unless you want to make a fight out of it."

"Okay, let's just forget it. Okay?" Skip adjusted his legs. "Have you heard from Georgetown?"

Becky shook her head. "No, still wait-listed."

"Bummer. But, hey, you have three other colleges to choose from. At least you're set. If I don't bring up my average, well...you know I can't go to college unless I get this free ride. I need this scholarship."

"Anything I can help you with?"

"Not unless you want to write my term papers. Gosh, I'm really behind in one of them. You don't think—"

"No. Don't even say it. Cecil Gray just got expelled for selling term papers."

"I feel so *pressured!* I can hardly wait for this year to be over. I wish I were smart like you, Becky. Everything comes so easy for you. You don't have to work at things like I do." Skip turned to the side window and sulked for a few seconds. Then he shoved his hand in his front pocket. "I gotta go soon. I don't want to rush, but I promised coach."

Becky opened the door to move to the backseat. She noticed Skip frantically jamming his hand into one pocket after another. Then he cursed.

"I don't believe it! I don't believe how stupid I am. I left them in my other pants!"

Becky closed the door. "All right, maybe we'll sneak back later."

"Nothing will happen, Becky. I promise. Trust me."

"Are you insane? You think I'm going to have sex without a condom?"

Skip made a frantic lunge toward the glove compartment and rummaged through it. In a matter of minutes he pulled out a small packet and smiled. "I almost forgot about this. Tommy told me to always keep an emergency stash."


Thor had been at the Brockston clinic for over an hour on a dual mission. He wanted to make certain his staff was cooperating with the new tech from Second Chance. He also wanted to check out the new tech himself. He liked the way Adam Bender operated. Thor had already watched Adam fill four purchase orders, mostly livers from fetal cadavers of twelve-weeks gestations, which Adam had carefully submerged in 4 percent paraformaldehyde with a cacodylate buffer, and several pair of eyes, which were safely in OPTISOL. He only had this one left, a twenty-three-week fetus, from which he was to extract both femurs and tibias, the spleen and thymus. Thor decided to watch the last harvest then head back to his office.

Just as Adam raised his scalpel, Thor saw the small body in the metal pan move.

"What the…hey…this fetus is alive!" Adam said.

Immediately there was a flurry of activity. A white-clad attendant and another technician came over and looked.

"The dreaded complication," the attendant whispered and walked away.

Thor continued watching the small body squirm in the pan and cursed.

"I don't do this!" Adam said as the baby gasped for air. "I don't work on live babies!"

The tech and attendant had disappeared, and Thor tried leading Adam away from the table. But Adam only became more anxious.

"Somebody! Come here and help this…this baby!"

Suddenly Dr. Newly stood beside them. "Keep him quiet. He's alarming the patients."

"You brought me a live baby!"

"Just calm down," Thor said and pulled on Adam's arm, but he wouldn't budge.

"That baby's alive!"

"It's a good specimen," Dr. Newly said. "It's what you needed, a twenty-three-weeker. What's the problem?"

Thor glared at Newly. "You're not helping any."

Adam backed away from the large metal table. "For heaven's sake, man, can't you see it's moving!"

Dr. Newly bent closer to the pan. "So it is." He went to the linen closet, pulled out several large terrycloth towels, then dropped them on top of the pan. "But not for long," he said and walked out. Adam scrambled behind him.

Thor reached for the towels, then stopped and also fled the room. By the time he got to the bathroom, Adam was kneeling over the toilet, throwing up. Thor helped him to his feet, then brought him over to the sink.

"You're a pro," Thor said as Adam splashed water on his face. "You've got to act like one. You know in our business this happens sometimes. It's part of the job."

Adam dried his face and said nothing. Thor followed him back to the specimen room and watched Adam collect his containers. He never looked at the towel-covered pan.

"Go have a cup of coffee and settle down."

Adam breezed by him and out the room.

"Will you settle down? Just go and…" Thor followed Adam past Flo's office and indicated with a jerk of his head for Flo to come out. They stopped Adam at the front door.

"Are you all right?" Flo asked Adam, but her eyes were riveted on Thor.

Adam Bender turned toward the concerned face framed by cotton-ball-white hair.

"What's wrong?" she said.

Adam shook his head. Already some of the ladies in the waiting room were staring. Thor gestured for them to go out the front door. When they did they saw a large group of people on the sidewalk. Many of them held posters of bloody babies. Others stood quietly praying. Thor positioned himself between them and Adam.

"He's crazy! He's absolutely crazy! Somebody should do something about him," Adam blurted.

Flo groaned. "Dr. Newly? Tell me it's not Dr. Newly."

"He killed…he killed a baby! I saw him. He just killed it, just threw some towels over it and…killed it."

Thor looked around nervously. "Lower your voice." Then he turned to Flo. "A dreaded complication."

*"What?"*

"You're not going to call the police, are you?" Thor asked.

Adam gave him a strange look. "You want to protect him?"

"No, just the clinic. I want Newly out, but I don't want to hurt the clinic doing it."

"A thing like this could really damage us." Flo moved closer to Adam, her hand resting on his shoulder.

Adam cursed under his breath. "I'm a little disappointed, Flo. I thought you, at least, were for the girls, on their side."

"I am. But how can we help them if we're closed?"

"Go home and relax. Give yourself a chance to calm down. You'll see there's nothing to be gained by calling the police," Thor said.

Adam hesitated. "I'll think about it." Then he flew

down the stairs, clutching his specimens and moving in a wide arc around the picketers.

Maggie raced down the hall of her apartment and opened the front door. She shoved the envelope with her rent payment into the small black mailbox over the doorbell, then rummaged in her purse for the car keys. She seldom got to the Center after eight, and it was already eight-thirty. She had stayed out late with Kirt, much later than she had planned. Three-thirty and they were still on the park bench talking. He was so easy to talk to, and they had so much to talk about.

She knew she was going to be dragging all day. She smiled. It was worth it. If the truth were known, she would have sat on that bench until morning. But it was Kirt, the practical one, who insisted on bringing her home.

She walked briskly down the sidewalk and was about to turn the corner into the parking lot when she noticed a black BMW slowing beside her. When she spun around, the BMW stopped and the door opened. A slender, dark-haired woman stepped out.

"I'm sorry. I didn't mean to frighten you," the woman said. "But I waited for you last night. I waited until midnight, then I left. I'm sorry. But I really need to talk. Should I make an appointment? I don't know what to do. I just need to talk...to you."

Maggie noticed the expensive leather shoes, the two heavy gold bracelets, the large diamond ring. "Do I know you?"

The woman shook her head. "I…I need to talk. Will you give me a little of your time?"

Maggie moved closer. "Do you know me?"

The woman nodded. "You're Maggie Singer, director of the Life Center."

Maggie smiled and reached for her hand. "Why don't you follow me to the Center? I'll fix you some coffee and we'll talk."

"No, not the Center. I couldn't go there. Please, someplace else. Anyplace you say, but not the Center."

Maggie looked at her watch, then into the woman's eyes. "Okay," she said with a sigh. "Okay, we can go to my place. It's right back there."

Maggie retraced her steps to the apartment, quietly praying all the way. By the time she inserted the key into the door, she felt the peace of God fill her. She ushered the stranger into her small kitchen and invited her to take a seat. "Coffee or tea?"

"No…nothing. I'm sorry to put you out, really. I'm sorry for the inconvenience."

Maggie began brewing coffee, making it extra strong. Finally she sat down next to her guest.

"I'm Teresa," the stranger said slowly. "Teresa Emerson."

"Dr. Emerson's wife?"

Teresa nodded. "I've been debating for days whether to come here or not. I feel really silly, embarrassed. You must think I'm a mad woman."

"What's wrong?"

"I'm having trouble sleeping. All I do is think. And the questions—I can't get the questions out of my head. It's hard when you've been married for fourteen years and then it's over. It's like you're not all there. I mean you're there, but only partly there. Am I making any sense?"

Maggie shook her head.

"I know. I'm babbling. I'm sorry. I'm not myself. It's shattering to leave someone...someone you love."

"You've left your husband?"

"I had to. I didn't want to. You understand?"

Maggie nodded.

"But now I'm so messed up. I just can't stop thinking about him. Not that I could do anything for him. I can't help him. I can barely help myself. That's the problem. I need to get my life back."

"How can I help?"

"I have so many questions. And they're all running into each other. Someone I know said you might be able to answer them."

"What questions?"

"This friend read an article somewhere, an article about abortion...actually about abortion providers. She said that abortion hurts them. I mean does things to them. I mean..."

Maggie placed her hand over Teresa's. "Your friend was right."

"I hope you're a person who can be trusted...who doesn't say things...I mean tells..."

"Whatever you say here is confidential. I'll not tell anyone."

"It's Thor, my husband. He's so unhappy. I want to know it's not because of me. I need to know...because he has other women. I'm sure I didn't drive him away. But I can't really be sure, can I? He's so unhappy. He works too hard, always trying to prove himself, but then he gambles so much of it away. It's doesn't make sense, does it? And I so desperately need it to make sense. Sometimes I think I understand. I think I've got it all figured out and then it gets all jumbled in my head and I get confused and then I start thinking it's all my fault and then..."

Maggie squeezed Teresa's hand. *My grief is beyond healing; my heart is broken. Listen to the weeping of my people; it can be heard all across the land.* "Abortion affects everyone involved. Those who get them and their families; those who provide them and their families."

Teresa dabbed her eyes with her fingers. "Yes, that's what my friend was saying." Maggie pulled out a napkin from the blue ceramic holder on the table and handed it to her. "What...what are some of the things that happen?"

"If you want, I have a book you can borrow that will explain everything I'm telling you, but in greater detail. Generally speaking, most abortion providers are unhappy. They suffer from anger, depression, fatigue, low self-esteem."

Teresa nodded. "Thor is angry all the time. And he's afraid. Afraid he'll end up a failure like all the other Brockstons. He's always had that fear. Even before he started doing abortions. We used to talk about it all the time. We used to talk...a lot. Before...we talked a lot."

"Maybe his insecurity paved the way. The desire for control and money, the desire to succeed, all compelling forces that could've made his decision to become an abortionist easier."

"I tried to talk him out of it. I wanted him to go into general practice. Open a little office somewhere. But he told me my thinking was too small. He wanted to open up a chain." Teresa laughed sadly. "He always did love business more than medicine."

"Does he drink?"

Teresa shook her head. "No. Why?"

"Because compulsive behavior is common: drinking, drugging, gambling."

"He gambles. A lot. He owes so much money to Lou—he owes a lot of money. But I never made the connection. I never thought there was one."

"These are deeply damaged people, Teresa. Hurting people who are desperate to forget, to erase from their memory the reality of what they're doing. Sometimes they subconsciously want to destroy themselves, so they choose drugs or alcohol or gambling. And some of them choose suicide."

"Suicide?" Teresa's eyes grew large. "I never thought...I never considered Thor capable of suicide."

"All destructive behavior is a form of suicide."

"I've tried to help him, tried to talk to him."

"Is he difficult to talk to?"

"Very."

"Maybe he's closed down already. In time, they do. They become desensitized, dehumanized, and finally close down emotionally."

"He closed down to Eric long ago."

"Eric?"

"Our son. He's in boarding school." Maggie noticed the

tender look on Teresa's face. "Thor never goes to see him. He used to. But not now. It's been...years...at least three years since Thor went to Oxlee. And he allows Eric to come home only for holidays, the major ones like Christmas and Easter. I've begged him...but only the major holidays. It's like he can't stand the sight of his own child."

"Does Thor have nightmares?"

"No, I don't think so."

"Many of them do. Many of them say they see babies and blood in their sleep. Many have insomnia because of it."

"No. I don't think so, not Thor."

Maggie rose. The coffee was finally ready. She poured herself a cup, leaving out the customary cream. "You sure you don't want some?"

Teresa shook her head. "I still don't understand why he cheats. And it seems like he wants me to know, that he wants to get caught. Like he's flaunting it in my face. Sometimes... sometimes they even call the house..." Teresa's voice broke.

Maggie sat down next to her. "Often abortionists become hostile and resentful toward their patients. They're angry with them. They blame the women who come to them for making them do the abortion, for getting pregnant in the first place. Some even develop a deep disrespect and hatred for women."

"Yes, I think that's happened to Thor. The way he talks, yes, sometimes I think he dislikes...hates his patients. I've told him so. But what does that have to do with him having so many affairs?"

"Some abortionists will go out of their way to degrade their patients—to punish them, in a sense. Inappropriate speech, sexual assault, molestation, and even rape at abortion clinics are not uncommon, and all are punitive actions by the abortionist or his staff. This desire to degrade women can spill over into their personal lives. Some abuse their wives, some cheat."

Teresa began to cry. "It hurts so much. I know it shouldn't anymore, but it does."

Maggie leaned over and embraced her. "I know. I'm sorry."

"He just doesn't see it. I've talked to him a thousand times about it, but he just doesn't understand."

"They rationalize, Teresa." Maggie released her. "They become masters at rationalization."

"How you must hate him. How you must hate all of them…the providers. They call you such horrible names, say such awful things."

"I don't hate your husband or any of them. I just hate what they do."

"I don't believe you." Teresa stared at Maggie for a long time. "Maybe…maybe you are telling the truth about the hating part. But right now, I think I hate you, just a little. Because you and the others, the other pro-lifers, you understand what's going on, what happens to the doctors and staff…how they suffer…how they make their families suffer, and yet you never tried to help Thor. You never tried to help, did you?"

Maggie nodded. "Yes. Every day when I pray for him, when I ask God to show your husband the truth about what he's doing, to show your husband that he was not made for this kind of life, for such an ignoble purpose."

Teresa reached over to the napkin holder and pulled out another one and began dabbing her eyes. "Can God…can God ever forgive someone like Thor?"

"Yes. If Thor wants forgiveness. Nothing is impossible for God."

"I'm not very religious. I had some church when I was young, but it didn't really stick. I never thought it was important. Now…well, maybe I'd like to try it again."

"Then meet me here Sunday morning, ten to nine, and I'll take you to mine. It's a little Baptist church around the corner. It has a wonderful pastor, and the people—you'll love them."

"You mean it?"

Maggie smiled. "I never say things I don't mean."

"Adam's pretty shaken, Thor. And he's the best in the business. I've given you the best because I know how big and how important this contract is to both of us. But he says he doesn't want to go back to your Brockston clinic. Now what can be done?"

Thor Emerson took a deep breath. "Is he going to the police?"

Carl Langley laughed into the phone. "I've discouraged that. Persuaded him it wasn't the best course of action. Not good for him, not good for us. So no need to worry there. But what you should worry about is getting your facility under control. If my techs are so rattled they can't do their work, how's that going to be good for business? You know what I mean? You need to ensure that this kind of thing doesn't happen again. Instruct your staff to take care of all complications prior to delivering the specimens to my techs. It shouldn't be that difficult, Thor, to establish procedure. And if you have any loose guns on deck, it would be wise to rid yourself of them."

"You mean Newly?"

"You know what they say about bad apples infecting the bunch. Rotten things smell; smells attract attention."

"Well...I'll try—"

"And one more thing. It's bad business, Thor, to get fined by the Health Department. Makes clients nervous. Makes them think you're running a slipshod outfit, unable to provide quality specimens."

Thor stopped his pacing and sat down on the leather sofa. Suddenly he felt very tired. "Carl, I can make things right. You're not to worry."

"Remember what I said at the onset? Once I pull a contract, it stays pulled."

"No need for that kind of talk. I'll straighten everything out. You'll see."


After he hung up, Thor went to his desk, opened the top drawer, and removed a folded newspaper article with the headline "Local Abortion Clinic Bomber Canon Edwards to be Released from Jail." He had torn it out on some whim, some gut feeling that this information might prove useful. Thor fingered the edges of the paper and thought again about a plan he had once discarded as unattractive.

# 5

BECKY TAYLOR CREPT UP the stairs clutching a Greenbrier Pharmacy bag, which she tried to keep hidden. She had spent the better part of her Saturday morning driving the seventy miles back and forth to Greenbrier so that no one she knew would see her buy this. When she heard the clanking of dishes in the kitchen, she paused, then tiptoed to her bedroom and closed the door. She tore the blue and white box from the plastic bag and shoved it under a pile of clothes on the floor. Then she opened her door, very quietly, and slipped into the bathroom. From a pink floral dispenser mounted on the wall, she pulled out a small paper cup.

Moments later, Becky crept from the bathroom, carrying the cup filled with urine. Once inside her bedroom, she retrieved the box from under her clothes, opened it, and pulled out the plastic tester. A small cup fell out with it. With a shaky hand, she deposited three drops of urine into the sample window, then waited. One minute, two minutes. It felt like an eternity. Three minutes. She paced the room, not caring that she stepped all over clothes and shoes. She watched the pulsing second hand of the Bulova on her nightstand. Five minutes. She closed her eyes and held her breath, afraid to look at the plastic container, afraid of what it would tell her. Another full minute passed with Becky standing in the middle of her room, eyes shut tight.

Finally, she opened them and stared at the tester. A red stripe cut across the sample window. Without knowing how she got there, Becky found herself on the floor weeping into a pile of dirty clothes. How could this happen? They had used protection. She picked up her head and looked at the tester again, hoping, praying that she had misread it. But the color had not changed.

Suddenly, she heard her mother's voice. "Becky. Becky!" Footsteps were coming her way. *Not now. Oh please not now!* She threw some clothes over the pregnancy kit, then buried her face under the bed just as her bedroom door opened.

"Becky, I've been calling you."

Becky continued to pretend to look for something.

"Get up, Becky. I have something for you. A letter from *Georgetown.*"

Becky could hear the excitement in her mother's voice. Quickly, she wiped her eyes, then grabbed a shoe she had not seen in months and pulled it and herself out from under the bed. She remained kneeling on the floor.

Nancy Taylor waved the envelope in Becky's face. "This is it. The one you've been waiting for. Open it. I can't believe how nervous I am. "

Becky took the envelope, ripped it, and pulled out a letter. Her eyes scanned the page until they hit the word *accepted,* then she handed it to her mother.

"Oh Becky! I knew you could do it. Wait till your father hears, he's going to be overjoyed. This is the day we've both dreamed about. You're the first Taylor to ever go to college. But *Georgetown*...I'm so proud."

Becky looked down at the one shoe still sitting in her lap and squeezed her eyes closed. If only her mother would go away. She didn't know how much longer she could keep herself together.

Nancy Taylor bent over and gave her daughter a hug. "You've always been my delight."

Becky began to sob.

Her mother bent down and put her arms around her. "I had no idea how stressed this was making you. I wish I had known. I would've told you that no matter what college you went to, it would've been all right with your father and me. It didn't have to be Georgetown. I'm sorry if I...if we made you feel so pressured."

Becky only sobbed harder, and Nancy pulled her daughter's hands away from her face.

"What is it? What's the matter?" Nancy was on the floor, now, beside her daughter, and when Becky wouldn't look at her, she forcibly lifted Becky's chin. *"What is it?"*

Becky just shook her head.

For a long moment the mother's eyes bore into her daughter's.

"No, oh no, no. Don't tell me you're...?" Color drained from her mother's face.

"What should I do, Mommy? What am I going to do?"

Nancy Taylor had already risen to her feet, had begun backing away. Her right hand was behind her feeling for the doorknob. "I'll discuss this with your father," she said in a near whisper. "We'll come up with some...thing." Her voice trailed off as the door closed. Then all Becky could hear was the sound of her own sobs.

Around 2:00 A.M. Maggie had awoken with a pressing desire to pray for Teresa Emerson. So when the doorbell rang at 8:15 the next morning, Maggie wasn't surprised to see a timid but smiling Mrs. Emerson at her front door.

"I've decided to take you up on your offer for church. I hope you don't mind."

Maggie returned the smile, then invited her in. "I'm thrilled you came. We have a little time yet, so how about some coffee?"

Teresa laughed nervously. "I guess I am a little early. I just didn't want to make you late...or miss you."

Maggie led her guest into the kitchen, poured freshly brewed coffee into two cups, and handed one to Teresa.

"I read that book you gave me, *The Centurion's Pathway*. I don't understand it all, but I see so much of Thor in it, so much of myself. I never realized how big a part I played, just by not speaking up. How I...how I..."

"Facilitated?"

Teresa nodded. "I've spent a lot of time soul-searching. I must tell you, I don't accept all of what it says, but I'd like to find peace, to put an end to this turmoil. To put it behind me. I think maybe if I stick with it and keep going over the steps in the book, then maybe…maybe I can heal."

"I'm sure of it," Maggie said, taking a sip of her coffee. *Please God, touch Teresa this morning.*

Throughout the service Maggie watched Teresa out of the corner of her eye. And every time she did, she felt God reminding her that it was *not by might, nor by power, but by my Spirit.* Her prayers increased in fervor. *Please God, don't let Teresa leave the same way she came. Please help her, comfort her, give her peace. Bring her into the saving knowledge of Jesus.* But the more Maggie prayed, the more restless and uncomfortable Teresa seemed.

The choir led the congregation in singing "Amazing Grace," "Rock of Ages," then "Our God Reigns." When they finished, Pastor Summer stepped behind the podium. "Two men," he said in his clear voice, "come into church to pray. One man sits upright in the pew, thinking about how good he was all week, how he tried to do everything right, how all his problems and troubles were because of someone else. The other man, the man next to him, barely looks up, but keeps his head down, wishing he were better, knowing how far short of God's standards he has fallen.

"There are people right here, right now, that fit these descriptions. People who are burdened by their sin and know of no way out, and others burdened by their pride and looking for no way out. But both are burdened and both lack peace. Both need a healing touch. Both need to come to the feet of the One who died for them, who freely gave Himself for them. *Both need Jesus.*"

Maggie watched Teresa begin to rise, then sit back down. *Is she leaving, Lord?*

"'For it is by grace you have been saved, through faith—and this not from yourselves, it is the gift of God—not by works, so that no one can boast.'"

Maggie reached for Teresa's hand, but she pulled away.

"I feel the Lord wants me to open up the altar early today. I believe He wants us all to spend time around it, on our knees. Don't leave here burdened by sin or burdened by pride. Jesus said, 'Come to me, all you who are weary and burdened, and I will give you rest.'"

Teresa shot up from her seat and stepped into the aisle. But instead of running out the front door, as Maggie expected, she ran up to the altar, dropped to her knees, and began to weep.


Sounds of a ball hitting the side of the brick building floated through the slightly open window of Maggie's office. From time to time, she'd put her pen down and just listen to the laughter of the children, their feet slapping against the asphalt alley. The kids had come straight from school and had been playing stickball for hours.

She listened as one boy accused another of cheating, then held her breath waiting for a fight. She peeked out the window and watched as the boys settled their differences. One bloody nose and it was all over. Soon, Maggie heard the whack-thump-whack of the ball and once again she picked up her pen.

She had been working on her Bible study for the next Project Rachael group, but she kept allowing herself to be distracted by the children outside. She felt the familiar stab. No children of her own. *You'll never have children of your own.*

She hated when she got stuck in that rut, the wheels of her mind spinning and spinning but going nowhere. *Wallowing in self-pity again, Maggie? Yes, it just isn't fair.* She had been through this with God a thousand times. And lately, she was having this argument with Him more frequently. Not an argument, but a complaint. She had been complaining and whining about it a lot lately.

Why couldn't she let it go? Kirt said it didn't matter. But she knew differently. She had seen it before. In the end it always mattered. It wasn't his fault that he couldn't see it. It would be up to her to be the strong one, to maintain the balance in their friendship and keep it from teetering over into love. But even now, she knew it already had. *It just isn't fair.*

When she looked up, she was startled to see a large man scowling down at her. He had crept in so quietly she hadn't noticed. Where was Agnes? How had he slipped past the receptionist? Maggie began to pray silently.

"Hello, Canon." He looked even more disturbed than the last time Maggie had seen him. His eyes were dark, brooding, and moved in nervous jerks as he studied the room.

"Don't like open windows." Canon moved to the

window by Maggie's desk and closed it.

Maggie again looked toward the door. *Where is Agnes?* "Why don't you sit down?" She pointed to the chair across from her desk.

But Canon continued to stand by the window, watching the kids play in the alley. Just then Agnes appeared at the door, holding a cordless phone. She mouthed something about calling 911.

Maggie shook her head.

"I used to play stickball when I was a kid," Canon said. "The psychiatrist in prison kept askin' me about my childhood. Wanted to know if it was happy or was I abused or somethin'. As if they know anythin'. They thought I was crazy. Practically said so." Finally, he walked over to the empty chair and sat down. "You think I'm crazy?"

Maggie shrugged. "You can't go bombing abortion clinics. You can't go doing some of the things you've done without people thinking you're a little off."

Canon smiled, then nodded. "They're all liars, you know. Them doctors. They tell you things that ain't true. They know what they's doin'. They see, they *see*, but they lie just the same. They're all liars. But I don't care what people think. I don't much care about that. Don't matter anyway. Don't matter one bit."

"Why not, Canon?"

"Because the whole world's goin' to hell in a handbasket, that's why. Because it's all topsy-turvy anyway. Because when people start killin' babies and nobody doin' nothin' about it, that's when we's finished."

"I know how you feel, Canon. But we have laws. We

have to work with and by the law. You just can't take the law into your own hands."

"Why not? They do. They take God's law and switch it to suit theirselves."

"Yes, they do. But you *can't*. Because if you do, you're just like them. You can't go around threatening someone because you don't like what they do."

"Maggie, I respect you. I always have. You do good here. But you're a woman, and God never give no woman the same mandate of warrior as He gave a man. He don't expect you to do what I do. But we're in a battle and I gotta fight for the right thing."

"Canon, this is a spiritual battle. We must fight this thing with prayer and fasting, without violating God's laws."

"I don't see where David fought Goliath with prayer and fastin'. No sir. He picked up a stone and hurled it. That's what I am. A David. It sure would be nice if you could understand that."

Maggie shook her head. "I can't, Canon. I'm sorry."

He knotted his eyebrows and began clenching and unclenching his fists. "Then you can't use me?" he finally said.

Maggie shook her head.

"You won't let me stay, maybe do some good here at the Center?"

Maggie sighed and leaned across her desk. "I can't, Canon. We get fifty girls a week here, and most of them are frightened and confused. We must maintain a peaceful atmosphere if we're to help them. Sometimes just a little thing can set them off. You're unpredictable, Canon, and I can't—"

"Unstable. That's what the psychiatrist said. But what does he know? I ain't, though, Maggie. I ain't unstable. You just don't understand. I ain't blamin' you. Can't be helped that you're a woman and don't see it the way a man would. In all the other wars, the men went out to battle and the women always stayed behind. Can't be helped that you don't understand. And I ain't holdin' it against you either. Don't think I hold a grudge." Canon Edwards slid a piece of paper across the desk, then rose from his chair.

"That's my number. If you ever need me, Maggie, for anything, ever, you just call. You hear? You just call."


Becky sat on the couch holding her mother's hand. She wished she could just roll up in a ball and die. She couldn't bear to look at her mother's face, which was all twisted and red. Her father's was even worse, with large sparkling tears that hung at the corner of his eyes like suspended glass, threatening to shatter all over his face. That was the worst part. Seeing her father like that. Knowing she had reduced this tough mechanic to tears. How her parents must hate her! Maybe if she'd just die, her parents wouldn't be in so much pain. They wouldn't have to be sitting here trying to figure out how to solve her problems for her.

Becky had not gone to school, but had spent the day in her room, crying and waiting for her father to come home. Her mother had told her they would talk about the "situation" tonight. No one had talked about it since Saturday, when Becky had first told her mother. It was now Monday night. She was sure it had taken her mother a full day and a half to figure out what to say to her father. She was sure her mother had not dropped the bombshell until this morning when Becky had heard them arguing. She imagined her mother telling him all about it, all about how his daughter had messed everything up, how she had gone and ruined all their plans and the family's hope of sending someone to college.

And when her door had finally opened and her mother told her to come downstairs, Becky had been numb with fear. Whatever her father did to her, she deserved that and more. Maybe he'd hit her, although Becky had no memory of her father ever hitting her. But if he hit her now, it would be okay. Anything would be okay, only she wished he'd stop sitting there looking so sad. She wished he'd stop looking like any minute he was going to bust out crying, because she couldn't handle that. Not that.

"You're careless, Becky. You're careless." Jim Taylor's voice faltered. "Just look at the way you keep your room."

"I'm sorry, Daddy. I'm so sorry."

"Well, it's too late for that, isn't it?"

"Yes, Daddy. It's too late. I've ruined everything."

Becky could feel her mother's labored breathing, as though she was weary of life and all its burdens, as though this new burden was the one that would finish her. Becky buried her face in her hands and began to sob. "I'm sorry. I'm so sorry." Then she felt her father's hand on her head.

"Okay, okay. We'll just have to make the best of it. No use going on and on with this. We'll just have to make it right.

There are things that can be done. We'll just have to make it right."

Becky could feel her mother tense. When she looked up, she saw a new terror on her mother's face."

"No, Jim, please."

"There's no other way. You want her to ruin her life like you did?"

"Jim, not now, for heaven's sake."

"I don't see any other way. We've got to get her back on track. Help her get her life together."

"Please, Jim, there are other ways. We could—"

"No. History's not going to repeat itself here. Not in this house."

Frantically, Becky looked from her mother to her father. Her mother's eyes were pleading, begging, while her father's face was like flint. When her mother looked down, Becky knew she had lost some secret battle.

"It's best," her father said. "I believe it's the right thing... the only thing. I want you to get an abortion."

Becky sank back into the couch. She felt as if someone had just drilled a hole in her heart. She just sat with her head against the pillows of the couch praying that something in the night would take her life, that she'd go to sleep and never wake up.


All the way home from the Life Center Maggie prayed for Canon Edwards. She felt a deep sorrow she couldn't pinpoint. Was it because of him? Or was it because of those kids outside her window? She suspected it was both. Her heart broke for Canon. But it also broke for herself. It bothered her that her inability to have children kept coming up, kept rising to the surface like oil in a pot. This thing she wouldn't let God put His finger on. *Not fully.* She had to stop thinking about it. Thinking about it wasn't going to do any good, wasn't going to change things.

Before she even got to her apartment door, she could see them, red and full, crammed into a cheap plastic vase. In spite of herself she smiled. Roses. She looked from side to side to see if Kirt was around, and knew he wouldn't be there because he was at the capital—yet felt disappointed anyway. Funny how it was getting harder and harder to say good-bye. She knew for him too. But that gave her little comfort now.

She bent over the flowers and pulled off the florist's card. "Roses are red, violets are blue, I think I could conquer the world if I had you. Love, Kirt." He always seemed to be there when she needed him, his funny cards, his flowers, his voice on the phone. She unlocked her door, then scooped up the bouquet and brought it inside.

She deposited the flowers and her purse on the kitchen counter and dialed the phone. She held her breath until she heard the click of the receiver on the other end.

"The flowers are lovely. Thanks, I needed that."

"Rough day?"

"Ummm. And yours?"

"My fists are sore from duking it out with some of my peers in the Assembly."

"What's going on?"

"A few of my esteemed colleagues are trying to create a

catchall piece of legislation that will incorporate DNA iden-
tification, falsely reporting a bomb on school grounds,
stalking, clinic access, and religious freedom."

"No."

"I kid you not."

"Sounds like I should have sent you roses."

"Your voice will do just fine. Thanks for calling. Now
tell me about your day."

"Nope."

"Okay, then you'll have to sit through one of my jokes.
Did I tell you the one about three boys in a schoolyard?"

Maggie smiled, then closed her eyes as she listened to
Kirt. She tried to visualize his face, the arch of his eyebrows,
the tilt of his head. She missed him so very very much.


Becky sat curled on the front seat of the car, as far from
Skip as she could get, her back against the door. The door
handle jammed into her spine, but she didn't change position. Her eyes were swollen from crying most of the night.
Around 3 A.M. she had changed her wet pillowcase, but in
no time it was wet again. Around four her thoughts turned
to Skip. How was she going to tell him? What would he
say? She had wondered if he'd want to marry her. Then
decided, not likely. Then realized *she* didn't want to marry
him.

Her parents had said little to her this morning. Her
father hadn't even looked at her when she left, not even to
give her his two-second inspection, which he always did,
as though he needed to stamp his seal of approval on her

whenever she went out into the world. Well, his seal of approval had been revoked. Of that there was no doubt.

Becky looked over at Skip, so eager, so carefree. He hadn't even noticed how grotesque she looked from her sleepless night, that her eyes were sunken and puffy. Was he thinking it would be just like always? Just another fun afternoon in the backseat? As she watched him look out into their secluded thicket, she felt a twinge of hatred. His smooth bright face looked so relaxed, so rested. His lips curled into an easy smile; not a hint of red anywhere in his eyes. Suddenly the injustice of it all overwhelmed her. Was she the only one who had to cry? She curled her feet underneath her, shrinking into an even smaller ball. All the way to Lover's Cove she had been trying to string together the right words, the right way to tell Skip. She had tried to think how she could soften it, how to make it easier. Now, she didn't want to make it easy.

"I'm pregnant," Becky said, so matter-of-factly it startled her.

Skip spun around, jamming his knee into the steering column. "*What?*"

"I'm pregnant." She stared defiantly at him.

"How? How did that happen?"

"How should I know! Maybe that emergency stash of yours was just too old or maybe it was defective."

Skip's face reddened. "You know, Becky, that's not fair. You're putting all this on me. You could've taken some responsibility, you know. You could've taken the pill or something. Why did it always have to fall on my shoulders?"

"This is a rather silly argument now, don't you think? I mean, it's done."

"What are your plans?"

"What do you mean?"

"Oh, Becky, come on. What are you going to do about...about the pregnancy?"

Becky could feel the tears begin to well up. "I don't know. I thought we should discuss it."

"What's to discuss? It's your body, it's your choice."

"Now isn't that a nice little cop-out!"

"What are you talking about?"

"It's *your* baby too."

Skip began rubbing the knee he had just injured. "It's not a baby yet, Becky, it's just tissue. And I don't think we should let a little tissue ruin our lives, do you?"

"So you're saying I should get an abortion?"

"It's the sensible thing. Neither one of us is ready for marriage, and we both have college to think about."

"I don't know if I can handle an abortion. It scares me, Skip, and deep down—"

"You do what you want. Okay? But if you're asking me for advice, I'm telling you you're crazy if you don't get an abortion. You can't seriously be considering having this kid? How are you going to support it? I can't help. Even with the scholarship, I'll have to work part-time. You're not thinking straight at all."

Becky slumped against the seat. "I guess not."

"Tommy's girl went through this, and she's all right. Nothing happened to her."

"Loraine had an abortion?"

"Yeah. Remember when I told you he was having all that trouble with his dad? Well, it was really Loraine. Tommy made me promise not to tell. Loraine didn't want an abortion either. She wanted to get married. But Tommy finally talked some sense into her and everything's fine now. She had it and she's okay."

"But Tommy and Loraine have split up."

"That's my point. It shows you how wrong Loraine was. She wasn't ready for marriage and neither was Tommy. Now she's dating another guy, and it's better for everyone. Everyone's happy. See how things work out?"

Becky closed her eyes. She felt utterly exhausted.

"When this is all over, you'll see that you did the right thing for everyone." Skip leaned closer and put his hand on her ankle. "I'll get the name of that doctor that did Loraine, then we'll put this all behind us." His hand slid up her leg. "If you want, I could help you relax a little."

Becky uncurled her leg to push his hand away, but kicked his injured knee instead.

"What!" Skip said, rubbing his knee. "What did you do that for?"

Becky just looked at him and said nothing.

"Man, that hurts! And the playoffs start this week. Coach'll be mad if I'm not out there giving it my best."

"I'm sorry. It was an accident," she said weakly.

"Sometimes, Becky, you're so careless."


"Did Skip give you the name of that doctor yet?" Paula asked, lounging on her yellow Laura Ashley-ensembled bed.

"Yes." Becky sat curled on the companion patterned loveseat.

"Are you going?"

"No. My dad said he doesn't want me to go there. He said he has the name of the best clinic in Brockston and that's where I'm to go."

"At least you have your dad looking out for you. You're really lucky. A lot of dads wouldn't be this helpful."

"I guess."

Paula rose from the bed, walked over to where Becky was sitting, and plopped down on the matching stuffed chair. "You don't seem very grateful. I mean, your parents could've been really hard on you. I mean really, Becky, think about it. Most parents would've had a hissy fit. I still don't know how you could've been so stupid."

"So what do you want from me? It's done, isn't it!"

"You don't have to bite my head off. I know your hormones are all messed up, but you don't have to take it out on me."

Tears began running down Becky's face.

Paula got up and retrieved the tissue box. "Here."

Becky grabbed a handful and wiped her eyes, then blew her nose. "I don't know what's the matter with me. I feel so lousy, and all I do is cry."

"You're pregnant, that's what's the matter."

"Paula, would you think I was crazy...would you believe me if I told you I don't want this abortion?"

"You can't be serious. You have your whole life ahead of you. You want to ruin it?"

"I'm just so scared. I think about it all the time. I'm so scared."

Paula threw the box of tissues on the floor, then pushed them closer to the love seat with her foot. "I heard it was nothing. Just a simple procedure. Someone told me it was like scraping plaque off your teeth."

"You think so? I don't know—"

"Don't think about it so much. That's your problem, you think too much. You've always thought about things too much."

Becky laughed a sardonic laugh. "Yeah, except when it counted. Why didn't I think a little more then?"

Paula shrugged. "You notice how it's always the girl that takes the fall? How come no one is asking Skip why he didn't do a little more thinking?"

"Yeah. It stinks."

"Just like this room."

"What?"

"It's so feminine, so predictable. It's what you'd think a girl's room should be. It's the same as a girl acting a certain way, the way people expect her to act."

"You're babbling, Paula."

"No, listen. I'm saying something important. It's like a girl who lets her guard down, once, just once, because she's so crazy in love with a guy. Then the guy turns out to be a jerk. But now everyone thinks she's easy, because that's what the jerk tells them. So when she's with other guys, they start expecting things. Things she doesn't want to do. But it's out of her control now. Because it's expected, you see. And she goes along, and that, of course, reinforces what everyone thinks anyway, and then there's more expectations. It's like you're in a trap and don't know how to get out. Are you getting what I'm saying?"

Becky nodded slowly and handed the box of tissues to Paula when she saw her friend's tears. "How did we end up like this?"

Becky knocked softly on the door marked Guidance Counselor. It had taken her two days to get the courage to make an appointment to see Mr. Harding. She knew the kids all liked him and considered him cool, easy to talk to. She needed that. An adult who would be easy to talk to. An adult she could trust with her secret and maybe help her feel better about what she was planning to do. She didn't know anyone other than Mr. Harding who could fit that bill.

The door opened and a smiling youthful face peered out. "Come in, Becky. Come in." With his hand he gently guided her in and directed her to take a chair. Then he took the one next to hers rather than going back to sit behind his desk. "Before you came, I checked your grades and saw that you're doing very well. I also understand that congratulations are in order. You're the only student this year to be accepted to Georgetown. Your parents must be very proud."

Becky bit the inside of her mouth. She just couldn't cry. *Please not now, not here.* But even so, tears began to roll down her cheeks.

Mr. Harding pulled a clean handkerchief from his pocket and handed it to her. He allowed her to cry and just sat quietly patting her shoulder.

Finally, Becky looked into the kind, caring face. "I'm pregnant."

The way Mr. Harding bobbed his head up and down made Becky wonder how many times he had heard this. He rose quickly and went to his desk. "I understand. You don't want your parents to know, but you need advice on who to see." He opened a drawer and fumbled among the papers, then pulled out a card, walked back to the chair and handed it to her. "This is the best abortion clinic in town. If you need transportation, I can arrange it. And if you do it on school time, I can get you excused from your classes. Your parents will never have to know."

Becky stared horrified at her counselor. "You don't understand. My parents do know. My dad...my dad has already made arrangements."

Mr. Harding frowned and sat down. "Then you're right, I don't understand, Becky. What's the problem?"

"I don't know if I want an abortion. It seems wrong somehow. It seems—"

"Now you listen, Becky. We're not talking about a moral issue here. We're talking about a procedure...just a little procedure. A little tissue gets scraped away. There's nothing wrong about that. You're making too much of it. You have to look at the realities. You're young, unmarried, on your way to college and the rest of your life. Don't you *want* the rest of your life, Becky? You owe yourself that."

"Yes, I guess—"

"And Georgetown? How many kids get into Georgetown? That's not an opportunity you can throw away."

"Yes, but—"

"There are no 'buts,' Becky. You're a smart girl with a bright future. If you don't have an abortion, you'll be letting yourself down and your parents too. What about them? You already said your father made arrangements. That means he's in favor of you doing the right thing. You have to consider his wishes. This thing could ruin all your lives."

Becky pressed the handkerchief to her face again. Why was it clear to everyone but her what the right thing was? "Yes, of course," she finally said. "Of course you must be right."

Mr. Harding sat back in his chair and nodded. "I am right, Becky, and time will bear me out. Years from now, when you look back on this whole thing, you'll wonder why you made such a fuss."

# 6

"CANON EDWARDS?"

"Who wants to know?"

"A friend."

"I ain't got no friends."

"You've got a few."

"Say, who is this?"

"I told you, a friend…actually a friend of a friend."

"You got somethin' wrong with your mouth, mister? You sound funny."

"No…I'm…I'm just upset. This friend of ours…I can't name names…but this mutual friend says I can trust you. She says you'll know what to do."

"What friend? I told you I ain't got…you say a woman gave you my number? Was it Maggie? Now why would Maggie go and give you my number?"

"Because she thinks you can help me."

"Maggie wants me to help you?"

"She said you would, that you'd know just what to do."

Thor could hear the sound of Canon lighting a cigarette, then heard him take a deep drag. After that, complete
silence.

"Canon? Are you there?"

"Don't know why I bother with these, just nails in my
coffin. Prison does that. Gives you bad habits."

Thor heard Cannon fumble the phone, then make an
irritating scraping sound. He pictured the ex-con smoking
his cigarette in a small dirty room, gazing out a grease-
stained window. Thor thought he heard the creaking of bed-
springs.

"Canon? Why don't you answer? Are you still there?"

"Yeah, I'm here."

"I'm in trouble and I need help."

"I ain't in the habit of helpin' people I don't know."

"Well, Maggie thought—"

"You just said we shouldn't mention her name, so why
you keep sayin' it?"

"Sorry. I'm upset. It's my daughter...she was butchered
at the Brockston Clinic. Dr. Newly did it. They say she's not
the first. She's in bad shape. In the hospital now. They don't
know if she'll live or die. I have money. I can pay you. I can
pay whatever you want. Only you have to do something
about those people there. You have to do something about
Dr. Newly. You have to scare him or something—"

"Why did you let her go?"

"What? Well...I didn't know she was going for an abortion. I only found out later, when the hospital called." Thor
heard Canon curse.

"Don't you people know nothin'? Don't you know how

to love and protect your kids and keep 'em out of the hands of monsters like this Newly fella?"

"I've got money. I can pay you anything you ask. Only please, you've got to stop this monster from ever doing anything like this again. Just name your—"

"Let me call Maggie first."

"No! You can't call her. Don't you see, if you do you'll make her an accomplice. And you don't want to do that. Think of the Center, of all her hard work." Thor could hear the phone being fumbled again.

"Maggie never approved of the way I did things. Why should she tell you to call me?"

"Well—"

"Unless she does approve. You tryin' to tell me that mister? You tryin' to tell me that Maggie understands what I do?"

"Well—"

"I guess it's possible. I mean, why would she tell you to call me? Course she could never tell me that, on account of the Center and all. The law would shut her down. Then what would happen to all those frightened, hurtin' girls? Yeah, I guess she really must understand. If she told you to call, I mean. You got twenty thousand dollars?"

"Well...yes—"

"I know that's askin' a lot, mister, but after I do what I gotta do, then I gotta leave town and I'll need me some cash."

"I'll put it in a locker at the bus station, along with Newly's schedule. I...I'll do some checking and find out when he's at the clinic. After you pick up the cash, I'll expect you to do your part."

"Yeah, okay."

"What...what will you do?"

"You leave that to me. I'll do what I gotta."

"Well...all right. But I don't want anyone to get hurt. Just scare Dr. Newly a little, maybe threaten him so he'll leave town."

"You want me to do this or not, mister?"

"Yes, of course—"

"Then stop askin' questions and let me be. I *said* I'd do what I gotta."

"Well, yes...okay, you handle it. I'll need your address, though, so I can mail you the key to the locker."

Canon rattled off his address. "Just do me a favor. Don't tell Maggie you talked to me. You're right...we gotta leave her outta this."

"Naturally. I don't want to hurt her any more than you do."

Thor Emerson hung up the pay phone, then removed the four large gumdrops from his mouth. He had been facing the corner with his back to the other phones and turned around to see if anyone might have overheard. The phone stall next to him was empty, and the few people he saw were scrambling to catch their buses. He glanced at the yellow lockers bunched together in groups of six. He had already rented one, using a phony ID, compliments of Louie.

Thor adjusted his sunglasses while trying not to dislodge his wig. That was a stroke of genius on his part about using Maggie. It would be nice if Thor could tie the two together in this. Strike a blow against the Life Center. Yes, this was going to be a real win-win situation. And it was only going to cost him twenty thousand. He had expected to pay ten times that much. Would wonders never cease? His luck was definitely changing. He could feel it, like a warm sliver of joy, slicing through his body. Soon all his problems were going to be over—Newly, the pro-lifers, Louie. And once that happened, maybe, just maybe, he'd try to get Teresa back.

Thor sat behind the mahogany desk in his command center. For the first time in a long while, he actually felt in command. He watched his pair of Clowns swimming contently round and round in the seventy-eight-degree water. The bloated female swam vigorously past the seaweed and looked in good health. She was larger than his hand now. Any day the tank population would increase, defying the maxim that Clowns don't breed in captivity. It just proved that with the right stimulation—the proper manipulation—anything was possible.

He tapped his fingers on the desk, then looked at the number in front of him. He had to play it cool. Sound natural. He rehearsed again what he would say, then cleared his throat before dialing the phone.

"Hello, Adam. Carl tells me you're not feeling well."

"To tell you the truth, Dr. Emerson, your Solutions Clinic in Brockston leaves a lot to be desired. I'm...finding it increasingly difficult to work with Dr. Newly. Every day, it's something else. The man defies all protocol. He contaminates my specimens by using unsterilized dilators. He's unbelievable. I've seen him use the same dilators on half a dozen girls! I don't know how he gets away with it, how he calls himself a doctor. I can't work like this. I can't do my job. Our clients will not pay for contaminated samples. It's all so counterproductive. I've told Mr. Langley about it. Quite frankly, I'm frustrated."

Thor smiled. "I understand, Adam. That's why I'm calling." It was amazing how everything was working out to his advantage; how things were just falling into place without that much effort on his part. "I think it's best you stay away from the Brockston clinic for…for the next few weeks anyway. Concentrate on my other clinics. I've begun interviewing doctors to replace Newly. I feel confident that in a short time, things at Brockston will be under control. Just give me a few weeks."

"All right. Anything is better than what's going on now. Should I send my assistant to Brockston to see if we can salvage anything in the meantime?"

"No. Like you said, it's counterproductive. Let me get Newly's replacement, then when everything's under control, you can come back." Thor could hear Adam sigh.

"A sound plan, I think. I'll explain everything to Mr. Langley."

"Feel free, but I've already discussed it with him."

There was a brief pause. "Of course, this'll make it impossible to satisfy all the POs we've gotten. None of your other clinics are nearly as productive as Brockston. But maybe I can partial fill. Sort of spread the wealth by filling only part of the orders with a promise the balance is coming. I can't guarantee it'll work. It's worth a try, though."

"Okay, Adam, do your best. But don't worry about it too much. If everything goes well, pretty soon you'll be able to fill all the purchase orders you can get."

After he hung up, Thor pulled from his drawer a sheet of lined paper that had been torn from a three-ring note-book. In poorly written, almost childlike penmanship, the word liar had been written four times in large lettering and filled the page. Stapled to it was the envelope it had been mailed in. Thor folded the paper and envelope, then slipped them into his pocket. *Could things get any simpler?* Now, just the right stimulation—the proper manipula-tion—that's all that was needed.

Thor walked up the gray concrete steps of the Brockston Police Station and pulled open the ornately carved maple door. Inside, a four-and-a-half-foot-high wooden desk stretched wall to wall and separated the large entrance room from the metal file cabinets, half-wall partitioned offices, and angular corridors that led to private offices in the back. The entrance room, the room where civilians entered, was at least two feet lower than the rooms behind the desk barrier, so when people came in, they had to look up at the officer behind the desk.

An officer, looking very close to retirement age, smiled when he saw Thor. "Can I help you?"

"I need to see Lieutenant Tooley."

"And you are?"

"Dr. Emerson. Thor Emerson."

The officer nodded. Almost everyone in Brockston knew Thor Emerson, at least by name. The officer dialed a three-digit extension, and within minutes Thor found himself on the second floor, standing in front of Lieutenant Tooley's desk.

"Hello, Dr. Emerson. No trouble I hope?" It was Tooley who had apprehended Canon Edwards after he had bombed Thor's Brockston clinic six years ago.

"Not yet, but that's not to say there won't be." Thor noticed there was a lot more gray in Tooley's hair now.

"What seems to be the problem?" Lieutenant Tooley indicated that Thor should take the empty seat beside the desk.

"Canon Edwards. He's back in town. Did you know?"

"Yes, sir. Very little we don't know around here."

"I'd like some protection."

"Has he threatened you?"

Thor pulled a paper from his pocket. "Does someone always have to get hurt before you can do anything?" He handed the officer the paper and watched as Tooley unfolded it, then scanned the page.

"What's this?"

"An anonymous note—I think from Edwards. Who else could it be? I mean—the man was just released from jail and I just got this—you figure it out."

"Okay, maybe it's from him, but it doesn't say anything threatening, so what makes you think you need protection?"

"Because Edwards doesn't like my kind of business. Because he has a screw loose and you know what he's capable of. And because he's done it before and no telling if he's planning to do it again."

Tooley shook his head. "Dr. Emerson, I understand your concern, but unless you have some concrete evidence that you or your clinic is in danger from Canon, there's nothing we can do."

"I don't have any evidence. Not the kind you want."

"What kind have you?"

Thor hesitated, then shrugged. "Only a gut feeling, an uneasiness."

"Can't say I blame you. Tell you what. Suppose I ask the boys to cruise by your clinic from time to time. Can't help you with your other clinics, out of our jurisdiction, but maybe we can keep an eye on your Brockston place, unofficially of course."

"How about a plainclothesman staked outside the building?" He tried to sound desperate.

Tooley shook his head. "No can do. It's a swing-by in a squad car or nothing."

"All right. Just try not to intimidate my customers. They might get nervous if police cars start circling the clinic."

Lieutenant Tooley laughed. "Nobody's going to circle your clinic. Just a casual—and not too often, either—look-see. I'd be grateful for what you can get, if I were you."

Thor nodded and extended his hand, which Tooley took. "I feel better already. I know you'll do your best to keep my clients and staff safe."

"Now don't go off half-cocked. I didn't promise anything.

Just a drive-by every once in a while. I can't promise anything more. You understand?"

"Come fund-raising time, there'll be a big check in the
mail."

Tooley's face reddened. "Now we don't look kindly at
people trying to bribe us. We try to do our best for everyone—no matter who they are—no strings attached."

"I just wanted to show my appreciation, that's all. No
harm intended."

Lieutenant Tooley mumbled something and shook his
head. Thor turned and walked out the door, feeling fairly
confident that Tooley would not be sending any squad cars
to his clinic.

Becky had cried all morning. She had screamed and argued
with both her parents, but they had held fast. She was to
have an abortion at the Brockston clinic at two o'clock. The
closer it came to two, the more dread Becky felt, and the
more she realized she didn't want to have an abortion.

She had gone over all the arguments in her head, then
replayed them for her parents. Nothing worked. The fact
remained: She was unmarried and unable to support a
baby on her own, and her parents as well as Skip had driven that fact home. If she had this baby, she would be on
her own.

She kept hoping and praying that somehow some miracle would stop these wheels from rolling over her and
grinding her onto this path not of her choosing. She didn't
know why she felt so strongly. It was almost irrational, this

feeling of panic and dread. Everyone was telling her this was the solution to her problems, yet all she wanted to do was run the other way.

Could she be mad? Had she plunged over the edge? Why was she so out of step with everyone else? Why couldn't she feel the way they all felt about this abortion? See the need for it? *Want* it?

All she knew was that a life was growing inside her and she was about to kill it. They kept telling her it was a blob, a pink blob, nothing more. She wanted to believe them. She wanted to embrace this act of murder and call it by another name, but she couldn't. Her body wouldn't let her. Neither would her mind, her emotions. Already, she had begun to think about what the baby looked like. Would it be a boy or a girl? What color were the eyes, the hair? These were dangerous thoughts for an assassin.

She looked at the clock on her nightstand and winced as the minute hand jerked to 1:15. Slowly, she pulled off her tank top and replaced it with a clean white Oxford shirt. She didn't bother tucking it in. Then she went to her dresser, found the jar of cream under a headband, and began creaming off her makeup. Her eyes caught sight of Raggedy Ann slumped against the mirror's edge. She should throw it out. It was dirty and torn and worn—a worn-out child's toy and she was no longer a child. Children didn't have babies and children didn't have abortions. *Did they?*

She tied back her hair with a rubber band. When she looked at herself, she appeared so young, so antiseptic, even virginal and pure, that she had to laugh. What a joke!

What a cruel joke it was to be a woman and get caught.

She thought of Skip and wondered if he had cried this morning. She doubted it. He hadn't even called her. He had called her last night when it was safe. He had avoided mentioning anything about what she was going to do today, only spoke to her for a few minutes, just long enough to ask her if she still wanted to go to the prom next week, because if she did, he needed to rent his tux. *The prom?* She could hardly believe it. Was she going mad? Or was it everyone else?

"Becky? Becky, we have to leave now or we'll be late." Her mother was at the door, and after one sharp tap, opened it. Her mouth was taut, like a soldier who had been shot in battle but was somehow mustering the strength to go on.

Becky wished she didn't look like that, so wounded. She began to cry, and her mother came over and gently cradled her in her arms.

"I'm so sorry, Mommy. I'm so sorry. I just wish…I just—"

Nancy Taylor's mouth tightened even more. "I know, darling. I know."


Classical-sounding music piped softly through the stereo system and was the only thing heard in the otherwise silent waiting room. Becky sat next to her mother but refused to look at her. From time to time Becky stole timid glances at the handful of women waiting with her. Girls, most of them, like herself. But there were a few older ones, in their twenties and thirties; one actually looked forty. Many waited alone. Some, like Becky, had a companion. But nobody looked at anyone else or spoke a single word.

Becky's throat felt like it was closing, and she kept wiping her palms on her jeans. She thought about running out the front door and into the small crowd that held pictures of dead babies in one hand and packs of literature in the other. She had seen another small group huddled together praying. At least that's what it sounded like.

These strangers were the only people in the world who seemed to want Becky to keep her baby. She had tried to reach for one of their flyers, but her mother had blocked her hand and forced her up the three concrete steps and through those awful brown unmarked doors. She wondered if the strangers outside were praying for her now. She hoped so. Maybe a miracle would happen and something, someone would stop her from doing this. Maybe someone would tell her there was another way.

She heard muffled sobs. A young girl sat shivering alone in a corner chair. Becky wanted to scream, "We can't let them do this to us!" But no words would come out. She felt almost faint from terror. One of the staff had given her a sedative when she first signed in, but it didn't seem to be doing any good. She had never been so frightened in all her life. When an attendant called her number, Becky was unable to respond.

Her mother nudged her. "That's you. That's your number."

Becky looked confused. "What?"

The attendant walked over and Becky grabbed for her

mother's hand. "Come with me!"

The attendant shook her head and pulled Becky from her mother, then down the hall. "I'm sorry, your mother can't come. It's against the rules."

Becky felt her knees go weak and clung to the stranger. "What are they going to do to me in there? What…what are they going to do to my baby?"

"I'm sure this has all been discussed with you before-hand, dear. Now is not the time. Just don't think about it. It'll all be over soon."

Becky didn't have the strength to tell the attendant that she knew nothing about what was going to happen in that room, that she knew nothing about what was going to hap-pen to her baby. It was taking all the strength she could muster just to put one foot in front of the other, to keep herself from keeling over.

The attendant had a strong grip on Becky's arm and led her gently but firmly toward a closed door. She opened it and ushered Becky inside.

"Everything off. Put on the gown, opening in back, then get on the table."

Becky nodded and began undressing even before the attendant closed the door.

Within minutes, Dr. Newly appeared. He grinned broadly when he saw her.

"Don't be nervous. It'll all be over soon. Six minutes. I can do these in six minutes flat. So lie down and relax."

Becky sat on the edge of the table, trying to keep the blue gown from flying open in back. Dr. Newly's grin widened as he watched her. He patted the end of the narrow table. "Come on, rump down here and spread your legs. We both know you've had practice with that."

Becky's face reddened and she tried to maneuver to the table edge without the gown riding up, then suddenly felt herself being yanked and her feet jammed into stirrups. Dr. Newly stood over her and began running his hands up and down her body.

"What…what are you doing?"

"Examining you. I like to do quick pre-procedure check-ups."

"I don't want to be examined. Stop…stop that!"

Dr. Newly laughed. "You're not going to be one of those screamers, are you?"

The door opened and in came another attendant. This one was younger than the one who had taken Becky down the hall, and she looked very angry.

"You should've waited for me, Doctor!"

"It's your job to keep up. I don't wait."

"I'm sorry, but I was helping clean the other room. You left a…I know how you insist that the patient and room be ready before you enter. It's very difficult to maintain three rooms at the pace you keep."

Dr. Newly laughed. "I don't think our little patient here wants to hear your problems, do you?" He looked down at Becky, winked, then moved to the end of the table.

Becky could feel him prep the area with a cold antiseptic solution. Then she felt an excruciating pain as the doctor inserted something hard and cold into her cervix.

"You didn't sound the uterus, Doctor."

"No need. I did a pre-exam."

"But doctor—"

"You want to do this procedure?"

The attendant took Becky's hand and began rubbing it. "This part may hurt a little, but your cervix must be dilated so the doctor can insert the suction tube."

Becky blinked back her tears. She had never felt so much pain. It was like he was tearing her body apart. She felt horror, dread, fear. She couldn't speak or even look at the attendant.

"It's okay now," the attendant said finally, letting go of Becky's hand. "The tube's in. Soon it will be over." Then the attendant flipped on the suction machine.

A noise like the sound of a vacuum cleaner filled the room, and Becky gasped. A short time later, Doctor Newly began swooshing the tube around inside her uterus. Becky felt her insides being torn from her and began to scream.

Dr. Newly cursed loudly. "I knew she'd be a screamer."

"Stop! Stop it…please stop it!" Becky yelled.

"Shut up! You'll scare the other patients." Dr. Newly's hand began moving faster.

Becky couldn't believe the pain. It felt as if her entire insides were being ripped apart then sucked out of her body. Her arms flailed in all directions, and her hands grasped for something solid. She struggled to sit up. That's when she saw it. From the tube leading out of her came fluid and tissue, all being pumped into a glass cylinder. She could clearly see the contents. Floating among the pulpy flesh was a tiny arm and a miniature hand with perfectly formed fingers. How could this be? She was only ten weeks pregnant. She began screaming again and tried to get off the table, but the attendant restrained her.

Dr. Newly cursed again. "Shut her up! Do you want everyone to hear?"

The attendant clamped her arm around Becky's neck and covered Becky's mouth with her free hand. "You have to stay quiet. If you move about, the doctor could slip and injure your uterus."

Becky's eyes grew wide with terror. Just as Dr. Newly flipped the switch to stop the suction, Becky felt the meager contents of her stomach come up and fill the attendant's hand. The attendant helped her up, handed her a paper towel, then walked over to the little sink in the corner and washed.

Dr. Newly threw his rubber gloves into a small basket near the suction machine, then glared at his patient. "No tub baths and no *sex* for a few weeks. Think you can handle that?" he said, and stormed out the door.

Becky lay crying on a little metal table. They had put her in the supply room, a tiny room down the hall far from everything so she wouldn't bother anyone. A dingy curtain served as a door. Immediately after Dr. Newly had left her, Becky began bleeding heavily. The attendant insisted that the doctor examine her, and when he did, he told Becky it was her fault for thrashing around during the procedure. He also told her not to bother coming back to him the next time she got "knocked up." Then he instructed the attendant not to let Becky's mother see her, but to send her home and have her come back in three hours "when the bleeding stops and the girl calms down."

Now, crying and frightened and wedged between shelves of sheets, gauze, rubber gloves, and antiseptics, Becky felt totally alone. She couldn't get the picture of what she had seen in that glass jar out of her mind. She had killed her baby. She was a *murderer.* The sheets beneath her were sticky and wet with her blood. Was she going to die too? She hoped so. She deserved to die. But she didn't think she wanted to die alone, even if she did deserve it.

She could still feel the tearing, the ripping. She could still hear the suction machine. It seemed so loud in her ears. She would remember that sound to the day she died. *If only that day were soon.* When she let that doctor rip her baby apart, that suction machine scooped out her life as well. And now she felt empty. Terribly, terribly empty.


A man walked slowly past the small group of pro-lifers outside the Brockston Solutions clinic. His left hand clutched the neck of his tan trench coat. His right hand and arm remained rigid at his side. A baseball cap, pulled low, and a pair of oversized sunglasses covered most of his face. He kept his head down and ignored the attempts of one of the picketers to give him literature.

When he entered the clinic only one girl was in the waiting room. He heard voices coming from one of the rooms down the hall, but saw no one. He removed a steel rod from his inside coat pocket and shoved it into the two looped handles of the front door.

Next, he removed a snub-nosed semiautomatic rifle

from inside a special pocket he had sewn into the coat lining. For an instant he hesitated, then squeezed off several shots and killed the girl. Next he moved down the hall, shooting at anything that moved. A white-haired lady slumped over her desk; her blood splattered the wall behind her. More shots, more bodies fell, as he opened one door after the other. Finally, he came to the last door and flung it open. A man wearing bloody rubber gloves stood holding a coat tree like a weapon. Cowering behind him were a white-uniformed attendant and a pale woman who half-sat, half-lay on a bloody table.

"Who are you? What do you want?" asked the man with the bloody gloves.

"You Newly?"

"Yes—"

"Then this is for you." The gunman fired three shots into Dr. Newly, then shot the women. He reloaded and sprayed the room with bullets. When he was finished, he picked up the patient's chart that had fallen out of its plastic holder on the door, ripped off a page, wrote something on the back, and shoved it into the bottom of the holder pocket. Then he stripped off his bloody trench coat and wrapped it around his rifle. With one hand he opened the window, then punched out the screen. With his foot, he pulled over a small stool and positioned it under the window. And in a matter of a minute he exited the building.


Becky Taylor lay shivering on the metal table. Any minute she expected the curtain that separated her from the massacre to be ripped aside and to see someone with a gun standing in the doorway. She hoped he would come quickly and that death would be swift. It would be a perfect ending to the day. When no one came, she thought of crying out, "Here I am!" But she was too scared and weak to say anything and instead lay frozen beneath a thin sheet. She had not heard a sound for some time and wondered what could be happening. She lifted her head and dropped it again. It felt unusually heavy, like the end of a hundred-pound dumbbell. Then she heard sirens, then crashing noises and wood splintering, then shouts and feet running down the hall. She held her breath. She felt dizzy, weak and cold, so cold. She would not fight. Whatever this person was going to do to her, she would not stop it. Let the avenger come. Let him send her to where her dear baby awaited her.

"Merciful heavens!" the policeman said as he pulled back the curtain. "Here's another one, but it looks like she's still alive."

Becky stared at the friendly face and wondered why the police officer thought she had been shot.

The officer pulled the metal stretcher out of the closet. From her position in the hall, Becky could see bodies everywhere lying in pools of blood.

"Don't worry, we'll get you to a hospital. Hang in there, lass."

Becky raised her head to tell the officer she was fine, that she had not been shot, but when she did, she got a look at her sheet. It was covered with blood almost up to her chin. She dropped her head and closed her eyes. Maybe she'd be seeing that little baby of hers after all.

# 7

WHEN MAGGIE SWITCHED ON the light and saw a man lurking in the corner by the file cabinet, her heart did a flip. Stubble covered his face and his eyes had a haunted, faraway look. His clothes were wrinkled and dirty. A large blue backpack lay at his feet. When a breeze caught his blond hair and rearranged it, Maggie turned to the open window. The screen had been cut and the window jimmied open. Her hand went to the phone.

"Don't do it, Maggie," Canon said, stepping from the shadows.

"I've got to call the police. You must turn yourself in."

Canon's rough hand covered hers and forced it away from the phone. "I ain't never goin' back to prison. They'll have to kill me first."

"You murdered seven people, Canon. Seven innocent people."

"I thought you'd be mad about that. About me getting all seven, I mean. But they weren't innocent. They all had

SYLVIA BAMBOLA

blood on their hands in one way or other. I knew soon as I walked in that door they all had to die. I was just the sword of God, Maggie, the avenger, and I had to do what needed to be done."

Maggie shook her head. "This is not God's way. You're piercing the heart of God with that sword of yours."

"I didn't come to argue. But they're all liars, you know, those abortionists. They know what they're doin'. They see...they see and they know, and they do it anyway. And their lies...their lies kill people."

Canon shuffled uncomfortably on his feet. His head was bent low, his eyes fixed on his shoes. "They ought not to have done it. They ought not to have broken her like that."

Maggie sighed and walked up to him. Who was Canon talking about? Twelve years ago, after his wife died, he started going to pro-life demonstrations. But everyone saw how unstable he was, how fragile his emotions were, and tried to discourage him from coming. He would weep uncontrollably in front of the abortion clinics whenever he saw a young girl or woman go in. He would mumble to himself as he walked back and forth on the sidewalk. But he was harmless in those days. He hadn't turned to violence yet.

"They ought not to have done it," Canon repeated.

Maggie put her hand on his shoulder. *Is he talking about his wife?* "It was a long time ago." She began to pray for wisdom, for protection, for Canon.

"That big ugly policewoman just busted her fingers. I heard it. It was disgustin'. I wanted to throw up."

Maggie sighed. *Beatrice Younger.* Canon was talking about Beatrice Younger.

"She was goin' on eight months. They could see that, with her belly big, stickin' out like a watermelon. They knew. They oughten've treated a pregnant woman like that. Like she was some kind of criminal. And she wasn't doin' nothin' but counselin' someone on the sidewalk, quiet like, real quiet like. But I heard it. They tried to lie about it later. But I heard it. That big ugly policewoman arrestin' her, then breakin' her fingers, right there on that sidewalk."

Maggie closed her eyes. "I know Canon." That was the day, outside the Solutions clinic at Brockston, that Canon turned. That was the moment his unstable mind twisted itself onto a new path of violence. That had been almost ten years ago, and Canon had been in and out of trouble since. But he had never done anything like this last unspeakable act.

"Turn yourself in, Canon. For the love of God, *please* turn yourself in."

Canon shook his head. "Ain't no good talkin' about it Maggie. I'm lightin' out. I just wanted to stop and say good-bye and to thank you for understandin'."

"For understanding what?"

"Nothin'. Don't want to speak about it. No good if it gets you into a bad fix. But I just wanted to tell you thanks and good-bye. That's all."

Maggie sat down behind her desk and dropped her head into her hands.

"And I wanted you to know I got regrets. I did my best,

but I ain't finished, Maggie. I didn't finish the job. I'm sorry about that."

"You have to leave now, Canon, and I have to call the police."

"I know that. Don't think I don't know that. You do what you gotta do and I'll do what I gotta. I don't guess I'll be seein' you again." He gave her a strange, sad smile and crawled out the window and into the alley.

Maggie picked up the phone and dialed 911. And after she was finished, she began praying for Canon, for the grieving families of those who lost their lives at Solutions, for the young girl found alive and her parents, for the police who would have to bring Canon in, and for the Life Center that was now sure to face a firestorm. *What Satan has meant for evil, please God, turn and use for good.*

But even after she prayed, Maggie found her thoughts consumed with the young girl they found alive. There was an urgency in her spirit she couldn't explain. Slowly, Maggie dropped to her knees and resumed praying.


Maggie spent most of the morning answering Lieutenant Tooley's questions about Canon Edwards. "Where was he going?" was the one Tooley had asked the most—a dozen times or more. But never had the Lieutenant asked Maggie why she hadn't tried to stop Canon. After her time with Tooley, Maggie couldn't face going back to the Center and had called her receptionist and told her she would be away for the rest of the day. Then she had called Kirt.

⋘◦⋙

Becky tried to open her eyes. Her lids felt like they had been nailed shut. It took all her effort to open them into slits. She saw a silver pole next to the bed and plastic bags hanging from a small crosspiece on top of it. Plastic tubing traveled from the bags and into one of her arms. She tried to move that arm, then realized it was strapped to a board. She could see dim outlines of people in white, moving about in the hall outside her room. A *hospital.* She closed her eyes and tried to remember. *Why am I here?* She lay there for a moment, then the horror of what had happened returned. *O God, why am I still alive?*

Maggie sat smiling into Kirt's face as he held her hand. The afternoon had been wonderful, but too short…for both of them. He had shown her his office, introduced her to his staff and new secretary. They had walked and talked and then had an early dinner.

Maggie pushed her empty dessert plate away, then took a sip of coffee. They had been lingering over their food for two hours. It was almost seven, and she needed to head back. Being with Kirt made her feel much better about things. *And He called His twelve disciples together and sent them out two by two.* Two by two, two by two. Maggie was beginning to see the wisdom of twos.

"I still can't get over the fact that you drove to the capital to see me. It's a first."

"Next time, I hope the weather will be nicer. The

forecaster's calling for 'a copious amount of rain.' You should've seen the drops on my windshield. They were the size of quarters."

Kirt brought Maggie's hand to his mouth and pressed it against his lips. "That road through Hunter Mountain gets pretty slick when it's wet. There are plenty of hotels in town. You could stay over."

Maggie shook her head. "I want to be at the Life Center tomorrow when it opens. There's going to be a lot of back-lash because of what's happened. I don't want people to think I've run away."

"Anyone who knows you understands you never run from anything." Kirt gave her a strange look. "Except when it comes to…"

"Comes to what?"

"When it comes to marriage."

"I'm trying, Kirt, honestly I am."

"I know. But I want you to pray about something. Will you?"

"Okay."

"I want you to ask God if I'm to be your husband."

Maggie pulled her hand from Kirt's. "Why are you doing this?"

"Because I know that if God says yes, you'll tell me."

"This sounds like manipulation."

"No, Maggie. I just need to know if I'm really hearing from God or hearing what I want. Sometimes, when you want something so badly—sometimes you can get con-fused. So I need you to pray. Okay?"

"And what will that do?"

"If you say yes it will help me wait it out. I don't know anymore if I can wait it out, not unless I know for sure that it's of God. I don't think I can bear the disappointment later...if it should come to that. So, will you? Pray about it, I mean?"

Maggie nodded. "What...what did God say to you? About us? About our future?"

Kirt studied her, his eyes intense and sparkling. "You really want to know?"

"Yes," Maggie said, almost inaudibly.

"He said you were my Eve. He said for me there would be no other. He said you were going to be my wife."

Becky's long black hair hung loosely around her shoulders, obscuring most of her face as she looked down at the little bundle in her arms. Tears dripped from her chin and onto the rag doll wrapped tightly in a towel. It had taken several tries, but she had finally bundled the doll just like she had seen the nurses do in the hospital. She swayed back and forth on her bed.

"Rock-a-bye, baby, in the treetop, rock-a-bye, baby, in the treetop." She didn't know any more of the lullaby and repeated these few words over and over. Then she stopped singing and broke into sobs. She had been doing this for hours now: rocking, singing, crying. The dull ache inside her seemed to grow larger by the hour. There was no escaping it. Some giant, invisible vacuum was sucking out her insides. The pain was terrible. But she had to submit to it. It was the only way. Because soon, very soon, she would be empty. And then she wouldn't feel anything. Then the hurting would stop.

It would have been easier if she had died. But nobody would let her. Why did they have to meddle? Why had they gone and spoiled everything by giving her all that blood? She wondered whose blood it was, then began to sob all over again. No wonder she felt so odd. She had a stranger's blood flowing in her veins. She would never be the same again. Never. With her free hand, she knocked the empty box of DayQuil onto the floor. She didn't want her parents to see that until it was all over.

She took Raggedy Ann's red yarn hair and ran her fingers down each strip, strand by strand, smoothing it as she went. When the entire head was done, she clutched the doll to her chest. "Rock-a-bye, baby, rock-a-bye…" Becky closed her eyes. She could still hear the sound of the suction machine, but it was getting fainter. The work was almost done. Soon it would all be over.


After Becky puked into the toilet bowl, she sank down onto the floor. The cool ceramic tile made her feel better, and she just lay there in a fetal position, wondering when the next wave of nausea would hit. She felt as if she had been throwing up forever, and couldn't imagine there was anything left inside her. It wasn't supposed to be like this. The twelve softgels she had swallowed were supposed to put her to sleep forever. She felt another wave of nausea and scrambled to her knees, reaching the bowl just in time. Her hair and her clothes and the room all smelled like vomit. *You can't even do this right! You can't even kill yourself!*

She heard footsteps in the hallway, then a rap on the door. "Becky? Becky, are you all right?"

Becky groaned and lay back on the cool tile. "Go away, Dad."

She heard the knob rattle and a thud as her father pushed against the door.

"I said, go away!" She had never in all her life talked in that tone to her father or her mother. But she didn't care how she spoke. What were they going to do? Ground her? She would have laughed at that thought if she didn't feel so sick.

"Open this door, Becky, or I'll break it down!"

"I'm all right, Dad. My stomach's just upset."

He stopped turning the doorknob. "Well...okay...anything I can do?"

The hard tile floor had begun to hurt Becky's back, so she turned to her side and resumed a fetal position.

"Becky? I said is there anything I can do?"

"No, Dad, not unless you can give me back my baby," she answered in a near whisper.

"What? What was that?"

Tears began to puddle beneath Becky's cheek as she pressed it against the tile. "I said I want my baby back! Can you hear that? I want my baby back! I want my baby back!"

The next thing Becky heard was her mom, coaxing her father away from the door. "Leave her. She needs time. Give her time. She'll be okay." Then Becky closed her eyes and began to sob.

ᖇᖇ

Hours later, after Becky had risen from the floor and washed, she went back to her room and pulled out her diary from its hiding place. She had not written in it for a long time. Certainly not since the abortion.

She tried to think of what day it was and decided it must be Tuesday, but she wasn't altogether sure. Saturday she had gone to Solutions, then a few days at the hospital getting someone else's blood forced into her. Did everyone think that all they had to do was fill her up and she'd start running again? Okay, so she'd been out of it for what? Two days, three? Or was it more? When Becky realized she really didn't care what day it was, she settled on Tuesday and wrote that date in the top left corner of the page.

Then she began twirling the pen between her fingers. But if it was Tuesday, then why were her parents home? They had been home all day. Were they worried? *About her?* She crinkled her eyebrows in anger. Let them worry. She didn't care about them anymore. Why should she? They hadn't cared about her. About how she felt or what she wanted.

She glanced at her rag doll. It was still wrapped tightly in a towel and lay close by her side. She smiled down at it.

"You just stay quiet, like a good little girl," she whispered, "and let Mommy get her writing done."

Then Becky turned her attention to the open diary on her lap.

*Dear Diary,*

*I'm scared and I don't feel well. And I did something horrible. I killed my baby. Do you think God could ever forgive me? I don't think I'll ever be able to forgive myself. It was awful. I was terrified. The doctor was disgusting. He touched me and it made me sick. But that wasn't the worse part. The worst part was when I saw my baby's arm and hand. It was so tiny! It was so perfect! It looked just like a real arm and hand, only it wasn't attached to anything. The doctor had torn it off my baby, then sucked it out of my body. I don't think I'll forget the sound of that machine as long as I live.*

*I feel empty now. And sad. So terribly sad. I'd do anything to change things, to make things right. But it never will be right. And I don't know how I'm going to live the rest of my life with that.*

*While I was there, someone came, a man I think, and killed everybody. They're calling it a massacre. Only he didn't find me. I was in a closet with a curtain on it—they put me there because I was crying too much and they didn't want me around the other girls— so I didn't see what happened. I only heard shots and I was afraid, but not the same way I was afraid when I was in the other room with that machine.*

*Everyone thinks I cry all the time because I'm remembering that massacre. The truth is I hardly think about it. It's like a dream and doesn't seem real. The other truth is that I wish the gunman had found me.*

*I don't like myself much anymore. And all I do is cry. I just can't seem to stop crying. I'm feeling pretty useless.*

*I don't even care about going to college. I don't care
about anything right now. Maybe it will go away in time,
this feeling. If it doesn't, then I'll have to make it go
away. Right now, the strongest feeling I feel is hate.*
    *I hate myself so much.*

Becky sat propped in bed, staring at the wall in front of
her. After finishing her diary entry, she had fallen asleep.
She looked at the clock on her nightstand. She had been
napping for almost an hour. But what was that sound—the
sound that woke her? It took several minutes before she
realized it was her mother vacuuming downstairs. She
noticed her heart was racing and that she was drenched
with perspiration. Then she noticed the rag doll. A towel
hung in disarray around the doll, as if it had also had a fit-
ful sleep. Becky pulled the towel off, then dropped the doll
on the nightstand. What was Raggedy Ann doing on the
bed and why was she wrapped like that?

A timid knock on the door made Becky jump. "Who is it?"

"Dad."

"Come in." Becky watched the knob turn and her father
step cautiously through the doorway. He walked as if he
were on tiptoe. He wore an anxious look, and Becky followed his eyes to the rag doll sprawled across the night-
stand.

"Feeling better?"

Becky shrugged. "I guess so." She vaguely remembered
throwing up in the bathroom. She watched her father's face
relax a bit.

"You want to talk?"

"About what, Dad?"

"About…about things. I know you had an awful scare, with that madman in Solutions. It might help if you talked about it."

"I don't want to talk, not to you, anyway." She could see by his face she had hurt him.

"Becky, I love you. All your life I've been looking out for you and trying to do what I thought was best, in your best interest. I'm sorry I picked Solutions. I know you trusted me and I picked a place where some nut job almost killed you. I'm *real* sorry about that. But you have to let your mother and me help you through this."

Becky turned her face to the wall. "I don't want your help. I don't want your help ever again. Not as long as I live!" In spite of herself, she began to weep softly.

"I know you were frightened. I know how traumatic this has been, and it's natural for you to blame me. I blame myself as well. I could've gotten you killed."

Becky faced her father once more. "You just don't get it, do you? I wish that maniac had killed me. I wish I had died. I wish I was dead!"

"You can't mean that. You have your whole life ahead of you. You—"

"I want my baby back!"

Jim began backing out of the room. "I know it's hard, but in time…in time things will get better, you'll see."

"I hate you! I'll hate you for the rest of my life for what you made me do!"

# 8

"MAGGIE, I'M NOT BLAMING you. All I'm saying is that there's an ugly mood in town. Nobody's going to breathe easy until Canon Edwards is caught. People are edgy. And word has gotten out that you were the last person to see him before he left town."

Maggie stared at her friend. "Where did they hear that from?"

"Well, not from me, if that's what you're thinking. Whatever way they found out, it's out, and it's not sitting well with some folks."

"You still think there'll be trouble, don't you?"

Lieutenant Tooley scratched his scalp. "I've seen people get ugly over less."

"What about police protection?"

"What about it?"

Maggie laughed. "Come on, Tooley—can I have some?"

"I'll tell you what I told Doc Emerson. Unless someone threatens you, I can't do one thing about it."

"Dr. Emerson asked for protection?"

"Right after Canon got out of jail, the doctor came running over. He was mighty nervous, too. Wanted me to post a guard, a plainclothesman outside his clinic. Course I couldn't do that. No provocation. But I did tell him I'd send a squad car around his place, now and again, for drive-by surveillance."

"Seems strange that he'd run right to you before Canon even tried anything."

"Come on, Maggie, the Doc had every right. You know Canon blames him for Patsy's death."

Maggie shrugged. "Partially, yes, but deep down Canon blames himself. And that's just one of the demons he's fighting. He can't forgive himself."

"Canon didn't spend the last six years of his life in prison because he tried to blow himself up, Miss Smarty Pants. He's got it in for Doc Emerson. First he went after his clinic, and now this...this bloody massacre. I never thought I'd see a thing like that, right here in my own backyard."

"I know. As mixed up as Canon is, I never thought him capable of this. But it's gotten more jumbled in his head—Patsy, Beatrice Younger, the whole thing."

Lieutenant Tooley wrinkled his forehead. "Now don't you go trying to dig up that skeleton. This department had a spotless record, until—and since, ever since we got rid of...but that's not the issue and don't go making it one. Your daddy must be turning over in his grave, that's all I've got to say. You, the daughter of a cop, defending a killer."

"I'm not defending him, Tooley—"

"Lieutenant Tooley to you, you turncoat." He reached over and brushed her hair away from her eyes.

"Doesn't it seem a little strange that Dr. Emerson would come to you, out of the blue like that?"

"It wasn't out of the blue. He had a paper—a note he thought was from Canon and it made him nervous."

"What did the note say?"

"Just the word *liar* written over it."

Maggie sighed. "That's Canon, all right."

"So, Doc Emerson was right, wasn't he? Said he had a feeling. Must've been one of those premonitions."

Maggie toyed with the paperweight on Lieutenant Tooley's desk. It was a baseball carved out of stone, and on the edge was a small gold plate with the inscription: 1975 Champs.

Tooley took it from her and placed it back on his desk. "I hate people tinkering with my stuff."

"I remember when you won that," Maggie said.

"How could you? That was twenty-five years ago. You were in diapers."

"I was ten. And I watched every inning."

Tooley shook his head. "Where has the time gone?" Then he leaned way over the desk. "And if you're so old, why aren't you married?"

"I'm not so old. But if you plan on dancing at my wedding, maybe you'd better give me a little protection until this thing blows over."

Lieutenant Tooley laughed and showed a good set of teeth.

"Well? Can you at least give me the same protection you gave Dr. Emerson?"

Tooley looked away. "We're releasing them today."

"What?"

"The bodies, the seven people. The ME has finished all the autopsies, and they're going to be released today."

Maggie looked at her friend sideways. "Are you all right?"

"I never thought I'd see it get like this," Tooley said wistfully.

Maggie squeezed his hand. "Will you give me some coverage? Will you have someone drive by the Center a few times a day?"

"Sure. I owe that much to your daddy." He looked down at his baseball trophy. "I never thought I'd see the day that I'd have to protect one of our own like this. A lot has changed in twenty-five years."

By the time Maggie left police headquarters it had started pouring again. According to the weatherman, a wide band of rain had stalled over the Brockston area and that meant rain for the next several days, and plenty of it. She opened her umbrella and headed for the Munch & Lunch, where she was supposed to meet Kirt at noon. It was already ten past. She saw him through the window, sitting at their favorite table, and waved when she caught his eye. Within minutes, she was sitting beside him, blotting her wet face with a napkin, the dripping umbrella by her feet.

"Have you ordered yet?"

He shook his head. His eyes danced when they looked at her. "Did you do what you promised?"

Maggie wrinkled her nose. It was only because of Kirt's insistence that she had gone to Lieutenant Tooley for protection.

"I was right, wasn't I?"

"As usual."

Kirt laughed and handed Maggie a menu. "Lieutenant Tooley still thinks there might be trouble?"

"Yes. Said the mood of the town was ugly. Although no one blames me directly. But still, Canon did come to see me before he left. So, in a way, he stained the clinic and I guess me with it."

"Why don't you take the rest of the day off? Come away with me up to the mountains. Relax a bit."

Maggie peeked over the top of her menu and laughed. "Impetuous man. Ever hear of appointments? Schedules? Not everyone is a recovering workaholic. You can't stay here forever, you know."

Kirt placed one hand on top of hers. "If you can't take the afternoon off, then we go to plan B."

"Which is?"

"Dinner and a movie."

Maggie nodded. She felt the warmth of his hand as he squeezed hers. "How's A2792? You should be there, you know, to help ramrod it through." She saw his face tighten. "I don't need a baby-sitter. That's an important bill, Kirt. You've been working on it a long time. But if you don't try to sway the fence-sitters, you could lose."

Kirt removed his hand from hers. "The turkey burger sounds good. Think I'll get that."

Maggie tossed her menu on the table. "Me too. So tell

me, how long will you be in town this time?"

"Four days. Getting my rest before the big battle. A2792 goes to vote next week. This morning I convinced the last fence-sitter of the importance of our parental-consent bill. Don't worry, Maggie, we have enough votes this time to make it illegal for underage girls to get an abortion without their parents' permission."

Maggie blushed and looked away.

"That's the problem, Maggie. You just don't trust me. You think I'm some schoolboy who'd jeopardize something this important? To do what? Baby-sit? Impress you?"

Maggie shook her head. "It boggles my mind that a minor needs permission to take an aspirin at school or to get her ears pierced, but she can get an abortion without her parents knowing anything about it."

"Don't change the subject. We were talking about trust. And like I was saying, I don't run from my responsibilities. I don't crumble when things get tough. And I know how to work things through. You can trust me, I'm not going to fall apart when things get hard."

The waitress appeared and took their order. When she was gone, Kirt leaned closer to Maggie.

"Did you do the other thing that I asked? Did you pray about us?"

Maggie nodded.

"And?"

"And I'm not sure. I need to pray more."

"But you got something from the Lord?"

"Yes."

"What?"

"I still have to pray, but the only thing I got was that Jesus sent out his disciples two by two."

"Well, that at least is a start in the right direction. Don't you think?" There was a big grin on Kirt's face. "Now, *I've* got news."

"By your face, I'd say it was good."

"I've been approached by some influential Republicans in our state and asked if I'd like to run for Congress."

Maggie flew out of her chair and hugged his neck. "You'd make a wonderful congressman!" When she saw people staring, she blushed and returned to her seat. "I'm so proud of you." Her eyes glistened with joy. "I guess your dad will just have to take one Fergason off of Fergason, Fergason, and Fergason."

"Not so fast, Maggie. I said I was *asked*. I haven't been elected."

"You will be. If you run, you'll win. I'm sure of that."

"What makes you so sure?"

"Because of who you are. Because you're a wonderful man. I believe when people in this state get to know you, they'll just fall in love with you."

"Like you have?"

Maggie smiled, her eyes meeting his. "Yes, like I have."

"If I'm elected, you realize I won't be able to visit like I do now. Not as often, anyway. We won't get to see each other very much. How do you feel about that?"

Maggie could feel tears fill her eyes and tried to hide them from Kirt. But he saw them and pulled two napkins from the chrome dispenser on the table and handed them to her.

"Sorry. I don't know what got into me."

"Don't you?"

"Well...yes...of course I do. I'm just not ready for all this."

"I know you're not. I just want you to know I'll still be around when you are."

Maggie entered the Life Center and saw Agnes rise from behind the receptionist's desk and clasp her hands together the way she always did when she was worried.

"What's wrong?"

"There's someone in your office."

Maggie watched her receptionist's face pale. "What is it?"

"I tried to keep him out, but he was wild...said he had to see you, and not to try to stop him either. He said he would wait and that...and that people like you should not be allowed to ruin other people's lives and that someday you could get hurt too, just like you hurt others. I was going to call the police, but I didn't know if I should...if that would make bad publicity for the Center, especially with that Canon Edwards thing and all. I hope I did—"

"You did the right thing. It's okay. I'll go see him. Did he give his name?"

Agnes shook her head. "You be careful. No telling who he is. I'll stay by the phone, and if I hear the slightest ruckus, I'm calling the police."

Maggie smiled and gave Agnes a hug to reassure her, but even as she began walking down the hall toward her office, she was composing urgent prayers for help. And when she saw the large, angry man standing in front of her desk, the fervor of those prayers increased tenfold.

"How can I help you?" she said with a forced smile as she moved across the room.

Before she could reach her desk, the man thrust his hand inches from her face.

"I have never...I have never intentionally hurt anybody." His voice quivered and the hand came closer to her face. "But I could hurt you lady. It would be real easy to hurt you."

"I'll call the police!" Agnes yelled in a high-pitched voice from the doorway. "You leave her alone or I'll call the police!"

Maggie waved Agnes away. "No need. I'm sure Mister... what did you say your name was?"

The stranger appeared confused as he looked first from one woman to the other. Finally, the hand dropped to his side. "Mr. Taylor. Jim Taylor."

"I'm sure Mr. Taylor just wants to talk, Agnes. Don't you, Mr. Taylor? Just want to talk? Perhaps you can get Mr. Taylor a cup of coffee, Agnes. How do you like it?"

"Coffee? I don't want...maybe...just one teaspoon sugar. Thank you."

Agnes shook her head, but Maggie gave her a stern look and waved her out. Then she went and sat behind her desk. "Now, how can I help you?"

Jim Taylor sat shaking his head, not saying anything for a while. "She hates me," he finally blurted. "My own daughter hates me. She tells me so all the time. And the way she looks at me! She glares, and she never smiles any-more. Most of the time she just sits in her room and cries. My wife and I are at our wits' end."

Agnes returned with a steaming ceramic mug and placed it on the desk where the man in the chair could reach it. Then she gave Maggie a nervous glance. "I'll be by the phone."

Maggie nodded but didn't take her eyes from the man slumped in front of her. "Why don't you start at the begin-ning."

When Jim Taylor looked up, there were tears in his eyes. "My daughter was the sole survivor of that abortion clinic massacre."

Maggie's heart jumped. "And you blame me?" she found herself saying.

"What? I…well…you and your kind, that's what did it to my girl. That's what tore the heart right out of her and made her hate me. She's damaged. I don't know if she'll ever be the same. She went through a lot of trauma. All those dead bodies all over the place. You crazy lifers! What right do you have to go shooting up a place and killing everyone, just because you don't agree with what they're doing?"

"No right at all."

"So why did you do it?"

"I didn't."

Jim Taylor eyed Maggie, then picked up his coffee. "Well… you know what I mean."

"No, Mr. Taylor, I don't know what you mean. There are eighty volunteers here at the Life Center and not one of them was at that clinic when your daughter was there. Neither inside nor out."

"But your people picket that place all the time!"

"Some of the volunteers at the Center also sidewalk counsel outside Solutions from time to time. But I was told that not one of them was there that day."

"Well…what about that madman? Canon Edwards?"

"He's not, nor ever has been, part of this Life Center."

"But they say you were friends. And you're both *lifers.*"

"I suppose I'm as close to a friend as Canon has in this town. But that doesn't mean I condone what he does or did. I'm truly sorry about what happened at Solutions. And I'm so very sad to hear about your daughter. I've been praying for her and—"

"How could you have known who she was? Her name was kept out of the papers. To protect her from that madman. How did you find out?" He began to rise out of the chair.

"Sit down, Mr. Taylor." Maggie's tone was soothing. "I didn't know her name. God just placed her on my heart. By the way, what is her name?" Maggie watched the man's face contort with pain. For a moment, she didn't think he was going to answer.

"Becky. My little girl's name is Becky. She's seventeen and she's the sweetest girl in the world. And so smart. She's going to college. Been accepted into Georgetown. The first Taylor ever to go to college. At least I think she's going. She says she's not sure. Can you imagine that? She just doesn't seem to want to do anything. This whole business ruined her. May have ruined her for life."

Maggie sat for some time, saying nothing, just praying silently and staring at Jim Taylor. She watched him fumble his ceramic cup, then shuffle his feet back and forth beneath his chair, then finally drop his head against his chest. All the while she prayed. Finally, she took a deep breath.

"The shootings at Solutions were tragic, and have probably deeply injured Becky, but not nearly as deeply as the abortion itself."

"Now listen here, you're not going to give me some of your lifer double-talk, because I'm not going to listen."

"How badly do you want to see Becky get well?"

Jim Taylor put his cup down, and Maggie thought he was going to get up and walk out. Instead, he leaned over the desk, his eyes glaring. "You people have to push and push and stir each other up until one of you gets so crazy he goes and kills a buildingful of people. Then you want to turn it around and blame it on someone else."

"Will you just listen to what I have to say?"

"The blame should fall where it belongs." Jim pulled a handkerchief from his back pocket and wiped his face. "That's what I came here to tell you."

"Every day in this country, forty to fifty women are either critically injured or killed by abortion and—"

"Maybe neither you nor your people went into that building and pulled that trigger, but you had a hand in it. You have to be held accountable."

"Every day, 416 additional women are added to the list of those suffering from post abortion syndrome."

Jim Taylor wiped his hands on his handkerchief.

"I'll spare you more statistics, Mr. Taylor, but believe me, there are a lot of hurting, damaged women walking around, hurt and damaged by their abortions. The more pressured a girl is to have an abortion, the more severe her post abortion syndrome."

"You're saying this is all my fault!"

"When did you hear me say that?"

"You said if a girl is pressured. I just tried to help. I wanted to do what was best for Becky. I wanted to make sure that she had a future...college...she's only seventeen."

"So you're saying you pressured her?"

Jim dropped his head into his hands. "You lifers are the ones who messed Becky up, shooting everything in sight. Not me. Why are you trying to turn this on me?"

"A girl who has been pressured will blame and even hate the ones who pressured her, be it boyfriend, husband, parents, friends."

Jim looked up and stared into Maggie's eyes. "She hates me. She tells me that all the time. She blames me. I thought it was because of all those killings...the trauma and all..."

"A woman who has had an abortion can feel confused, sad, guilty, betrayed, angry...ashamed. She can become depressed, even suicidal. She could develop nightmares, have flashbacks, develop eating disorders, abuse alcohol or drugs or both, act psychotically—"

"Stop! I don't want to hear this!" Jim rose to his feet but seemed unable to move.

"Sometimes she'll engage in self-degrading or self-punishing behavior. She may cry often and for no apparent reason. She may lose the ability to have close relationships with others, especially with a husband or boyfriend. Often a woman will go through a five- to ten-year period of denial, and even twenty years is not uncommon, during which time she'll repress her feelings. But sometimes, like in Becky's case, the abortion is so horrific to her that these things come upon her almost immediately. She seems…" Maggie watched as Jim Taylor sat back down in the chair and bent in half at the waist. His head hung between his knees.

"I was just trying to help her. She's only seventeen."

Maggie rose from her chair and went to him. "Why don't you bring her to the Center? We see girls like Becky all the time. We have a program, Project Rachael, that has helped many women like your daughter." Then Maggie put her hand on Jim's shoulder. "But now, may I pray with you?"

Jim shrugged. "I don't believe in that stuff. You pray if you want, but it's not going to make any difference."

"Mr. Taylor, prayer makes all the difference in the world."


The man with the clipboard scribbled something on his paper, and Thor strained to see what it was. He was sure the insurance agent was going to try to minimize the damage, and Thor wasn't going to stand for that. Ever since they had started their walk-through of the clinic, the agent had been noncommittal and visibly unimpressed by what Thor believed was extensive damage. It was bad enough the police had dragged their feet in declaring it no longer a crime scene and had only this morning removed their yellow plastic tape from around the front of the building. And getting competent people to fill all the empty staff positions was another problem. But now, to have this pipsqueak of a man try to cheat him by downgrading his insurance claim was just too much.

"Look, just look at that wall," Thor said, stopping in the waiting room. His finger pointed out a series of bullet holes that had left little caves in the Sheetrock. "Spackle won't do much there. That whole section will have to be pulled down and re-Sheetrocked. And paint. Everything will need to be painted. And we'll need new wall-to-wall carpeting. Even if we could get the stains out, we'd never get rid of that stench."

The insurance agent continued writing as Thor talked, but he said nothing. Finally, they stood outside Flo Gardner's office. The desk was splintered in two places, and the wall behind the desk was pockmarked. The carpet around the desk squished beneath their feet.

"That maniac hit a pipe. Ripped it right in half. Flooded the bathroom on the other side of that wall and this room as well. I'm going to need new plumbing. And then there's the matter of a new tile floor in the bathroom. The water lifted the tiles right off. You never get what you pay for. I spent good money on those tiles, told them to put them on a mud floor. But it's obvious they didn't use mud, just some sort of glue. And the water stains on the wall! Look at that wall! All the walls in the bathroom will have to come down. This one too. Once water gets into a wall like that it just disintegrates the Sheetrock."

Thor guided the agent out of Flo's office and down the hall, pointing to bloodstains and bullet holes as he went. Then he began inspecting the first of his three operating rooms. His voice went up several decibels. "Look! Just look at my suction machine! Look what that madman did to all my equipment."

In each succeeding room it was the same. Except the last, where not only was the equipment blown apart, but also the windows and furniture.

"Just look at this. Just look at this mess! This is going to cost me a bundle."

By this time the agent had stopped writing and just stood with his mouth open. "I've never seen anything like this," he said with a tremor in his voice.

"It's bad," Thor said. "You agree it's bad?"

"The worst I've seen in my twenty years in claims."

"Then make sure that's how your report reads. I'm not going to pay for all this. Not after paying those outrageous insurance premiums all these years. You got that?"

"Well…I only survey the damage. It's not up to me to determine the actual reimbursement. That job belongs to—"

"You just make sure that everything you see is on there." Thor stabbed the papers on the clipboard with his finger. "Everything. And we're not leaving here until it is."


Jim Taylor had not been gone five minutes when Agnes came bustling into Maggie's office, her face tight.

"Someone here to see you. He won't give his name either! Is there supposed to be a full moon tonight or something?"

"Another angry parent?"

"No, I don't think so. But he won't tell me anything. Insists on speaking only to you."

Maggie sighed and closed her eyes. "Show him in." *I can do all things through Christ who strengthens me. His grace is sufficient.*

Within seconds a man with an inordinate amount of blond hair appeared. The hair was so dense and voluminous that it made him appear tall, though he was actually rather short.

Maggie rose from her chair and bent over the desk with her hand extended. The man hesitated, then gave it a limp shake.

"I'm Maggie Singer. How can I help you?"

The man sat down in the only chair by the desk. "My name is…my name…perhaps that can wait. I feel…I mean, I'd like to…to talk first."

Maggie nodded and watched the stranger pick at his cuticles. "What would you like to talk about?"

The man's thumbnails turned white as he folded his hands and pressed his thumbs together. "The Solutions massacre."

Maggie watched the thumbs compress even tighter and worried that they, like a pencil under too much tension, would snap. She couldn't see his face because he had dropped his head, and his thick blond hair had formed a curtain. Maggie could almost hear the seconds tick noisily away amid the silence. Finally his thumbs relaxed and he looked up.

"You must promise me that when you use the information I'm about to give you, you'll not implicate me in any way."

"That's a difficult—"

"I'm afraid for my life. If they...if the people I work for knew I was talking to you...I have a family. I need to protect them and myself. You understand?"

Maggie sat very still and nodded. "I promise I'll not implicate you without your permission."

"They're selling baby parts...all kinds of parts...all ages. I get POs every day for eyes, kidneys, livers, ears, bones, brains—everything, you name it. They use everything."

"But that's illegal."

"Not if you know how to do it. There are ways around the law."

Maggie stared in disbelief. "How?"

"It's like a chain, a chain that on the surface appears very legal." The man began picking his cuticles again. "First you have a buyer, a researcher from a government agency or a university or a pharmaceutical company. This buyer sends the wholesaler a list of wanted baby parts, then the wholesaler faxes the order to the provider or source, which is the abortion clinic. The wholesaler has installed its techs in the various abortion mills it uses as its providers, and the techs harvest the requested parts."

Maggie shook her head. "I don't care what name you put on it—wholesaler, provider, tech—selling aborted babies or their parts is *illegal*. How are they getting away with it?"

The man smiled wryly. "That's just it, nobody sells the baby parts. They donate them. The abortion mill donates the parts to the wholesaler, and the wholesaler donates them to the researcher. Money changes hands only as a 'fee for service.' The wholesaler pays the abortion mill a site fee for using their premises and for access to the baby parts, and the researcher reimburses the wholesaler for costs incurred for the baby parts' retrieval."

Maggie narrowed her eyes. "Who are you? Is this some kind of perverted gag, because if it is I'm calling the police and—"

"No, don't do that. Please." He pulled a piece of paper from his pocket. "Just look at this and then tell me if I'm playing a sick joke or not." He flipped the paper onto the desk.

Maggie picked it up and began reading. "Second Chance Foundation, Subsidiary of Total Health Corporation, Fee for Services Schedule. Eyes—eight weeks, (40 percent discount for single eye), $75; ears—eight weeks, $75; bone marrow—eight weeks, $350; spinal cord, $325..." Maggie dropped the paper on the desk. She felt sick to her stomach.

"Who are you?" she asked again.

"A tech for Second Chance Foundation. My name is Adam Bender."

Maggie fingered the paper in front of her. "May I keep this?"

"Yes, and I can...I'd like to get you more information, purchase orders, invoices, the works. But it'll take time."

"Why are you doing this?"

"I thought—once I really did believe—I was doing

some good. Helping in my small way to maybe find a cure for a disease or something like that. You know what I mean?"

Maggie nodded.

"But now…after seeing how they operate…after seeing it for so long, I can't anymore. They're dangerous, these people. The money's too big, and now you have huge legitimate corporations with their fingers in the pie and it's…well…it's become like a runaway train."

"Forgive my saying this, but that answer sounds a bit too pat. For all I know you could be someone sent here to set me up, make me and the Life Center look foolish. This is pretty explosive stuff. Why should I believe you're willing to risk your career and your life simply because, according to your own words, you've had some "change of heart"? I'm sorry, Mr. Bender, but I don't buy it."

Adam Bender began picking his cuticles then pressed his thumbs together. "Once, at the Brockston clinic, I saw Dr. Newly kill a baby. It was horrible. Have you ever heard the term 'dreaded complication'?"

Maggie nodded.

"Well, Dr. Newly had one…a dreaded complication. It was after that that I found out what a loose cannon he really was and that he was a real problem…a *real* problem for the clinic. All the staff said so, and he had at least one or two lawsuits pending against him and at least two pending against the clinic as a direct result of his unethical behavior. They say he actually carved his initials into the abdomen of a girl he did an abortion on. Can you believe that?"

"What does this have to do with—"

"Dr. Emerson was trying to get rid of him. He'd been trying for a while, but I think there was a problem because no matter how many times Dr. Emerson promised Flo—Florence Gardner, she was the office manager at the clinic—he never actually did it. Not until the massacre."

"What does that have to do with Dr. Emerson?"

"Don't you see? The massacre was the perfect solution to Dr. Emerson's problem with Newly."

"You can't be suggesting that Dr. Emerson had anything to do with that?" Maggie stared at the anxious man. "You are suggesting it."

Adam didn't flinch. His eyelids didn't even flutter. His blue eyes just stared sadly back at the woman across the desk.

"But *why?* Why would you think such a thing?"

"Because he worked it with my boss that I wouldn't be at the clinic. He made sure I'd be somewhere else. After the 'dreaded complication' I was pretty upset, and I let my boss know it. I couldn't, wouldn't be party to that sort of thing. Dr. Emerson suggested that I work at one of his other clinics for a while, until he could take care of the situation. Well, he took care of it, all right."

Maggie shook her head. "For that to be true, Dr. Emerson would've had to talk Canon Edwards into doing this for him, and I don't think that's possible."

"Why not?"

"Because Canon would never do anything for Dr. Emerson. It was Emerson's botched abortion that killed Canon's wife."

"I didn't know that." Adam shrugged. "It just seemed

strange to me, that's all—too much of a coincidence. Maybe I'm wrong. But...I don't think so."

Maggie rose from her desk. "Believe me, Mr. Bender, there's no connection between Canon Edwards and Thor Emerson. But you've convinced me about the baby parts. I'd like more information, if you can get it. Some purchase orders, some of those invoices you spoke about, then maybe I can pass them along to where they'll do the most good."

Adam Bender rose from his chair and stood facing Maggie. "Don't ever try to find me or contact me. When and if I get something, I'll come and see you. And don't forget your promise. You must never use my name or tell anyone about me."


Shortly after Adam's visit, Maggie heard a series of loud bangs. *Now what?* She left her office and headed down the hall toward the reception area. Agnes stood by a partially opened front door yelling through the crack. "Stop that! You just stop that right now!"

Maggie looked out and saw two boys, teenagers. It had been raining off and on for most of the day. A steady drizzle was soaking the boys, but they didn't seem to mind. They had a bucket of rocks at their feet and were hurling them one by one at the Center. She pulled Agnes from the door and bolted it.

"Call Tooley and tell him to send a squad car. That should frighten them away." Then Maggie headed back to her office.

"And what are you going to do?" Agnes said.

"I have my own phone call to make."

Maggie dialed the familiar number and sighed with relief when Kirt and not his machine answered.

"Hi there," she said. "Got any good jokes?"

"Well, sure! Have you heard the one about two neighbors who…"

Maggie closed her eyes and listened to his strong, comforting voice.

After seeing the insurance agent to the door, Thor Emerson began walking around the clinic with his own notepad. What could he salvage? Maybe Flo's desk could be puttied, sanded, and restained. It was solid oak and would be costly to replace. He jotted that down, then wandered along the hall.

The pictures were still okay. No damage there. That was good, because he had spent a bundle on those. All original watercolors, matted and framed, a soothing distraction for the women on their way to the procedure rooms. But the large four-hundred-dollar artificial fern in the corner was spattered with blood and would have to go.

He dreaded going into the operating rooms again. That's where the most damage had occurred; that's where his wallet would be hardest hit. How could Thor have anticipated this? How could he have known that Canon Edwards would do something so extreme?

He entered the first operating room and after poking around, found a stainless steel sterilizer in perfect condition. He also noted that the procedure table was salvageable. It had a bullet hole, but a fresh vinyl cover would make it like new. No need to tell the insurance company, either. He'd just let them pay for a new one.

He spent several minutes in the second room but found only a medicine cabinet intact. He walked back into the hall and stared at the partially opened door of the last procedure room. He wasn't even going to bother to go into that one. It was a nightmare. Thor shuddered at the carnage. He already knew nothing had survived there. He even found himself feeling sorry for Newly. He hadn't wanted it to be like this. *If only Newly had listened! Then I wouldn't have had to hire someone like Canon.* But this. He never expected this. He never wanted this.

Thor was about to turn and head back to Flo's office when he noticed a piece of paper with a bloody smudge on it, stuffed into the bottom of the chart holder on the door. Slowly, he pulled the wadded page from the plastic holder and unfolded it. There, in childish printing, a printing Thor instantly recognized, was a single sentence.

*The job ain't finished yet.*

# 9

DR. THOR EMERSON SWORE under his breath as he nodded for the attendant to flip on the suction machine. This was his twentieth abortion today. He ignored the young girl's soft whimper, and when she began to moan louder, he became agitated and forced himself to work faster.

"It'll be over soon," he said, trying to comfort her, but his words sounded more like a rebuke. He had forgotten how much he hated doing abortions, how utterly angry and depressed they made him feel. What did they want from him? All these girls with their problems? You'd think they'd know better. Use birth control pills, something. But no, when they found themselves in trouble, they came to him, then complained because it hurt a little. Never showed any gratitude either. Just whined and complained. *What do they want from me?*

Dr. Emerson found himself almost recklessly probing the uterus with the plastic cannula and finishing the procedure much faster than usual.

"Next time, use birth control!" he said, stripping off his surgical gloves and depositing them in the waste can. Then he stormed out of the room, scowling at both the patient and attendant as he left. In the hall, he bumped into Clara Jackson, his new office manager, then brushed by her in a huff.

"Not so fast, Dr. Emerson. A word, if you please!"

Thor darted into the small kitchenette and began pouring himself a cup of coffee. Everything smelled new—the walls, the rug. Even the small white Formica table and four chairs he had added as an afterthought were new. It had taken two crews, working day and night for three weeks, to get the clinic back on its feet.

"You're running way behind, Doctor," Clara said, "and two of the girls in the waiting room have gotten nervous and left. Giving them too much time makes them nervous, makes them *question*. We can't allow that, now, can we?"

Thor looked at Clara's pockmarked face and saw her wince from his stare. A man-hater. He could see it in those raven eyes. The boys must have been cruel.

He thought of Canon Edwards and that blood-smudged note. He had brought it to the police and was given around-the-clock protection. He drew the line when a female detective wanted to work undercover at his clinic. *That's all I need, the police under my feet.* But he had agreed that police should be staked out twenty-four hours a day at his clinic, at his home. There was no way Canon would be able to get to him without being seen.

"Dr. Emerson!"

Thor turned his back on Clara. But if Canon did hit the

clinic again, and Clara got injured, it wouldn't be that dras-tic. Not like Flo. That had really hurt. He was really sorry about that.

"A coffee break is hardly in order! What if more girls walk out?"

"I think you're forgetting that I own this clinic." He took a big swig of coffee, and turned just a bit so he could watch her black eyes narrow, like a bird of prey ready to swoop. "I'll take breaks whenever I please."

"Well, if you run your business this way, no telling how long it'll be yours. You hired me to keep things organized, to keep the sled in the ruts, as it were."

"Yes, but I didn't hire you to ride me." Thor watched the eyes harden even more. "The best thing that could hap-pen for both of us is that the police find Canon Edwards."

"Why do you say that?"

"Because no doctor is going to step foot in this clinic until Edwards is safely behind bars. And I don't want to be here, Clara. And you want to be in charge. Once I get someone to replace me, you can ride roughshod all you like."

"I suppose if it weren't for your Dorianna Gray and Second Chance contracts, you wouldn't even bother com-ing in?"

"If it weren't for those contracts, I'd keep the clinic closed until we found someone."

"I'll put a new ad in the paper tomorrow, perhaps list more of the job perks…but for now, since you are it, I need to remind you that Adam is still here and that not all his POs have been filled."

"You're going to make a great office manager, Clara," Thor said, then drained his cup. "Thank God I won't be here."

When Thor passed the alcove next to Clara's office he saw Adam Bender by the copy machine stuffing a handful of copied pages into a folder. "What are we looking for now?"

Adam reddened. "Ah...what? Oh...I need...ah...an eight-week spleen and pancreas, the ears and brain." He began following the doctor down the hall.

Thor stopped in front of procedure room one, then pulled out a chart from the plastic file holder attached to the door. When he glanced at Adam he noticed the tech's face was as red as a strawberry.

"Sorry, but I've got a twelve-weeker here. Need anything?"

Adam fumbled through his pile of unfilled POs, and almost scattered them all over the hall floor. "Ah...yes, the skin."

Even through the crowd, Becky could see Skip coming toward her, and she spun around in the opposite direction. She didn't want to talk to him, not now, not ever. She felt a loathing she had never thought possible to feel for anyone.

"Hey, where're you going?" She felt fingers grasp her right upper arm. "Didn't you see me coming?"

Becky shook her head and kept walking.

"Slow down, will you?"

With an exasperated sigh, Becky stopped and leaned against one of the lockers. *"What?"*

"You got PMS or something? I mean, what's with you? You act like I'm diseased, like you don't want to see me anymore. What is it? I mean, if that's how you feel, the decent thing would be to tell me."

*"Decent* thing? What do you know about decent?"

"Look Becky, I've had just about enough—"

"You, you, you. That's all you ever think about, isn't it, Skip? What about me? What about how I feel?"

"I don't know what's eating you, but if you don't tell me, how can you expect me to understand—"

"Understand? You don't understand anything! And do you know why, Skip? Because you're a selfish, self-centered moron. You didn't even come to see me when I was in the hospital. Not once. Not one time!"

"Are we back to that? I've already told you how sorry I was. I can't help it that I had practice and then a big game. Why are you still harping on—"

"Because I almost died! That's why. Because I almost bled to death getting rid of your…our baby while you were busy dribbling a stupid ball around the gym."

"I never knew how bad it was…never…I swear. They told me it was a simple procedure. Like getting your teeth cleaned or something. I didn't know you were in such bad shape, or I'd have come, game or no game I would've."

"Well, you didn't. And nothing can change that."

Skip's head dropped as he began tracing a circle with his sneaker. "I'm sorry, Becky."

"So am I."

"I don't know what else to say. Tell me what to say and I will."

"Say good-bye, Skip. Just say good-bye."


"Becky Taylor, please stay after class. I need to speak to you," Mr. Hanson said just before the bell rang and everyone began scrambling out.

Becky tried to scurry out with the rest of the class and pretend she hadn't heard him. But he made his way to the door before she did and was waiting for her.

With a nod of his head, Mr. Hanson indicated she was to sit down in one of the front row desks. Then he waited for the last pupil to leave and took the desk next to her. For as long as possible, she avoided his face by staring into midair, but gradually his silence pulled her eyes to his. She noticed how tired he looked, how old.

"What's going on with you, Becky? You're one of my better students, actually my best. So when a teacher's top pupil gets an F on her last two exams and a D-minus on her term paper, that teacher must ask himself some serious questions. One—has said teacher failed to hold that pupil's interest? It happens. Sometimes by the end of the year a teacher is burnt out, doesn't always give his best. Is that the case, Becky? Have I lost your interest?"

Becky shook her head slowly.

"Then I must revert to two—that said student finds herself in some serious difficulty. So I repeat my question, what's going on with you?"

Tears began streaming down Becky's cheeks. "Nothing...

nothing that you can help me with."

"A high school is a small community. Not much happens that isn't common knowledge. There have been rumors…innuendoes…and if correct, then I understand how serious things are with you. And since I'm retiring at the end of the year, I feel freer to come right out and say what I want."

He paused and Becky could see a wistfulness on his face. "Becky, if things are serious, if they're as bad as rumors say, then know this, and tuck it away somewhere for later. I am praying for you and will continue to do so. And God, if you will allow Him, can reach into your deepest hurt and heal it."

Maggie picked up her cordless and a scrap of paper and walked into her living room. She glanced at the phone number in her hand. For the past three hours she had felt that familiar nudge from the Lord. She would wait no longer. She dialed the phone.

"Hello…Mr. Taylor? This is Maggie Singer from the Life Center. I just wanted to call and find out how Becky's doing." She heard a sigh.

"About the same."

"Since your visit to my office, you and your family have been in my prayers—"

"Listen, I'm not up to this right now. Okay?"

"Okay. But before you go, I just wanted to ask if you had thought about that Project Rachael program I told you about?" She heard another sigh.

"She can't go on like this much longer."

"What's going on? What's happening?"

"Her grades are falling. She won't see her friends. She's depressed, won't eat. And that crying…night after night. I've tried everything, but I can't make it right. I just can't make it right. Becky's whole world is coming down around her. My wife's afraid…she's afraid that Becky might hurt herself."

"Why don't you let her come to our next meeting?"

"I don't know…"

"We've helped so many girls like Becky."

"We've tried everything short of a psychiatrist."

"Then I can expect to see Becky next Sunday night at the Center?"

"I don't know…I'll think about it."


Thor Emerson swore under his breath as rain streaked his windshield. Overhead, a mass of clouds hung so low Thor felt as if he were driving in a cave. It had been raining off and on for over four weeks now. He couldn't remember Brockston ever getting so much rain, and he hoped it would end soon. It was making him feel out of sorts— despondent, gray. Maybe a few laps in the pool would perk him up.

As he pulled down his street he saw the familiar dark sedan parked across from the house. He supposed he should be grateful. They had never missed a day, not since he had given Lieutenant Tooley that paper. Still, Thor didn't feel too grateful. He felt more angry, disgusted. The

Brockston police force was one thousand strong. Surely you could expect more results. The quicker this thing was over, the quicker his life could get back to normal, and the quicker he could forget and put it all behind him. *Why can't they find Canon?*

When he drove up the circular macadam driveway, he was surprised to see his wife's car parked near the front door. The only correspondence he had had with Teresa in almost a month was from her bloodsucking lawyer. He was in no mood to entertain an estranged wife. As he got out of the Lexus, he bumped his head and let out a string of curses.

The Tiffany glass front door was unlocked, and Thor quietly entered. He stood for a moment in the marble hall-way, then heard noise in the kitchen and headed that way. From the doorway, he watched Teresa make herself a cup of tea. It annoyed him that she still felt so much at home, in the home she had chosen to leave.

"Hi there," he said, slipping onto the stool by the polished granite counter.

Teresa looked up from her tea and smiled. Thor could see he had not taken her by surprise, that she had known all along he was there, watching her.

"Mind telling me what you're doing here?"

"I want to talk to you." Teresa took a sip from her cup, then leaned her elbows on the counter.

"I'm surprised you'd want to talk to me without your sleazebag lawyer present."

"What I have to say is private."

"Okay, so say it. You have two minutes."

"Ever the arrogant, the egotistical—"

"I've had a hard day. I don't plan on having a hard night. Spill your guts, Teresa, like always, and get out."

"Okay, you want it short and sweet, so here it is. Don't try to take Eric from me. My lawyer says you're trying, along with everything else. I don't care about the house, your business, or your stock portfolio. You can have them all. I'll settle for alimony, child support, and Eric. You don't love him, Thor. You couldn't care less. But he's my life."

"Exactly, and that's why, no deal." Thor was surprised when he felt his heart racing, when he felt moisture on his palms. "You shouldn't have walked out on me. I can't forgive you for that. I've worked hard to make a name for myself, to elevate the Brockston family to its rightful place. You know how important that is to me. And you did it anyway. You made me look bad."

"I know you hate losing. But this is low, even for you."

"I've decided to leave you with nothing. By the time I'm finished you may have to pay me."

"Don't do this, Thor. Please. I'm begging you."

"You shouldn't have left. People are talking. You've made me look like a fool...a failure."

"Thor—"

"Now I'm going to rake you over the coals, Teresa, and watch the skin burn right off. I can hire a dozen men who will testify they were your lovers. I can produce hotel and restaurant receipts if I have to."

Teresa eyed him coldly. "You plan on keeping Louie busy."

Thor chuckled. "Everything can be bought for a price. You ought to know that."

"Yes, if there's one thing you've taught me it's that everything's for sale. But I just didn't want it to come to this."

Thor watched with satisfaction as Teresa blinked back tears. *Tears.* Nothing had changed.

Teresa wiped her eyes with the back of her hand. "Thor, you don't know how desperate I am. You're playing with fire. One way or the other, I'm getting Eric. Don't make it come to this."

"Come to what?"

Teresa grabbed a handful of napkins from the counter and began drying her face. "I have a complete folder on you. Pictures, everything. But I won't use them. All you have to do is give me Eric."

"You have nothing anyone would be interested in, so don't try to bluff. And don't try to pit yourself against me because then the gloves will come off and it will really get ugly."

Teresa's hand shook as she picked up her cup and took a few sips of her tea. "I thought I knew you. I still can't get over what you're capable of—what you did."

"What do you have, Teresa? A few pictures of me in the sack with someone? Well, just try to find those women. None of them will testify. I, on the other hand, can get as many men as I need to testify against you. So don't go there, Teresa. Just don't go there."

Teresa leaned against the counter as if bracing herself so she wouldn't fall. "I never thought I'd leave you, ever. But I couldn't stay. You were killing me. But I knew I couldn't leave, not without insurance. I've been collecting insurance, Thor."

"You're starting to bore me, Teresa."

"I don't think the newspapers will find me boring when I tell them about your connection with Three-Fingered Louie. Or how some of your clinics were funded by mob money."

"Don't be ridiculous, Teresa. Even you can't be that stupid. Louie values his privacy. He'll not take your shenanigans lightly."

"We're talking about you now, Thor, about what's going to happen when the good citizens of Brockston not only find out who's been backing your clinics but what you've been doing there. They're not going to like you selling baby parts."

Thor laughed. "Where's your proof?"

"I told you I prepared. I've been preparing for a long time. I've had a detective watching you for the last seven months. He's followed your every move. *Your every move.*" Teresa's eyes began filling again. "I never thought you'd be capable of it. Never. You've surprised even me." Her voice broke and she grabbed another handful of napkins.

"What's your bargaining chip? Come on. No more cat-and-mouse. Spit it out." Thor wiped his hands on his slacks.

"The detective photographed you at the bus terminal, in that disguise. It took me a long time to figure that one out. But I did, Thor. I did."

"What are you talking about?" Thor said in a near whisper.

"If you turn yourself in to the police, I'll stand by you. I'll stand by you every step of the way."

"Why should I do that?"

"Because of those killings at your clinic. Oh, Thor. *Why?* I should turn you in myself, but I can't face Eric and tell him that I was the one who sent his father to prison. But you…you can do it. Even now, it's not too late. *Please,* Thor. Do the right thing."

Thor lunged for his wife's throat, but she ducked behind the counter. He was about to go after her when he realized the stupidity of that action with the police outside. Thor shook with rage, and it took him several seconds to gain control enough to speak.

"I'll give you what you ask—alimony, child support, Eric. But you get nothing else. Not this house, not my business, not my investments, nothing, no part of them. Understand?"

Teresa had straightened from her crouched position behind the counter and now stood facing him. Her face was ashen and she flinched a little when he leaned over the counter to within inches of her face.

"Understand?" he growled again.

Teresa nodded.

"And don't ever, *ever* threaten me again."

"If I wasn't such a coward, I'd turn you in. So help me, Thor, I'd turn you in."

"And that's where I have you. I'm not a coward. I'm not afraid to do what's needed. So don't get in my way, because if you do, so help me, so help me I'll have you killed. And you know I can do it."

Teresa surprised Thor by leaning closer to him. Her eyes were fear-filled but they were also hard, unflinching. "I wouldn't do that if I were you. In fact, you better hope that nothing happens to me. Because if it does…if I should die…then my lawyer has instructions to take the dossier I have on you to the Brockston Police Department. So pray, Thor. Pray for my continuing good health."

"How do you spell supercalafragilisticexpealadocious?"

Maggie stood in her kitchen holding the phone and grinning from ear to ear.

"I can't find it in the dictionary. You'd think that a great word like that would be in there, wouldn't you?"

"You'd think so."

"So I take it you don't know how to spell it either?"

"Nope."

"So when I write it in my next card, you won't know if it's spelled wrong or not?"

"You just sent me a card."

"Did you like it?"

Maggie's grin deepened as she looked at the card on the counter. On the front was a cute calico kitten peeking out of a sewing basket.

"Well, what did you think?"

Maggie opened it. "Roses are red, violets are blue, I've never seen anyone as cute as you." She tried not to laugh. "Are you planning on doing a whole 'roses are red' series?"

"No, I'm branching out. Raising the standard. That's why I wanted to know how to spell supercalafragilisticexpealadocious. I'm going to use that in my next composition. You'll get it in a day or two, after I've really polished it."

Maggie bit the inside of her lip trying to keep her laughter in. "Could you read me your rough draft?"

"Sure, if you don't think that'll spoil it for you. It's a mini masterpiece. I'm really proud of this one. So here goes: 'Supercalafragilisticexpealadocious is the perfect word to describe someone so precocious.' Well, what do you think?"

"I think I love you."


For what seemed an eternity, Becky listened to the crying baby and wondered why no one went to pick it up. Finally, she decided she must do something and began walking down the unfamiliar hall. *Where am I?* Timidly, she opened the first door, both hoping and dreading to find the crying child, but the room was empty. Sheer, cream-colored curtains fluttered like giant wings around open double French doors that led to a withered garden. She moved toward the opening, but stopped when the sound of crying floated in on the breeze. It seemed the crying was everywhere…or maybe more than one baby was crying. She felt confused, disoriented, and quickly left the room. Then she opened another door, then another, only to find the same: empty rooms. She ran down the hall, flipping doors open one right after the other. *Where is that baby? Why doesn't someone help? Doesn't anyone care?* She was frantic now, clawing, pushing at closed doors, flinging them open then running wildly to the next one. She couldn't bear the crying any-more. *Help! Please, someone help that baby!*

Her hand throbbed. She could feel the pain move up her arm. It had to be from the banging, from pushing against all those doors. She rested against the wall, then closed her eyes. The crying was all around her now—in her ears, behind her eyes. She couldn't get away from it. She even felt it in her chest, moving up from someplace deep. It burned as it went, burned and hurt as though something were being torn, something that had never been touched before but was now mauled and bloody.

When she opened her eyes, it took her a while to real-ize she was on her back, staring at the ceiling. Her right hand ached, and when she turned to examine it, she noticed her arm was sprawled across the top of her night-stand. She blinked and rolled her eyes. She was in her bed. How long had she been sleeping?

She remembered the crying baby. She felt the tears on her face, and only then did she realize that she was the one who had been crying.

# 10

MAGGIE SINGER LOOKED UP from her notepad the instant she heard Lieutenant Tooley's voice. She watched the familiar face light up in a smile and returned it with one of her own. She finished scribbling something on the pad, then tossed her pen on the desk.

"You come from good people, Maggie, especially your daddy. You know what I thought of him."

Maggie nodded. "And?"

"Now look at you, how you turned out. Right smack dab in the middle of the ugliest controversy Brockston has seen in years. Leading a pack of hooligans."

"Now, Tooley, you don't really believe that?"

"I'm just telling you this for your own good, Maggie. Keep your people away from the Brockston clinic. Thor Emerson's got a temporary restraining order against protesters, though Lord knows how he managed that. But in the wake of all that's happened, sympathy's running mighty high in his favor, and I figure the judge thought it was right and proper to cut him some slack."

Maggie looked back at her notepad. "I guess the judge hasn't heard about free speech."

"I'm doing my best, and I promise I'll continue doing everything I can to keep the lid on and to end this whole ugly mess. Nobody wants to see this cleared up more than I do."

"I know." Maggie noticed the fatigue on Tooley's face, the strain in his voice. There were circles under his eyes, and Maggie wondered how many extra hours he had spent trying to locate Canon or coordinating the nationwide manhunt. "I know how hard you've been working."

"But if you keep this up, somebody's going to get a busted head."

"Tooley, I'm not doing anything."

"No, but your people are. You don't want to see them get hurt now, do you?"

"They're *volunteers*. They don't answer to me, they answer to a higher authority."

Lieutenant Tooley rolled his eyes. "This has got nothing to do with religion. This has to do with the law. You listen up and get your people in line. You hear? I've already had to haul in three of them. I don't want to drag in any more, but I will. You understand? No one's above the law. If someone breaks it, I gotta act. Simple as that."

Maggie smiled at her old friend, then saluted him, just like she used to when she was a child. "Yes, sir."

"Stop that, now. It galls me that I gotta come over here and lecture you about law and order. *You*, in the midst of this hornet's nest. Your daddy must be turning in his grave.

Can't imagine what he'd say."

"Can't you?" Maggie's eyes twinkled.

"No. And don't go telling me that he'd approve, because I'm not buying."

Maggie rose from her chair. "Tooley, you know perfectly well that Dad would've backed me all the way. He always insisted I follow my conscience. It only saddens me that a lot of good people haven't followed theirs."

Tooley reddened, making his round, soft face look almost like a plum. "Now, don't you go putting this on anyone else, like it was their fault. The law's the law. Abortion is legal and that's that. You want to change things, you do it through the courts, not in the streets."

Maggie walked around her desk and gave Tooley a hug. "It's God who's going to do the changing, one heart at a time."


Maggie heard a sharp tap on her wall and looked up to see Agnes leaning against the door frame. Her face was pinched and she kept looking over her shoulder as though expecting something unpleasant to happen any minute.

"You have visitors. That man...the one who was here about a week ago, Mr. Taylor...he's back, this time with his family." Agnes looked behind her once more, then tiptoed to Maggie's desk. "They all look so...so despondent. Can you see them? I know they don't have an appointment or anything, but do you think you can squeeze them in?"

Maggie looked at the mound of paperwork on her desk. She was already half a week behind. She had over thirty intake forms to process, not to mention the stack of permanent records she needed to enter into her database. Then she looked at Agnes's face and sighed.

"Take them to the kitchen, and I'll be right there."

Agnes squeezed out a frail smile, then disappeared.

Moments later, Maggie carried her empty coffee cup into the small kitchen and found the family of three sitting quietly, nervously around the table. The room was heavy with sorrow. It exuded from the three and pierced Maggie's heart. It was a gift from God, this ability to feel the anguish of others, although at times Maggie felt hard-pressed to call it a "gift." But she knew it was from God, His equipping, His provision so she could do the work she had to do.

"Good to see you, Mr. Taylor," Maggie said.

The large man rose and extended his hand, then introduced his wife and daughter.

After the introductions, Maggie turned to the coffee-maker on the counter and began rinsing out the old grinds. "Coffee, anyone?"

No one answered, so Maggie simply pulled out three clean cups from one of the cabinets and began preparing coffee for them all. She didn't speak while the coffee brewed, but tried to let the family get used to the room, the smells, the fact that they were here in a place they didn't want to be.

She filled a creamer with fresh milk and put it and a sugar bowl and some spoons in the middle of the table. Then she filled the cups and placed one in front of each of them. Finally, she poured her own coffee and brought it, steaming, to the table. Throughout the silence, she had been praying. Already she knew God was calling her to press hard.

"Your father told me you had an abortion, Becky," Maggie said, sliding onto her chair. "How do you feel about that?"

The teen absently began twirling strands of long black hair around her finger and said nothing. Maggie glanced at the parents.

"Don't you think you should tell her about your organization first? Ease her into—"

"My question was directed to your daughter, Mr. Taylor. Please let her answer."

All eyes were on Becky, and she hunched so low in her chair, Maggie was afraid she'd slide right onto the floor.

"I'd like to hear about it," Maggie said, her voice calm. "Take your time, but it's important I know how you feel."

Becky began to cry. Tears streamed from her brown eyes, eyes soft and crushed, the color of peat. Her shoulders heaved as sobs erupted from deep inside. She couldn't speak. The mother rose quickly to cradle her daughter in her arms. The father stayed seated, glaring at Maggie.

"You were supposed to help. You're only making her worse."

Maggie put up her hand to silence the father but her eyes never left the young girl. "Let her cry. When she's ready, she'll speak."

For almost half an hour Maggie sat quietly watching Becky sob into her mother's arms. She wondered if this was the first time the daughter had allowed her parents to see her anguish and decided by the look of concern on the father's face that it was. When it looked as though Becky was all cried out, Maggie reached across the table and took her hand. For several minutes, Maggie gently held it, crying inside as she watched the young face streaked with unbearable pain.

"You have lost a child and you are in mourning," Maggie said softly, squeezing the young girl's hand. "Your grief is a good sign, a healthy sign."

Becky looked up, surprise on her face. "It is? I…I thought I was going insane. I thought I was losing…" Fresh tears splashed onto the table. "My friends told me I was acting stupid. Making too much of it." She glanced at her father timidly. "Nobody understands how I feel…how I've been feeling these past weeks." Then she looked at Maggie. For the first time, a faint ray of hope shone on her face. "I'm not going crazy?"

"No." Maggie smiled. She felt Becky's fingers slowly curl around her own. "Believe it or not, you're beginning to heal. Your grief tells me you're facing some harsh realities—or trying to—instead of pretending they don't exist. A lot of women in your position will do that—pretend—then years down the road something will happen to trigger deeply buried emotions."

"Will I…will I ever get better? Will it ever stop hurting?"

Maggie nodded, ignoring the exasperation on the father's face and the look of helplessness on the mother's. "It will get better, but not before it gets worse. There are some hard times ahead. Some tough issues you'll have to face, to deal with. Are you up for that?"

The father jumped to his feet. "Now wait a minute. Becky has been through enough. You said you could help her. I don't see how making her feel worse could possibly solve anything."

"You'll need courage, Becky. Can you do it?"

Becky's lower lip trembled and fresh tears welled up in her eyes, but her fingers firmly gripped Maggie's. "I don't know. It hurts so bad now. I don't know if I could stand any more."

Jim Taylor began pulling Becky's chair, trying to make his daughter rise. "Come on, that's enough. I'm taking you home. You had your chance, lady, and you blew it. I'm not letting you mess with my daughter's head."

Maggie tightened her grip on Becky's hand. She could sense a spiritual battle being waged. "Tell me how you feel about your abortion."

Becky's fingers went limp, and for a second she rose slightly as though to go, then sat down and just stared into Maggie's eyes. "It was horrible..." Her voice splintered and she dropped her head to her chest. "I think I heard my baby scream. I know that's ridiculous...but I did...from deep inside...I heard my baby."

For the first time, Maggie could see tears in Jim Taylor's eyes, and without another word, he moved from behind Becky's chair to the empty chair next to his wife. Maggie watched as he put his arm around his wife and they both cried. Then Maggie turned back to Becky. "It's not ridiculous. Only once before have I heard of this happening, but it's not ridiculous. When a woman becomes pregnant her body and mind begin to bond with that child. One of the deepest, strongest instincts a woman has is the maternal instinct."

"I didn't want to do it. I didn't want to!" Becky began sobbing again.

"Do what?" Maggie said, her voice calm, tender.

"You know…you know what."

"Say it. You must say it."

"I can't say it! I don't want to say it."

"Please, Becky. You must."

Becky jerked her head from side to side, making her hair slap against her face. "No, it hurts too much. Don't make me. Please don't make me."

Maggie squeezed the teen's hand. "I won't make you do anything, Becky. You have to want to take it out of the drawer and look at it. Do you want to?"

Becky's hand pulled from Maggie's, and she rested her forehead on the table, then covered her head with her arms. "No…yes…I don't know. I don't think I can. You say it for me."

Maggie rose, walked around the table, and sat in the seat Jim originally occupied. She pulled it very close to Becky's. "Four little words, Becky, four little words. You have to open that drawer sometime. Try…to do it now."

"I had an abortion," Becky whispered.

"Yes, you had an abortion. And what did that abortion do, Becky? By having the abortion, what did you do to your baby?"

"I killed it! I killed my baby!" Becky screamed. "I killed my baby!"

Maggie leaned over and hugged the weeping girl, then

began weeping herself. "Yes, you killed your baby."

Jim slammed his large fist on the table, making it jump. "This is going too far. You're making my daughter crazy with your talk. Stop it, just stop it right now!"

Maggie held the young girl tightly, stroking her hair, brokenhearted from being with the brokenhearted. "Mr. Taylor, Becky killed her baby and she knows it, has known it all along. And she's willing to face it, come to grips with it. Are you?"

Jim looked at his wife and sighed. "I only wanted what was best for Becky. I did it for her…for her future. I *love* her. I wouldn't hurt her for the world. I only did what I thought was…best."

"Where do we go from here?" Nancy Taylor asked.

Maggie released Becky and smiled. "If Becky wants, she's welcome to join Project Rachael, the support group I told your husband about. It meets once a week for twelve weeks. The new group is meeting Sunday afternoons and has already started, but Becky can still join. For part of the session, she'll get a chance to listen and share with other women who've had abortions, and the rest of the time will be spent in Bible study."

"Bible study?" both husband and wife said at the same time.

Maggie nodded.

"We're not church people," Jim said.

"Becky, do you have a problem with that? With joining Project Rachael? Knowing there's going to be prayer and Bible study?" Maggie asked.

The teen looked at her parents. "No. I think I'm willing

to do just about anything to get through this."

Jim shifted uncomfortably in his chair. "What kind of things are you going to be filling her head with?"

"The mercy and grace of God."


"Did you know that assemblymen in New Hampshire only make two hundred dollars a year and no per diem?"

Maggie hugged the phone to her ear, savoring the sound of Kirt's voice that was beginning to soothe away the hurts of the day. "And you thought you were working for nothing."

"Of course," Kirt continued, "if I were in California, I'd be making about $72,000, plus per diem, and maybe a nice piece of change from some creative-accounting expenses, if I were so inclined."

Maggie pictured Kirt's paneled office: his gray, overflowing file cabinets; his piano-finish mahogany desk set that his father and brother had given him as a gift when he won his assembly seat; the polished gray marble paperweight she had given him, engraved with the Scripture "The fear of the Lord is the beginning of wisdom"; and next to that, her picture. She had not realized until the day of her visit that he kept her picture on his desk, a five-by-seven in a plain mahogany frame. She wished she were there now in his warm, friendly office, so different from her office, an office too often filled with heartache.

"And what, pray tell, got you started thinking about salaries?" Maggie asked. "I never realized the subject interested you so much."

"I was reading an old issue of *Governing* and I came upon the article "Legislatures and the Salary: Mismatch Syndrome" by Alan Ehrenhalt. It started me thinking."

"Is this an example of my hard-earned tax dollars at work?"

"Right now, I'm probably the only one who is working. The capital's a ghost town. It seems everyone has gone home for the weekend."

"Well, obviously not quite everyone."

"Know what I'm thinking right now? I'm thinking, why am I sitting here reading an old article when I can be with you? If I leave now, I can get to Brockston in time to take you to dinner. And then we'll have the whole weekend to discuss salaries and how two can live as cheaply as one. What do you say?"

"I like the dinner idea."

"And the other part?"

"It's going to be a long weekend. Let's just take one thing at a time."

As Thor Emerson raced by Clara's office, he caught a glimpse of Adam Bender and stopped short. He backed up to the doorway just in time to see Adam rifling through the file cabinet.

"What are you doing?"

Adam's mop of blond hair covered a good portion of his face, but even so Thor could see deep red streaks, like fingers, begin to creep over the young man's cheeks.

"I...I wanted to recheck an order...from last week. I

think I messed up on my report for Second Chance."

"Why didn't you just ask Clara?" Thor moved closer. "She won't appreciate you going through these files. And quite honestly, neither do I. These files are personal."

Adam barely missed slamming the metal drawer on his finger. "I…I'm sorry. I didn't think it mattered. I just wanted to verify…sorry. It won't happen again."

Adam picked up the black briefcase at his feet, backed out of the office, and disappeared. Thor reopened the drawer that had occupied Adam's attention. It was the client files, with *Second Chance* typed on one of the folders. *Maybe he was telling the truth.* Thor was about to close the drawer when he noticed another folder cocked and out of alphabetical sequence. The label read *Galaxy Cosmetics. And then, maybe he was lying.* But why would he check out the Galaxy file? Unless…unless Second Chance was ticked that he hadn't met his quota this month and wanted to know if Thor was satisfying his other clients before satisfying them—which he was.

"Why aren't you in room two? Your patient is waiting."

Thor spun around to see Clara Jackson. "And why weren't you here in your office where you belong!"

"I'm entitled to a ten-minute break every four hours. If you have a problem with that, contact the Labor Board."

"Well, next time you take a break, lock your office."

Clara swaggered up to the file cabinet. "What's the problem?"

"Adam Bender. You keep him out of this office, understand?"

"What was he looking at?"

"I'm not sure, maybe this." Thor flicked the Galaxy tab with his finger. "Or maybe you misfiled it."

Clara laughed. "Hardly."

"What? You never misfile?"

"That wasn't misfiled, that was shoved in the drawer by someone in a hurry." Clara snickered. "He couldn't have liked what he saw."

"Put a cork in it," Thor said and walked out.


Two hours later, Thor ushered Clara from her office and ordered Adam in. He noticed Adam fidgeting, his finger picking at his front belt loop. He watched as Adam brought one hand to his mouth and made artificial coughing sounds. Then he watched Adam wipe his palms on his pant legs.

"I notice you aren't carrying your briefcase," Thor said.

"It's in my car."

"Is that where you keep the copies?"

"What?"

"The copies of the Galaxy file."

Adam's hand trembled as he brought it up to his forehead.

"It doesn't belong to you. I could call the police and have you searched, maybe even arrested."

For the first time Adam smiled. "If you think I've done something wrong, go ahead. Of course if they find anything, they'd have to confiscate it as evidence."

Thor pushed himself away from the desk and began rocking back and forth in his leather executive chair. The chair creaked as he rocked. He found it pleasant, almost soothing. "You have a lot of responsibility—getting fresh, uncontaminated specimens, packing them properly for shipment. Yes, a lot of responsibility."

"What's your point?"

"I've always thought you were overworked and under-paid. I could make it worth your while if you forget what you saw in that file today. There's no need for Carl Langley to see those copies."

"Carl?"

"You have no idea what I'm up against. There just aren't enough specimens to go around. Everyone wants a piece of the action—no pun intended. And the Galaxy account is…well, it's got to come first. There's a lot of pressure to meet their quota, and I'm talking pounds here. They buy it by the pound. They're not people you want to fool with or say you can't deliver. You understand?"

Adams face looked like chalk.

"I'm a businessman, and I have to think like a business-man. It's a matter of putting things into priority. Who can hurt you the most if you don't deliver? Carl can pull his account, but Galaxy…it's different with Galaxy. It's more serious. See what I mean?"

Adam wiped his forehead but said nothing.

"Why get Carl upset? The clinic closing put us a little behind, but soon enough we'll be back on track. And everyone will get what he wants. Everyone will be happy. And you most of all, with your nice big bonus of 50K."

Adam's fingers got caught in the belt loop. "I don't take bribes. I never have. And there were many occasions when I…I don't take bribes."

Thor continued rocking, back and forth, back and forth. "Who said anything about a bribe? I'm talking bonus, for working overtime and getting the job done—filling those backorders. The only catch is that Carl wouldn't know. It serves no purpose, don't you agree?"

"I need time to think about it. I'll let you know."

Maggie loved Sundays in the park, especially Sundays in the park with Kirt. Today the sun was out, an added bonus. It was the first day in weeks that it had actually blazed, bright and bold like a golden shield, instead of ducking timidly back and forth behind the clouds.

Maggie felt Kirt's hand brush against hers as they walked side by side, then their fingers intertwined. It felt natural for her hand to be in his, for his shoulder to gently, playfully nudge her. When had they moved to this new level of intimacy? Of hand-holding and good-night kisses? It seemed like ages, but Maggie knew it hadn't been that long at all. Maybe that's why it still made her nervous. Why it still violated her better judgment. She loved the feel of his hands, so warm and strong. He made her feel safe, loved. But this couldn't last. Already she had allowed it to go too far. They were way past the friendship stage. Her heart was as entangled as their fingers. Still…how could it work between them? She was like one of those empty rubber dolls. She felt the familiar anger bubble up inside her. *Forgive me, Lord. Forgive me.* How many times had she said that? How many times had she asked the Lord to forgive her? But the anger kept coming back. Why did it keep coming back?

Kirt glanced sideways. His boyish smile made Maggie melt, and she soon forgot her anger. Kirt guided them to a park bench where they sat down. Maggie laughed when he pulled out a crumpled paper bag from his pocket. She watched with eyes full of delight as he opened it and scooped out a handful of breadcrumbs for the birds.

"I thought you forgot."

"Now how could I forget our little feathered friends?"

Maggie watched two peach-and-gray doves waddle up to the crumbs around Kirt's feet. The smaller one had an injured wing and it hung, partially open and useless, on one side. The other dove hovered nearby like a shield.

"Rosie looks a little better today," Maggie said.

"Yup. It'll take time, but she'll be fine. And Dan will be right there waiting until she is." He gave Maggie a curious look.

"Why do I sense there's a cryptic message in this?"

"Not cryptic, Maggie, blatant. An object lesson. If God can put such devotion and faithfulness into a pair of doves, couldn't He put the same thing into two people who love each other?"

Maggie watched Rosie maneuver awkwardly with the hanging wing and hoped it would heal quickly. *But it would heal.* Eventually, Rosie would fly again. Kirt had missed that point. You couldn't heal something that wasn't there, that would never be there.

"You do love me, don't you, Maggie?"

She nodded, keeping her eyes fixed on the doves.

"And you know I love you."

"It's not that simple."

"Yes it is."

"It's not that simple!"

"It's simple if you want it to be, Maggie, but you don't want it to be."

Maggie turned toward Kirt. "What do you mean?"

"You really want to know?"

"Yes."

Kirt studied his companion for some time. "I don't think so. You say you do, you pride yourself in honesty, but in this thing, Maggie, you're not honest at all."

"Your remark seems rather unfair, especially since you haven't told me what it is I'm being dishonest about."

Kirt sighed. "Okay, I guess it needed to be said sooner or later. Years ago, when you had that abortion, it did something to you. I understand that. But you asked God for forgiveness and He gave it, and then finally you were able to forgive yourself. That's why so much of you has healed. But…"

"But?"

"But you've never come to grips with the fact that you'll never again be able to have a baby."

"Yes I have! Why do you think I can't make a commitment to marriage? Because I'm a realist. I understand full well what it means to be unable to give a man children. I've resigned myself…I know marriage is out of—"

"That's not coming to grips, that's feeling sorry for yourself."

Maggie watched Kirt scatter more crumbs on the ground, then watched as the large dove continued to stand guard while his mate pecked at the meal. Then she watched Kirt's hand cover hers.

"You'll never be free, Maggie, until you've forgiven that abortionist who butchered you. I'm right, aren't I?"

Maggie couldn't speak. She just tightened her grip on Kirt's hand.

"Satan has stolen so much from you. Don't let him rob you of a future with me. Don't let him do that."

"It's such a part of me now—the anger, the outrage."

"I know."

"Sometimes I feel so empty as a woman. There's a big part of life that I'll never experience again. Sometimes when I think about it, when I realize the loss, the terrible, terrible loss, I'm filled with a hatred I can hardly believe possible. Then I'm down on my knees asking for forgiveness, but it comes back. It always comes back."

"This time, instead of asking forgiveness, you must extend it."

"He took so much, Kirt. He made me…he left me half a woman. How could any man love me now?"

"I can…and do."

Maggie turned toward Kirt, her eyes pleading. "Doesn't it bother you, knowing that I could never give you a son…a daughter?"

"By God's grace, no."

Maggie shook her head. "I want to break free, I really do…"

"If that's true, then you know what you have to do."

"I can't!" Maggie said like a sob. "I just can't."

❧

Maggie couldn't stop muttering to herself. She felt like the weather, grumpy and ready to erupt. Since that episode in the park with Kirt, she had felt an agitation that seemed to rise to her lips like acid reflux and produce a constant grumbling. All Sunday she had snapped at Kirt. By late Sunday afternoon she had insisted he take her home, where she brooded for the rest of the day and night. When the alarm went off this morning, Maggie could barely rouse herself out of bed. And by the time she got herself to the Center, she was almost an hour late. Through it all, she had felt God's displeasure.

Listlessly she dug through the mound of papers on her desk, taking pains to avoid looking at the little picture of two swans swimming in a blue-green lake and the caption beneath it: "Peace on the outside comes from knowing God within." Today, peace was a stranger she could not coax to her door.

*Lord, how many times have we gone through this?* She flipped on her computer and the soft beeps and buzzing broke the uneasy silence. A few minutes later, the colorful screen saver flashed on, along with a scripture: *The heart is deceitful above all things, and desperately wicked: Who can know it?* She turned off her monitor.

"Adam Bender's in the waiting room, chewing his fingers. Can you see him?" Agnes said, poking her head in the doorway.

"Can't I have five minutes to get some work done around here without an interruption?"

"What's the matter with you?"

Maggie looked down when she saw the hurt on Agnes's face. "I'm out of sorts today. Sorry. I didn't mean to snap."

Agnes pointed to the wall calendar with a picture of an indigo lagoon on some tropical island. "You need a vacation. I've seen those signs before. You're the first here in the morning—except for this morning—and the last out. Too much work, Maggie Singer, and not enough R&R. When was the last time you sailed off into the sunset?"

Maggie gathered up some papers on her desk and began reshuffling them. "Please, Agnes, no lectures, not today. I'm not in the mood. Just show Adam in."

Agnes muttered something about a cruise, then left the room. Moments later Adam Bender stood in front of Maggie's desk. He placed a briefcase on the floor, then paced around her office, nervously fingering objects on the shelf or on her desk. Finally, she got him to sit down in the armchair across from her. For a moment, he just sat there, immobile, like a wind-up toy that had run its course. Then suddenly he pulled his black leather briefcase onto his lap and took out a handful of papers.

"Here," he said, "it's all here. And now I'm done with it. There'll be no more."

Maggie called to Agnes to get Adam a cup of coffee and waited until she returned with a steaming mug before saying anything. "Why don't you start from the beginning?" She gestured for Agnes to sit in the corner and take notes. "Do you mind?" she said to Adam.

Adam shrugged. Agnes sat down quietly and picked up a notepad.

"Tell us what happened," Maggie said.

"I don't know, exactly. He caught me rifling his files. Dr. Emerson knows what I've been doing. I think he's suspected for some time, but today...today he caught me."

"Then what happened, after he caught you?"

Adam walked her through the entire scenario with Thor.

"So he thinks you're spying for Second Chance?"

"Yes, and I'm out of it now. I want nothing more to do with this. Did you know my hair is falling out? Nerves. It's from nerves. My hair's all over the bathroom sink, in the shower, on the floor, everywhere. Even my wife noticed it. I can't take it anymore. I want out. My wife and I talked it over this weekend. I'm leaving Second Chance. I'm resigning as soon as I'm finished here. If Dr. Emerson ever finds out that I *wasn't* copying those papers for Second Chance, I don't know what he'd do. But I know this, I'm not taking any more chances. I have a family to think about. So this is it. Okay? I don't care what you do with this stuff as long as you don't involve me."

Maggie reached over the desk and took the papers from Adam's hand. She glanced at the top page and began reading:

Confidential protocol, Dr. Jack Vancouver, tissue use: HIV pathogenesis in scid-hu mice. To study the in-vivio role of various genes of HIV-1 pathogenesis and to determine the molecular basis of differences in the pathogenic properties of various stains. Tissue requested: liver, thymus, brain, lymph 16-24 week gest., note sex if possible. Fresh, buffered media to be provided (RPMI w/10% fes, 5 units/ml superoxide dismutase and pen/strep/glutamine). Ship on wet ice.

Maggie noticed that the ship-to address was a major university in California. She tossed the page on her desk and began reading the next one:

Confidential protocol, Dr. R. Bersero. Tissue requested: liver 17-23 week gest. (whole). Specifications: fresh, UW's soln.

The ship-to address was a major Boston hospital, directed to the attention of Surgical Oncology. She tossed that page, then started reading the next:

Protocol, placenta & membranes (cord is wanted, if possible, but not necessary). Tissue use: human collagens. Protocol, prenatal cartilage of leg and hip. Tissue use: study of biochemical characterization of human type-X collagen. Dr. Beverly Blake, cut whole placentas into two- to four-inch-square uniform sections and place sections in individual Ziplock bags directly on dry ice. Whole intact leg, include entire hip joint, 22-24 weeks gest. Age of fetus must be determined and noted. Indicate footpad measurement. Four to five specimens per shipment in special media provided. Wet ice. Dorianna Gray—division of Galaxy Cosmetics.

She flipped through the rest of the papers. There had to be at least thirty purchase orders in her hand, split almost evenly between Second Chance Foundation (on behalf of various universities, hospitals, and pharmaceutical companies) and Dorianna Gray/Galaxy Cosmetics. She tossed the entire batch onto her desk. Her body trembled. She hoped it didn't show.

"You can't walk away from this. You must come forward. Without you, the story won't have the same credibility."

Adam shook his head. "Like I said, I have a family. My daughter's only two. She needs a father. A thing like this can cause a lot of trouble. We're talking big money here. Nobody wants to see their gravy train derailed."

"Maybe if you discussed it with your wife again and—"

"I told you from the beginning I didn't want to get involved. These people are dangerous. I've been in this business long enough to see and hear what happens when someone tries to monkey with the system. You have to understand how serious this is. I'm talking about people getting killed. It's happened before. In this business, threats are often backed up with action."

Maggie nodded. "I know that and I appreciate all you've done. I'm sorry for pressing so hard, but this is so big, so…horrendous. It has to be made public. But I understand your position. I'll use this information in a way that will do the most good—without compromising you. You have my word. You won't be linked with any of this."

"I trust you, otherwise I wouldn't have come here in the first place. And about that other matter, the clinic massacre. Just forget I ever said anything. Okay?"

"Why is that?"

"I don't know what made me say anything—what I was thinking." Adam rose to his feet. "But I don't want to get involved with any of it. I have a family…"

"You still haven't changed your mind about that? You still think Thor Emerson had something to do with those killings in his own clinic?"

"I'd stake my life on it."


"Shall I offer my firstborn for my transgression, the fruit of my body for the sin of my soul?" Maggie had been staring at the Scripture for over an hour. Since coming home from the Life Center, she had been sitting on her bed with her Bible open to this passage. Every time she tried to turn the page, to get on to something else, her eyes, her mind, her heart returned to Micah 6:7. She could not afford to be at odds with God. Too much was happening. But how could she go forward with God unless she dealt with this? Even as she stared at the Scripture, she knew there could be no shortcuts. Was she ready for that?

"Shall I offer my firstborn for my transgression?" Maggie had put the sin of her abortion under the blood of Jesus years ago. So why was God bringing it up now? The Scripture had come to her on the ride home. Maggie knew it wouldn't leave her until God was finished. She closed her eyes and leaned into the pillows propped against the head-board. She would not fight Him. She would give Him His way, let Him touch that spot she had kept protected under a shield of denial—yes, this time she would let Him touch it.

"But I have forgiven!" Maggie screamed into her bedroom. "I have forgiven." And even as she said it she knew it was only partially true. She began to cry. It had been part of her for so long—this hate, this anger—and whenever she felt it she always confessed it to God. She had forgiven the abortionist for destroying her child, for lying to her and telling her it was only a blob she was carrying, for brutalizing her body, but she had never, never forgiven him for making it impossible for her to ever get pregnant again, for ever being able to deliver a beautiful baby, to hold her baby in her arms, to smell fresh baby powder on its little body, to hug and kiss it, to weep and laugh and dream with her child. She had never forgiven the abortionist for taking away her promise.

She thought of Kirt's words: "Satan has stolen so much from you." Then, as clear as any voice she had ever heard, she heard the Lord speak to her mind. *Will you let him steal more?*

Maggie threw herself face down on the bed. She felt so wretched, so deeply miserable. This was not the full life God had called her to.

She felt a presence in her room and looked up, but saw no one. It was as if God was there, waiting patiently for her answer. *Will you let him steal more?* And this time she heard her own voice answer, "No, Lord. No more."

# 11

DR. THOR EMERSON PACED back and forth in front of his desk. Even though it was Sunday and no one was in the office, he wore a gray pin-striped suit and white shirt. The only concession he had made was that he wore no tie and his shirt was open at the collar. He had spent years building his image as a consummate businessman, and it was hard to break the habit even when he was alone. He had not been in his "command center" for a week. His abortions at the Brockston Clinic kept him too busy.

He was grateful to Clara for her tenacity in getting someone to replace Dr. Newly. After weeding through several undesirables, she began calling abortion clinics within a fifty-mile radius, polling doctors to see if they were satisfied in their present service and, if not, what it would take to change employer. In one day she had found her new recruit, a doctor with a good reputation who was unhappy over certain slipshod practices at his clinic. She assured him that the Brockston Clinic observed the highest standards, then promised him a substantial increase in salary.

Thor wished the new doctor could start tomorrow, but it would be at least four more weeks before he joined the team, two-weeks' notice and two weeks for an extended and, according to the new doctor, much-needed vacation.

Thor watched his adult Clowns, a swirl of yellow, white, and black, dart behind the staghorn coral. He loved it here, away from the sights and smells of the clinic, away from the constant whining of the suction machines. He had begun hearing them in his sleep.

He walked over to his desk and sat down. It irritated him that the only time he had now was on Sundays, his golf days. But he needed the day to see what his other clinics had been doing that week and put out any fires that inevitably sprang up in this business. *Fires.* He really had one this time. His stomach turned at the thought of having to call Louie. He had put it off, had saved it until all his other business was finished. Now, only one white card, pulled from his Rolodex, remained on his highly polished mahogany desk. He fingered it briefly, then placed it back on his desk and began pacing again.

Thor found himself standing by the tank, tapping the glass to force the half-dozen young Clowns from their hiding places among the seaweed. He had missed the long-awaited event. And even though it was an occurrence preceded by both great excitement and expense, his interest in the Clowns had ebbed. It was only with the mildest curiosity that he watched them now.

He looked with envy as the parent Clowns emerged from behind the coral only to dart into the hollow ceramic pirate's vessel. It was easy for them to hide from the outside world. If only his life could be that simple. His envy dissipated when he noted the symbolism of the sunken ship. No, he wasn't going to get morbid and entertain thoughts like that. His ship was not about to sink, and certainly not by the hand of Adam Bender.

Thor headed back to his desk, sat down, and dialed the phone. Within seconds, he heard the familiar baritone voice. He pictured the hand, with two fingers missing, holding the phone at the other end.

"Hello?"

"It's Thor, Louie. We might have a problem."

"No 'hello—how are you'? Just 'Louie, we have a problem'? What am I? A quasi-cleanup/problem-solving service? Why is it that you college types have the most despicable manners?"

"Sorry, Louie. It's Sunday and I didn't want to take up your time with small talk. I figured you had better things to do."

"I suppose I do. So what's the problem?"

"I'm not sure. I said we might have a problem."

"Enough with the semantics. Just come out with it, Thor."

"Well…you know how you asked me to make the Dorianna Gray POs top priority? And I did, but that meant I had to bump another large wholesaler to second position and—"

"You're not usually this long-winded."

"Well, unlike Dorianna Gray, where my in-house tech takes care of things, Second Chance Foundation has its own tech in place. And this tech, Adam Bender, helped himself to my files and probably made copies."

"Probably?"

"More than likely. At first I thought I could handle things because I assumed he was just doing some industrial espionage for Second Chance."

"What changed that?"

"I found out that Adam quit Second Chance. And when I spoke to Carl Langley, the president, no mention was made about me bumping him for you, so I'm sure he doesn't know. Which means—"

"Which means that Adam Bender is working for someone else."

"Probably."

"Probably?"

"More than likely."

"Why is it you never say what you mean, Thor?"

Thor jammed the file card back into the Rolodex. "I thought you should know, that's all."

"I've always believed that self-preservation was a marvelous incentive for communication. So, what did he pilfer? What did he get that could hurt us?"

"He got POs for collagen."

"Why is that a problem? It's not illegal. So Dorianna Gray acquires placentas for their wrinkle creams, so what?"

"He may also have gotten copies of POs for type-X collagen."

Louie rattled off a string of four-letter words. "How

could you be so stupid! You know how much money my friends have invested?"

"Don't get excited, it may—"

"Thor, for a college guy, you can be pretty obtuse. These investors want to keep low profiles. Any ripple, no matter how small, will be unwelcome."

"We may be lucky if ripples are all we get."

"For your sake, I hope you're wrong."

Thor shifted uncomfortably in his chair. "I think the question right now should be, what are our options?"

"Are you utterly stupid? You think I'm going to discuss options over my home phone? You let me handle things. I'll discuss this with pertinent parties and take it from here."

"What do you want me to do?"

"Maybe you should go back to college."


Becky Taylor brushed her long hair over and over. She could hear the static crackle between the bristles of her brush, could feel the strands of hair rise around her head. But she couldn't see it because she avoided mirrors. She just couldn't stand looking at herself.

Her mother had bought her a white oxford shirt for the occasion, but she didn't wear oxfords anymore, especially not white. The new shirt was on the closet floor, buried under shoes and an assortment of wrinkled clothes. Instead, she had chosen a gray cotton pique polo, which belonged to Paula and hung loosely over her jeans. Paula's shirts had always been a little big on her, but lately they drooped. She didn't tuck it in. Her ribs might show and then she'd have to listen to her mother complain about how thin she looked. *Who could eat?*

She continued brushing her hair, thinking about whether she really wanted to go. Her stomach felt queasy. What would they talk about? *Will I have to share, give my story like one of those people at Alcoholics Anonymous?* She didn't think she could do that. But if she could just sit and listen...if she could do that, then maybe she'd go.

Maggie Singer had given her hope. But since that meeting at the Life Center, her hope had been slowly leaking away, leaving her flat and more depressed than ever. And her insomnia had gotten worse. She was afraid to sleep, afraid she would dream and hear that suction noise, hear that baby crying. The only improvement at all was that she no longer felt like an oddity. She knew she was not alone. Other girls felt as she did. Other girls cried in their sleep, if they slept at all, and other girls also wished they could undo what they had done, would give just about anything to undo what they had done.

She heard footsteps down the hall and hoped they were not coming her way. When there was a light tap on the door, Becky sighed. Almost hourly her parents found some excuse to come to her room and check up on her. *What do they think I'm going to do? Slit my wrists?* She opened the door and stared into her mother's face. Her mother seemed to have aged ten years, her father fifteen. They both looked so old. She had done that. She had broken the hearts of the two people she loved most in the world.

"Are you ready?" her mother asked almost inaudibly.

Becky noticed that both her parents had started speaking softly. The words in their house had become too painful. "Are you ready?" her mother repeated when Becky didn't answer.

Becky shrugged.

"You are going? You haven't changed your mind?"

Becky looked into her mother's pleading face and nodded. When Becky did, she felt an inexplicable excitement that surprised her, and she realized for the first time how much she really wanted to go, how much she need to go.

Becky watched a smile break out on her mother's face. It wasn't a real smile though. Just a shift in her mother's face that said she didn't hurt so badly, for this one split second the pain had subsided. The next minute it was back.

Becky reached over and gave her mother a hug. She could hear a sob tumble from her mother's lips.

"Now remember, if it gets too weird, or if they say anything to upset you, you can walk out. You don't have to stay. But I'm glad you're going. Maybe...maybe they can help. I only wish I could go with you. I don't know why mothers aren't allowed. I don't understand—"

"It's better this way, Mom. I need to do this myself. Maybe later I'll ask if you can come. We'll see."

Nancy Taylor dabbed her eyes with a tissue. "I'm sorry, Becky. I'm so sorry. I never thought it would be like this. I never meant for you to get hurt. If we had only known, we would've tried...tried to find another way. I'm...so...sorry."

Becky put her arms around her mother again. "I know, Mom. So am I."

Becky sat at the same kitchen table where she had sat the first time she came to the Life Center. The large twelve-cup Krups machine was busy brewing coffee, and the aroma of Colombian decaf filled the room. She looked at the scratched pine cabinets, the faded green floral wallpaper, the clean but slightly cracked beige vinyl floor that was supposed to look like ceramic tiles. It was an eighties kitchen, so like her own. It could almost fool one into thinking she was at a friend's, except that no one spoke. All eight of the girls, many older than Becky, sat quietly around the table, nervously fingering their empty coffee cups, waiting for someone or something to break the tension.

"Hello!" Maggie Singer said, almost bouncing into the room, joy written all over her face.

*She looks like a grinning imbecile.* Becky looked around at the others. No one smiled. But that didn't seem to deter Maggie.

"Who wants coffee?" Maggie carried the coffeepot over to where the girls sat and began pouring coffee into each cup.

*Is this supposed to show that she just loves everybody, and that love, love, love will make everything go away?* But Becky could see that the women were beginning to relax.

Maggie took the one empty chair. "Since we have a new member with us, I'd like for each of us to introduce ourselves and give as much or as little information as you feel comfortable giving. This way we can get a sense of who's here, where we're from, and maybe, if you want, how things are going for you since your abortion. Most of you didn't share last time, and maybe you'll feel better about sharing today. I'd like to go first, if you don't mind. And then we can move clockwise around the room."

Becky anxiously counted the chairs. She was number three. What was she going to say? Not one single solitary word if she didn't want to.

"My name is Maggie Singer, I'm thirty-five, single, never been married. I had one abortion when I was twenty, and I'm just now really getting over it, by God's grace."

Becky straightened in her chair. *This holy roller had an abortion?*

"My pregnancy was a real shock. We—my boyfriend at that time and I—had always used protection. I didn't know then that among young people condoms fail over 20 percent of the time."

Becky gulped air.

"I didn't know the Lord then, when I was twenty. I believed that science and education held the answers to all of man's problems. I also believed in the innate goodness of man. And back then, nobody told the truth about abortion. Abortions had been legal for over thirteen years when I had mine, and it was very politically correct. No one ever said anything negative about them. It just wasn't done. I had never heard one word about post abortion syndrome, about how many women's bodies were mutilated by the violence of an abortion procedure, or that 25 percent of women who abort their first pregnancies will never have another child."

Becky leaned over the table toward Maggie. *Why does she have to speak in such a soft voice?*

"My abortion did not go well. The doctor lacerated my uterus. That night I called him with severe abdominal pain. He said it was normal and to just rest. Two days later I was hospitalized and underwent emergency surgery. I had a hole in my uterus and vagina, and significant intestinal and pelvic inflammation. The surgeon also had to remove…a mass of dead fetal tissue from my abdomen. The doctor had to do a complete hysterectomy in order to save my life."

Two girls began to cry softly, and one just put her head down on the table. Becky blinked back her own tears. She had overheard the doctor in the hospital say if her bleeding didn't stop he'd have to operate. *How close did I come to never being able to have another child?*

Maggie took a sip of her coffee. "When I was finally discharged, I tried to commit suicide. I overdosed on sleeping pills the doctor had given me for my insomnia. That meant another trip back to the hospital."

Two more girls began to cry. Becky could see large ugly scars running across the wrists of one of them.

"But my story doesn't end here. I want you to know it has a happy ending. Thirteen years ago, after my second suicide attempt, I came to know Jesus. I came to know the One who will never leave me or forsake me, the One who knows me for what I am and loves me anyway. The One who can reach into the depths of a soul and heal all the hurt that's in it. The One who can give you new life and new hope. It is my desire…my prayer…that before this twelve-week session is over, you'll come to know Him too."

Becky sank back into her chair. She looked at Maggie and tried to reconcile the story she had just heard with the joy and love she saw radiating from her face. All Becky's life she had heard her father scoff at the televangelists, scoff and hoot at them, saying the only thing they were interested in was money. *Is this a con?*

Maggie reached over to the woman sitting to her left and gently covered her hand with her own. "Would you like to share now?"

The woman's name was Evelyn. She looked much older than Becky, close to forty, maybe more, it was hard for Becky to tell. Evelyn kept her head dropped most of the time, even when she spoke. She never made eye contact with the others.

Becky leaned closer to Evelyn, trying to catch every word, hardly aware that her own heart was racing or that her breathing was quick, shallow.

"About four years ago, my husband and I separated. We had one son, then, who was eight. For a few months we tried getting back together. He ran around like he was still a kid, going to bars with the boys and...I knew he had other women. So after giving it one last try, I realized it was hopeless, that my husband wasn't going to grow up and I didn't really want to raise two 'boys,' so I filed for divorce. Right about that time I found out I was pregnant. Nine years with Mark had given me enough experience to know that he couldn't be counted on for support, no matter what the judge said. So I was on my own. Completely. I was already working two jobs just to keep a roof over our heads. I knew I couldn't stop now, not if I wanted to survive. It would take every ounce of strength I had and every dollar I could earn if I was going to be a successful single mom. There was no way I could have another baby. I never even told Mark about the baby, so I couldn't blame him, later, when things got bad for me.

"The pain was terrible. They said it wouldn't hurt, that I didn't need anesthesia, but I cried and screamed on that table. I thought I was going to die. By the time they were finished, I had. I knew something inside me died that day.

"I drank really heavy after that, just to try to forget. When that didn't help, I began using drugs. All the drinking and drugs eventually got me fired from both of my jobs. I couldn't blame them. I was pretty useless and I was messing up my work and that meant someone else had to come behind me and redo it.

"I had a pretty nice job during the day. I really liked it. I worked in an accounting office as a typist and file clerk, but they liked my work and were going to train me as a bookkeeper and give me a promotion...until the drinking and...everything. That's the one I lost first.

"My second job, my night job, was in retail, behind the perfume counter in one of those big mall stores. Eventually, I started taking a few bottles of perfume home with me at night, to pay for the drugs and alcohol, and when I was caught, they fired me. I was lucky, because they didn't press charges, and they could have.

"By then I had these two huge habits I couldn't support, never mind a child. I was finally evicted because I couldn't pay the rent, and eventually Social Services stepped in and took my son away and put him in foster care because nobody could find Mark. By then I believed I didn't deserve any children anyway, so I didn't even fight it. I was high all the time, and I really don't want to talk about how I got the money for all the alcohol and drugs.

"My son's twelve now and I've missed four years of his life. Four years I'll never get back. I've been off drugs and alcohol for almost five months, and I have a little job in a hardware store doing their bookwork and filing. It doesn't pay much, but it's a start. I want my son back…and I know I have to show Social Services I can hold a job and stay away from the drugs and alcohol. But I have a real chance now, because the social worker told me so.

"The problem is, I still feel the pain of what I did. Every day's a struggle and some days I think it'd be easier to just go back to boozing and drugging. I need to get a grip on this thing because I'm afraid of what I might do, that I might slip back into the old life. I don't want to put my son through that again. I don't want anyone to ever take him away from me again. But I need help. A friend of mine told me about this place, how much it helped her, so here I am. I figured maybe I can get my life back on track, get my son's life back on track too."

Evelyn finally looked up. Her eyes were hard and crimson from crying.

Maggie smiled kindly at Evelyn. "I'm so glad you're here. I believe in a God of miracles, and I believe He wants to do one for you and your son, if you'll let Him, and if you'll do your part."

Evelyn pulled out a tissue from her purse and dabbed

her tears, but Becky could see a faint smile on Evelyn's lips.

Becky straightened in her chair when she saw that all eyes were on her now. She felt embarrassed, nervous, excited. She jutted her chin and looked around the room. By the time she opened her mouth, her chin didn't jut so far, and her head began to drop ever so slightly. Her mouth remained open for some time, but nothing came out. She compressed her lips, took a deep breath, and tried again. Still nothing. Finally, she covered her face with her hands and began to cry. No one spoke.

When she finally looked up, she knew mascara had smeared down under her eyes. She knew because of the black smudges on her wet fingers, but she didn't care. She didn't care what she looked like. She opened her mouth, and words that sounded as wet as her tears finally came out.

"I hate myself."


When Becky got home she found her parents sitting in the living room, tight-faced.

"How did it go?" her father said.

Becky shrugged, then walked to the stairs.

"We've been waiting for you to come home, honey. Can't you tell us just a little of what went on?"

Becky had started upstairs to her room, but stopped and faced her parents. "I hate you—I hate you both so much!"

Thor had barely taken off his jacket when the phone rang. He stood next to his California king bed, debating whether or not to let the answering machine take the call. He had wanted to do a few quick laps in the pool before dinner. *Four o'clock Sunday afternoon. Who could be calling now?* On the third ring, he yanked the phone from its cradle.

"Hello?" There was static on the other end. He switched hands and put the phone to his other ear. "Hello?"

He was about to hang up when he heard a soft, female voice.

"Thank you."

"Teresa?"

"Yes. I just wanted to thank you, Thor, for Eric. I got the papers today. I couldn't believe…well, thank you. You kept your word."

"You didn't leave me much choice."

"I'm sorry I had to behave like that, using threats and all, but sometimes, Thor, you are so unreasonable—"

"If you want to do some husband bashing forget it. I just got home and I'm whipped already."

"Ex-husband. I just signed the papers. It's ex now and no, I don't want to do any bashing. I just wanted to say thank you. It means so much…" Thor heard his wife's voice break, then soft crying.

"It's a shame things had to work out like this."

"Yes. I'm sorry too."

"It wasn't my idea. Just remember that."

"Are you lonely, Thor?"

Thor watched rain streak down his bedroom window. "How's Eric?"

"He's fine. He won an award. Took first place in the class science project."

"He's smart, like his dad."

"Yes…he asked for you. Wanted to know if you'd be coming to pick him up this year."

"What did you say?"

"I told him you were busy and that I'd be coming alone."

"You didn't tell him about the divorce?"

"No, I wanted to do that in person."

Thor pulled a pair of burgundy lace-up trunks from his bottom drawer, then began unbuttoning his shirt. "You coddle him too much. You should've just come right out with it."

"He's still a little boy, Thor, he needs—"

"He's eleven. Time to grow up and learn the facts of life." He could hear Teresa sigh and for a moment thought she'd hang up. Strange how he didn't want her to, how he wished she were here right now, in the room with him.

"I don't want to argue," she finally said.

"Okay, so we won't. When are you picking him up?"

"Wednesday. Eric's last class is that morning."

"You driving up the night before?"

"Yes."

"Remember that old roadside inn where we used to have lunch?"

"Our halfway house to Oxlee?"

"You used to laugh a lot on those trips, Teresa."

"So did you."

Thor looked at the four-poster mahogany bed, at the matching dresser and armoire with its inlaid wood marquetry. "How come you didn't take any of the bedroom furniture?"

"Because you love it so much. Remember how it took you three months to find just the right seeded glass lamps for the nightstands?"

"Seems kind of silly now, doesn't it?"

Teresa sighed. "I think Eric will take it hard. I've put off thinking about it. I'll figure out something Tuesday night, after work, when I head for Oxlee."

"After work?" He slipped out of his suit pants and into the cargo surfer. "Since when did you get a job?"

"I've been working for over a month now, as a secretary."

"You never mentioned—"

"No. I guess I didn't want you to know about it until this divorce was over."

"What did you think I'd do exactly?"

"You know how you are."

"Well...just be careful going through the mountains. We've had a lot of rain and there may be some mud slides or maybe even—"

"You actually sound concerned. Like you really mean what you're saying."

"There you go, bashing again."

"I'm not bashing. I find it...well...sad, and...touching."

"You do? I mean, the touching part?" Thor walked to the closet to hang up his suit.

"It's nice to be thought of, to have someone show concern. Thor...I've been going to church. Don't laugh, I know it's been so long since I've been in one, but it's helped me a lot. I mean, I feel better about things. And I've been praying for you…that you'd do the right thing. You'll never have peace, Thor, until you turn yourself—"

Thor threw the jacket and pants on the floor. "You haven't changed a bit. Still weak, still looking for a crutch. All right, if that's what you need, okay, just don't try pushing that stuff on me, Teresa. And for your information, the only reason I was concerned at all, if you can call it that, is because I can't afford to have anything happen to you. You have certain…documents that I don't want anyone to see, so I plan on you outliving me. And one more thing—just remember our bargain. You've got what you wanted—you have Eric. But if you go changing your mind and decide to share those documents with someone—like the police, for instance—so help me, Teresa, I'll have you killed. And you know I can do it. If you try to take me down, I'll take you down first."

Thor could hear a soft gasp.

"Okay, Thor. I'll let you get back to whatever you were doing. I just wanted to say thank you, that's all. For keeping your word. Good-bye."

The phone went dead, and for the longest time Thor held the receiver in his hand listening to the irritating dial tone. Finally, he walked from the closet to the bed and hung it up. When he did, he was stunned by the unbearable silence.


Maggie lounged on the floral down sofa nibbling a large Red Delicious apple and reading an Agatha Christie novel.

She loved Sundays. She could spend the morning at church, in praise and worship with other believers, then the rest of the day luxuriating in things she didn't have much time for during the rest of the week, like reading and cooking. Any minute now she was going to head into the kitchen and try out that new recipe Agnes had given her: orange lamb stuffed with mint and pecans. Maggie cooked only on weekends and usually made enough to last the week, otherwise it was fast food, which she detested.

She bookmarked her novel, then stretched out on the couch. The only thing missing from her day was Kirt. She had not heard from him all week except for one card. On the outside of the card was supposed to be a picture of a lion in a jungle, but it actually looked more like a housecat sitting between two giant ferns. Inside it said, "Wild about you." *Where does he find these?*

When the phone rang, she jumped from the couch.

"Hello!" Kirt's happy, energetic voice boomed over the line. "I got your message to call."

"Kirt. I was just thinking about you."

"All good thoughts, I hope."

"Every one."

"Did you get my card?"

Maggie glanced at it on the coffee table and smiled. "Where do you ever find them?"

"No good?"

"Perfect, just like you."

"I'm glad you called. I haven't heard from you in a while."

"I know. I've been doing a lot of thinking and praying."

"About?"

"About how you're the best man I've ever known. About how all things are possible with God."

"Really? That means you're missing me, and *that's* a good sign."

Maggie eased herself back onto the couch. Her stomach was doing butterflies. She hadn't expected to be so nervous. "Actually, I'm missing you terribly, and I was thinking I don't want to miss you anymore, ever."

"You don't?"

"No."

"Of course there's only one way I can think of to prevent that."

"Me too." Maggie held her breath.

"You'll have to marry me now, for sure. I mean, I'm not in my apartment. I'm sitting in my office and decided to check my messages and that's when I heard yours. Anyway, you're talking to a duly elected representative of your state and that makes everything official. So, no taking anything back."

"No, I won't take it back."

"You're serious?"

"Absolutely."

"So you're going to marry me?"

"Yes." The word sounded so simple, Maggie wondered why it had taken her so long to say it. But there was silence at the other end of the phone. "Having second thoughts?"

Kirt finally said, "Never," and Maggie heard the break in his voice.

"Are you crying?"

"Yes," he said softy, "for joy, Maggie. For joy. This is

God's miracle, and I'm just so full of joy."

Maggie wiped at her eyes. "I guess it's contagious. By the way, what are you doing in your office on a Sunday night? Don't tell me the recovering workaholic has fallen off the wagon."

"Your special delivery. I've been looking it over for the past several days. I brought it home with me, but it was so disturbing I couldn't sleep last night and thought about it all day today. Finally, I decided to maybe try and work on some ideas, so I came in."

"What ideas?"

"Well, since Dr. Newly's dead, Adam's testimony about the killing of that live baby shouldn't be too hard for him and would go a long way in alerting the public about what's happening in these clinics. People have to know that babies are being murdered both in utero and out, then sold for their parts."

"He won't testify. He was adamant about that. He won't let his name be used in any way. The only thing we've got are copies of some purchase orders. I made you a set and mine is tucked away in a safe place, but that's all we've got—copies—not even originals."

"All the more reason we need Adam. There's no convincing him?"

"No." Maggie could hear an exasperated sigh on the other end. "And I gave him my word we would protect his anonymity."

"Then we'll have to do it."

"Do what?"

"Take this story to the media."

# 12

MAGGIE SAT IN HER swivel chair watching the pouring rain create miniature tributaries down the windowpane. Behind her, on the desk, was a mountain of paper that resembled Kilimanjaro. She just wasn't up to the climb. She had at least a week's worth of work, and though it was Monday morning and she usually felt ready to take on the world, this morning she felt sluggish. She was tired from not sleeping, tired of this incessant rain, tired of being apart from Kirt.

The realization that she was finally going to marry had kept her up most of the night. And just when she was getting used to the idea and was about to doze off, she began thinking about that other matter, the one concerning Solutions Clinic and Dorianna Gray Cosmetics and Second Chance Foundation.

She hoped Kirt's suggestion to take the copies of the POs to 50/50 was the correct one. Was this the vehicle God could best use? Kirt knew one of the producers personally and said they would get a fair shake, that *50/50* covered both sides of an issue, tried to give both viewpoints. But Maggie wasn't so sure…not without Adam's testimony. They might have only one shot at this, and she didn't want to mess it up. She had been praying that the Lord would open the door He wanted them to walk through, that He would use this piece to not only save the lives of the unborn and their mothers, but to expose the abortion industry. *Touch hearts and lives with truth.*

When the phone rang, she spun her chair around and picked up the receiver. She was facing Kilimanjaro now, and she groaned.

"I'll go public."

"What? Who is this?"

"I said I'll talk. But I name the time and place. I call all the shots."

Maggie's eyebrows went up in surprise. "Adam? Adam Bender?" The voice sounded so strange, so far away. She heard him cough, then moan as though he were in pain. "Are you all right?"

"As all right as can be expected, considering that last night could have been my last night on earth."

"Are you serious? What happened?"

"Two heavyweights, and I mean that literally and figuratively, took me for a little ride. They wanted to ask me some questions, the most important one being who I gave all those POs to. They tried taking me up Hunter Mountain. I don't think they were planning on driving me back."

"How did you get away?"

"Long story, but let's just say bodies do bounce, but not like rubber balls."

"You jumped from the car?" Maggie was up on her feet now, pacing the room.

"It wasn't too bad. All that rain made the ground soft. I think that's what saved my life...no, I'm sure of it."

"Don't you think that God may have had just a little bit to do with the fact that you're still breathing?" She could hear Adam chuckle, then moan with pain. "How badly hurt are you?"

"I'm pretty banged up. May have a broken rib or two, and my ankle is seriously sprained."

"I'll call 911, then an ambulance. Tell me where you are."

"No. I don't want anyone to know my whereabouts, not yet. I want you to contact a reporter or news commentator, I don't care, just make sure you can trust him. Tell him you have a big story, complete with an eyewitness who'll do an interview. I figure once I've done that, it'll be too late for damage control. It won't matter anymore who has those POs. I'll let you know where I am after you've set every-thing up. But for now, I'm staying undercover. I don't mind telling you I'm scared."

Maggie sat back down in her chair and began praying for Adam. "It so happens we already have something in the works with 50/50. Do you have any objections to them?"

"No."

"After I set up the interview, how can I reach you?"

"Make the interview for tomorrow, twelve noon. At 10:30 A.M. I'll call you and give you directions."

"What about your wife? She must be frantic. Can I call her? Do anything?"

"No. I called her last night and told her to go to her parents'. They shouldn't find her there."

Maggie was on her feet again. "Okay, I'll wait for your call. Just tell me this…do they know about me, about the Life Center? Do I need to be careful?"

"No, they don't know, and yes, you need to be careful. These people are dangerous. If they have the slightest inkling that you have the papers, they'll be all over you like white on rice."

"Thanks, Adam. Thank you for not telling them about me. By the way, how did you get to a phone?"

"I had my cell phone with me. Those bozos never checked!"


Dr. Thor Emerson stripped off his bloody surgical gloves and tossed them into the waste can. This was going to be a beaut of a day, he could tell. It was barely 11 A.M. and he had already done fifteen abortions. That was one every eight minutes. Two more girls were in stirrups in the remaining procedure rooms, and Clara had just told him the waiting room was packed. No doubt she hoped to inspire him to a new Olympic-level performance. What would make her happy? A six-minute job? He cursed his soon-to-be replacement who was off somewhere on vacation. He had to get out of this pressure cooker, then maybe he'd take a vacation too.

He watched a young woman, Adam's replacement,

bounce down the hall carrying two bottles of DMEM, the sterile media she would use to preserve the eyes of the sixteen-week fetus he had just aborted. This time Thor wasn't taking any chances. He had ordered Clara to keep all POs under lock and key.

Since Thor had spoken with Louie, Adam Bender had not been far from his mind. He wondered what Louie planned to do, then realized he didn't want to know. How did he get into this mess? How had things gotten so out of hand? One minute a friend was loaning him money to open up another clinic and pay off some gambling debts, and the next minute that same friend was calling the shots. There had to be a way to get free—to get out from under— to break from Louie. *Is it possible to break from Louie?*

"Your patients are backing up!" Clara said, coming toward him, huffing with exasperation, her face red.

Thor glanced down the hall in the opposite direction. From where he stood, he could see the entrance door. What was there to keep him from walking straight down the hall and out that door?

"Doctor!"

"Which procedure room next? Two or three?"

"First you have a call. I tried to tell him you *couldn't* be disturbed. That you were up to your eyeballs in patients, but you think that stopped him? Some people just don't—"

"Who's on the line, Clara?"

"Louie. Louie something, I didn't get his name."

Thor brushed passed Clara and into her office. "What's up, Louie?"

"You have an extraordinary office manager. I like her. I

could use someone of her caliber myself." Thor listened quietly while Louie chuckled. "But I won't keep you. Business is business, and this is an intrusion. I just wanted to tell you that my men...well, I hate to say it, but they bungled the job. I may need to take punitive action, send them out of town for a while—maybe permanently. I haven't decided yet. But I think it's imperative you do some damage control on your end."

"Like what?"

"Incinerate your files, at least all the files on Dorianna Gray. Delete any computer records. That way, when the POs show up you can say they're a forgery—those cowardly pro-lifers attempting to discredit your Brockston clinic."

"What makes you so sure the POs are going to show up?"

"I've received a tip that 50/50 is about to do a taping on a very hot issue, and that the interviewee is someone who's in hiding and afraid for his life."

"Adam Bender."

"An astute guess."

Thor looked at the matronly woman planted in the doorway, her arms folded across her body. With the thrust of his chin, he indicated to Clara that he wanted her to leave. But she didn't budge. "Isn't there any way you can stop Adam?" Thor finally asked, glaring at his OM.

"I'm not in the leg-breaking business, Thor. I'm an entrepreneur. Besides, no one knows where he is."

"And your associates? Anything they can do?"

"It's best that my associates never find out about this.

Understand? They're not as modern as I am. They still do business the old-fashioned way—with a heavy hand."

Thor wondered that Louie didn't see the hypocrisy of those words. He reddened when he saw Clara's eyes bore into his own. Already she knew too much about his business.

"Thor? You still there?"

Thor turned his back to Clara and cupped the phone. "Yes, I'm still here, Louie."

"Then I shall leave this safely in your hands? I can depend upon you to eradicate all paper trails?"

"Yes."

"You have my gratitude. And it will show up in your mailbox in a few days."

"That's not necessary—"

"Business is still business. Of course this doesn't affect our friendship in any way. Your carelessness, I mean…the fact that I had to mop up your mess. After all, what are friends for?"

Thor listened to Louie chuckle in that soft way of his and for the first time began to believe Teresa's words, "A man like Louie doesn't have any friends."


The news van bounced and swayed along the dirt road toward a hunting cabin deep in the woods. Large metallic-blue lettering identified the truck as belonging to *50/50*. Inside, Maggie sat nervously watching the three-member TV crew talk amongst themselves. The fourth member, the driver, sat quietly behind the wheel, popping his gum and blowing bubbles. They all seemed incredibly unruffled, as though going to meet a friend for a picnic rather than a fugitive who feared for his life.

She looked down at the folder she carried, then closed her eyes and prayed that the interviewer, a young man in his thirties, wouldn't try to trivialize what he was about to hear. She wondered why the host of 50/50, Don Marlow, hadn't come. Maybe he didn't do fieldwork anymore.

When the van pulled to a stop, the driver got out first, and Maggie noticed he held something in his hand, close to his leg. It took her a second to realize it was a revolver. Only after Adam Bender emerged from the cabin and spoke quietly with the driver did he put the revolver away and give the sign. Instantly, the others poured out of the van. The sound man carefully lifted his sensitive amplifiers, then a box of mikes. Maggie watched the cameraman struggle with a large duffel bag, two tripods, and a rack of lights. The young interviewer came over and grabbed the duffel bag.

It took a moment for Maggie's eyes to grow accustomed to the dim light inside the cabin. She looked around. She was standing in one large open room. A huge fireplace occupied one wall, and next to that was a small kitchen with a table and four chairs, then a sitting room. She saw Adam, in the corner, slumped in a plaid, overstuffed chair that had seen its day. He held his left side and took quick, shallow breaths. His shoes were off, and one of his ankles was purple and swollen to twice its size. She wondered if he hadn't broken it.

"You look terrible," she said, walking over to the chair. "You should've let me bring a doctor."

Adam nodded. "Yeah. Maybe…maybe after the interview you can take me to the hospital? I'm feeling pretty miserable."

Maggie walked to the sink and filled a large glass with water then brought it over to Adam. "How did you find this place?"

"Thanks." Adam took the glass and brought it to his lips. "How did you know I was thirsty?"

"Your lips; they're dry." She noticed he had clean clothes on, clothes that didn't fit. "So…did you break in?"

"This is my father-in-law's hunting cabin. We go here all the time."

Maggie watched Adam turn pale and was afraid he was going to faint. "Can you do it? Will you be all right for the interview?"

"When a man has a family to protect, he can do just about anything," he said, wincing as he reached for the folder in Maggie's hand.


"Hello! This is Jim Carney from 50/50!"

Thor had to hold the phone a few inches from his ear. He gave Clara a dirty look as she leaned against the door frame of her office. She had nabbed Thor just before he could go into procedure room three to do his thirty-first—or was it thirty-second?—abortion of the day. "It could mean publicity for the clinic," she had said. "*Free* publicity."

"Dr. Thor Emerson?" the voice boomed.

"Yes," Thor answered wearily.

"Jim Carney from *50/50*. We just finished an interview

with Adam Bender, and we'd like to give you a chance to rebut."

"Rebut what?"

"His claim that you've been selling baby parts and that he has witnessed the murder of a live baby in your Brockston clinic."

"I don't care what he says, the guy's lying."

"Then you won't grant an interview?"

"Why should I? These allegations are completely false."

"Well, Dr. Emerson, regarding the selling of baby parts, we do have copies of purchase orders from Second Chance Foundation, Dorianna Gray Cos—"

"Purchase orders can be forged."

"And why would anyone want to forge them?"

"You're the reporter. Why don't you try to find out?"

"Maybe you can help me, Dr. Emerson. Would you give it a shot? Tell me who in the world would want to forge purchase orders and stick them in your file cabinet."

"Who said they came from my file cabinet?"

"Well…Adam claims these came from your office and he copied—"

"How can he make copies of something that never existed?"

"Why would he lie about a thing like that?"

"How could I possibly know? But if you want, I'll take a stab at it."

"Please do."

"I think the right-wing fundamentalists saw an opportunity to try to discredit the abortion industry in general and my clinic in particular, and used him."

"You're saying this is all pro-life propaganda?"

"Exactly. Now let me ask you a question. Did Adam contact you personally or did someone else?"

"Well...actually it was someone else."

"Who?"

"Maggie Singer."

"From the Life Center?"

"Well...yes."

"Maggie Singer, a right-wing fundamentalist antiabortion bigot. I rest my case." From the silence, Thor could tell he had confused the reporter. Finally, he heard Jim Carney clear his throat.

"Just one more question. Adam was pretty banged up. He said two men kidnapped him and he was lucky to escape alive."

Thor forced a laugh. "It's hard to believe Adam capable of eluding two men, unless he's grown since he worked here. I mean, the Adam I knew came up to my armpit and could barely lift his briefcase. I don't think he's got what it takes to manage the type of escape he describes. Do you?"

"And his injuries? How do you explain those?"

"They're extremists, these people. They're capable of anything."

Carney cleared his throat again, then said, "Okay, thanks," and hung up.

As Thor replaced the phone, he heard clapping and turned to see Clara clapping and smiling.

"Nicely done. Very nicely done."

As he walked by her, he had the strongest urge to belt her in the face.

"I'm leaving, Clara. I'm taking the rest of the day off." He saw the look of panic on her face and felt sweet revenge.

"You can't leave! What…what about all your patients? Who's going to do the rest of the abortions?"

"Why you are, Clara. You are." Thor walked down the hall and right out of the building, leaving Clara with her mouth open and a waiting room full of nervous women.

# 13

TERESA EMERSON HOPED ERIC would understand when she told him the news. They'd have plenty of time during the trip home tomorrow to discuss it. Ever since she started her drive through Hunter Mountain, she'd been trying to think of the right words to say. She usually loved this ride, loved the beautiful forest of maple and birch, loved knowing that at the end of the trip she would be seeing her precious son. But this time she hardly looked at the scenery, and the anticipation of seeing Eric made a giant knot in her stomach. How did you tell an eleven-year-old that his parents were getting a divorce? That their one family was about to become two?

She had read all the divorce books, had read all about how kids tend to blame themselves when their parents split up. What was she going to do? She didn't want Eric taking on more guilt. He already had guilt enough. She knew all those years in boarding school had made him feel defective, unwanted, in the way. And he was, for Thor anyway. Not for her, and all her trying to make up for it in the summers couldn't erase the fact that Eric had a father who didn't love him. But how could Eric possibly understand that Thor was incapable of loving anyone?

Teresa glanced out the passenger window. Daylight had already slipped away and the dark shadows made the maples by the road look like a giant army standing in formation. She shuddered. She didn't like driving through the mountains in the dark. *Come on, Teresa, don't get spooked. Just pay attention to the road.* At least the rain had stopped. But the road was still wet…wet and slick, the shoulder soft and muddy. She'd have to be careful over Fool's Crossing Bridge.

She glanced at her bag of fruit on the seat and thought maybe she should have that Bartlett pear. She tried opening the Ziploc bag with one hand. As she did, she could feel the car get away from her, and she knew she was in trouble. She felt the car skid, heard the screeching of her tires. She was all over the road.

As the car spun in a circle she could hear herself screaming. Any moment she expected to feel another car crash into her. Instead, she found herself suddenly on the shoulder, stopped, the nose of her BMW pointing into the woods.

For a long while all she could do was sit behind the wheel, trembling. She looked around. The highway was dark, with no sign of any cars coming in either direction. The only illumination came from her own headlights. She gasped when she saw the huge maple only two inches to her right. Two inches more and she might not have been able to walk away. She shook off the fear and carefully opened the door.

As soon as her foot hit the ground, thick mud oozed over her shoe and up her calf. She struggled against the suction and finally yanked her leg free, then got back into the car. She leaned out the open door as far as she could and saw that her back tire was also buried in mud.

She slid over to the passenger side, trying to keep the mud on her leg from smearing all over the leather seat. She could open the door only partway because of the tree. She stuck her head out as far as she could. It was enough to see that her right tire was buried even deeper than her left. *What am I going to do?* She slipped her hand into her purse and felt for her cell phone.

"Looks like you got a real problem here, lady."

Teresa's heart went up to her throat. She turned to the voice and saw a man in camouflage clothing with a cap pulled low over his head. He leaned through the open door on the driver's side.

"Maybe I can help."

Teresa pulled the phone from her purse and pointed to it. "I've…already…called. A tow truck will be along…any minute."

The man looked confused, then smiled a strange smile. "No you didn't, lady. I was watchin' you."

"You were…*watching?*"

"Yeah, I was walkin' along the tree line and saw your car go out of control. You're lucky you ain't hurt. Some-body upstairs must like you."

Teresa clutched the phone wondering if she could

punch in 911 before he was able to grab it.

"What I figured we'd do was gather up these here broken tree limbs and build a ramp behind the back wheels. Then you put your car into reverse and floor it, and maybe free the tires. Might work. Ain't nothin' worse than Hunter Mountain mud, though."

"You really think it'll work?"

The man shrugged. "Worth a try."

Teresa began to slide to the driver's side to get out and help gather wood. "I'm really lucky that someone from these parts happened by. I don't know what I would—"

"Who said I was from round here?" The man's tone was harsh.

"Well…you seemed to know about the mud and all. And…you're not backpacking, and it is night, and—"

"Why you got to be so nosy, lady? I was just tryin' to help. I hate nosy people. I could leave right now and let you sit here in this mess. It makes no difference to me. That's the trouble. Nobody minds their own business anymore."

The stranger started to walk away, and Teresa felt unexpectedly relieved, then full of panic when she realized she would still be stuck in the middle of nowhere. She dialed 911 and took a deep breath when she heard the operator answer. "Hello!" she said, not meaning to sound so shrill. "This is Teresa Emerson and my car is stuck somewhere along CR 45. The mud's up to the hubcaps and I can't get out. Maybe…"

The stranger stopped in his tracks and turned toward her. From the headlights she could see a frightening look on his face. It was a look of madness.

"Help! Help!" she screamed into the phone.

"Calm down, Mrs. Emerson," came the response on the other end. "Just tell me approximately how long you were driving along 45 so we can get a better idea of where you are."

"Help!" Teresa screamed as the man bent into the car and reached for her. "Get away from me!" She tried to kick him backward.

"Please, Mrs. Emerson, just calm down!" said the voice over the phone.

"He's trying to grab me! He's—"

The man ripped the cellular out of her hand and pressed the power button, then slipped it into his shirt pocket.

"Not many Emersons round here. You must be related to that abortion doctor."

Teresa stared, wide-eyed, unable to speak or move. The man flattened her against the seat, then pinned her down with his knee. One hand wrapped around her throat.

"You related to that guy? That butcher?"

Teresa opened her mouth but nothing came out. The man lunged for her purse and began emptying it out. He still held her pinned with his leg, but he no longer had her by the throat. When he found her wallet, he rifled through the pictures. He stopped when he came to the one of Eric standing next to his father. Without a word, he ripped it out of its plastic holder and shoved it into his pocket.

"You're his wife," the man said, backing out of the car and pulling her with him. "You're that butcher's wife. Now don't that beat all? Ain't it somethin' how things work out? Now maybe I can finish the job."

"My friend is excited about the clip. He saw it about an hour ago and said he's going to give it the first spot on *50/50* this coming Saturday night. He said it's dynamite and should blow a hole in the entire abortion issue. He also said Jim Carney tried to give Dr. Emerson a chance to refute the allegations, but he refused to give an interview. Emerson claims it's all a lie made up by the pro-lifers to discredit him."

Maggie sat curled on her floral couch, her feet tucked under her, one hand holding a cup of coffee, the other holding the phone. She couldn't help smiling at the sound of Kirt's voice.

"Carney said Emerson was really frosted. Practically accused us pro-lifers of beating up Adam Bender so his abduction story would look realistic. He had some colorful adjectives for you too. Want to hear them?"

"Sure."

"How's right-wing fundamentalist antiabortion bigot sound?"

"Hmmm."

"Of course *50/50* will have to get someone else on the pro-abort side to rebut, probably Planned Parenthood or maybe another doctor with a chain of abortion clinics. And we know what they're going to say. But Maggie, this has got to make people sit up and take notice. It's got to make them think about what's really going on in these clinics."

"I'm praying God will use this to open hearts. He has to reach their hearts, Kirt. That's where the change will come from."

"You're right, Maggie. But maybe this is one of the tools God will use. By the way, how's Adam?"

Maggie closed her eyes. "Well, I think his heart's probably in better shape than the rest of him. He's pretty banged up: fractured ribs, broken ankle, lots of cuts and bruises, but no internal injuries."

"You sound like you read his chart."

"I did." Maggie listened to Kirt laugh and noticed how good his laughter made her feel. "He's lucky to be alive. But he's going to be fine."

"On a lighter note, I just want to say, I miss you."

"Me too." Maggie took a sip of her coffee feeling warmed by both it and his words.

"The session's almost over. I'll be home in a couple of weeks. We'll have the entire summer together." Kirt paused. "That is, when I'm not working at the law firm and when you're not working at the Center."

"Sounds like we're going to be busy."

"Not too busy we can't plan the wedding, I hope. Which reminds me, where are we going for the honeymoon?"

"I don't know. Have any suggestions?"

"I've started gathering information on resorts and cruises. Maybe you can do the same and then we can put it all together and come up with a place we both like."

Maggie put her coffee cup down on the end table and stretched out. "What have you got so far?"

"An Alaskan tour—a two-week combination of cruising and land trips to Anchorage and Fairbanks."

"Really? I've always wanted to go to Alaska."

"You haven't heard the best part. There's the El Dorado Gold Mine, a real chance to see a permafrost tunnel first-hand, and then there's the authentic tent camp. Also the reproduction of an Athabascan Indian village looks good."

Maggie picked up the five-by-seven color photo from the end table. It was a new picture of her and Kirt, which she had just framed. She traced his face with her finger. "But isn't the Alaskan cruising season almost over?"

"No, they have them all the way up to the middle of September."

Maggie laughed. "Have you looked at the calendar lately? That's barely three and a half months away. I guess you were planning this for next year?"

"Noooo. I thought since I was going to be around this summer and could help, we'd...we'd—"

"You want to get married before September? Before *this* September?"

"Would I be pushing it if I asked you to make it before September 11? That's the last date of the cruise that gives you two nights in Fairbanks instead of only one, plus an additional night at the Denali Princess Wilderness Lodge. That's assuming you really want to go, but you can look it over and decide. Oh, did I tell you the package also included cruising through Glacier Bay and—"

"I love you, Kirt."

"I love you too, Maggie."

◦◦◦

Thor lay sprawled on his burgundy leather couch. The only movement he made was his right thumb pressing the channel changer. But nothing he saw on the eight-foot screen of his projection TV held his interest. One channel replaced another in an endless monotony of sitcoms and movies. Maybe he'd get some sleep. It had to be after eleven because he had just flicked past the eleven o'clock news with that boring anchorman whose name he couldn't remember but who reminded him of a Ken doll.

He stretched and almost kicked over his plate of Chinese takeout, which he had barely touched. How could he eat with all that was happening at the clinic? He still hadn't gotten over the call from *50/50*. All night he had tried to rouse himself to call Louie, to let his friend know what was going on. *Friend?* No, not friend. No use in stretching the truth anymore. If push came to shove, Louie would take Thor down just as surely as he'd take down those two muscle men who botched their job.

Thor laughed sardonically as he pictured an endless cycle of the hunter and hunted, of the predator and prey. Big fish eating up the little fish. He pictured Louie's face, with its hanging jowls and pointy overlapping teeth, and thought of a barracuda. Then he dismissed the image. Louie wasn't a barracuda at all. He rarely gobbled up his prey in one fierce bite. He was more like a piranha—jabbing, tearing, taking little bites at a time until there was nothing left. The same way Dr. Newly had been...and now Clara. He remembered the smug look on Clara's face as she had listened in. He could almost picture her filing away the information she had gleaned in some mental filing cabinet. Was she collecting her own "fireproof insurance"? They were all piranhas, the lot of them, even the women who came for his services. All biting and tearing, wanting something from him.

He flicked off the TV, then picked up his plate and carried it toward the kitchen. When the doorbell rang, he almost dropped it. *At this hour?* His heart raced. He opened the door and saw Lieutenant Tooley and another uniformed man standing in the doorway.

"Good evening, Doctor," Tooley said, stepping into the gray marbled entrance without being asked. His partner hesitated, then followed.

"Sorry to interrupt your dinner…but I think I may have some bad news."

Thor began walking toward the kitchen. His hands were shaking and he needed to get rid of the plate. "Come inside." He could hear footsteps behind him. He disposed of the plate and turned to the lieutenant. "What's happened?"

"About three hours ago, one of our 911 operators got a call from your wife…uh…ex-wife, regarding—"

"Teresa? Has something happened to Teresa?"

"Now hold on there. I didn't say nothing about anything happening to Teresa. Just stay calm while I tell you what we do know. No use in putting the cart before the horse."

Thor could feel pieces of himself being gobbled up, as though a school of piranha were having a feeding frenzy. He felt terror of a kind he had never experienced before as

Teresa's words exploded in his brain: *You better hope nothing happens to me.* He swallowed hard and tried to compose himself. "Tell me what you know," he said weakly.

"Like I was saying, Teresa told one of our 911 operators that her car was disabled—"

"Disabled? How?"

"Then she started screaming into the phone and the line went dead, but not before she told the operator she was on CR 45—"

"Yeah, she was on her way to Oxlee to pick up Eric, our son. She always drives 45 through Hunter Mountain."

"Well, that's were we found her BMW, mud up to the hubcaps. Looks like she skidded off the road."

"She wasn't...she wasn't killed, was she?"

Tooley shook his head. "Nope. She wasn't even in the car. No blood either, just a lot of mud, so we don't think she was hurt or anything."

"I don't understand. Why would she call you, then leave her car?"

Tooley cleared his throat. "That's the question we kept asking ourselves. The 911 operator said Teresa screamed, 'He's trying to grab me,' just before the phone went dead. So we tried to cover a wide area around the car. Then Jake here found the footprints, big ones, not Teresa's. Someone was with her."

"Maybe someone saw her stranded, gave her a ride back into town or..."

"Nope. The footprints went into the woods, and it looked like Teresa was dragging her feet, like someone may have forced her along."

Thor pulled out a stool from under the kitchen counter and sat down.

"And we found her purse in the car. We don't think Teresa would leave her purse voluntarily. And the odd thing was all the contents were strewn around the floor and seat. Like someone was looking for something."

"I don't understand any of this, Lieutenant. What does it mean?"

"Nothing more we can do tonight," Tooley said, placing his hand on Thor's shoulder. "But first sign of daylight, me and my men will follow the trail. There should be decent prints with all the mud. We'll scour Hunter Mountain till we find her."

"Thank you," Thor said, his head cradled between his hands. "Maybe…maybe I can help, go with you and—"

"Nope. You best stay away. We don't know what's what right now. Could be all a big misunderstanding. Could be something serious. But I want you to call me if you should hear from Teresa." He handed Thor a card with his number on it. "Or if anything unusual comes up."

"Unusual?"

"Like if someone should slip a note under your door or something."

"A ransom note?"

Tooley shrugged. "I've seen it all. Nothing would surprise me. Which brings me to my last question. Do you know of anyone who'd want to hurt you or your ex?"

"No." *Only several dozen.* Thor thought of the nameless, faceless people who had sent him threatening letters over the years: fathers whose babies he had aborted, women who had had serious complications from their abortions, those other women who blamed him for killing their babies, as if he pulled them off the street and forced them into it. But as far as a name, only one name came to mind. *Louie Pardino.*

As soon as the door closed behind Tooley and Jake, Thor raced back into the kitchen, yanked the handheld phone from its cradle, and began punching in numbers. When he heard the sleepy voice, Thor began yelling into the phone.

"What have you done with Teresa?"

"Thor? Do you know what time it is? Why are you calling me at such an ungodly hour?"

"I'm warning you, Louie, you better not hurt her! Not one hair of her head, you hear me!"

"Thor, stop shouting. Calm down and tell me what this is all about."

"The police just left. They think someone's kidnapped Teresa."

"I'm sorry...very sorry to hear that. But what does that have to do with me?"

"The POs from Dorianna Gray, the *50/50* interview. I know how you operate, Louie, your object lessons, your ways of punishment. But this time you were really stupid. This time—"

"Thor, I'd be careful if I were you. You're swimming in dangerous waters. I don't know what you think happened, but I had nothing to do with any of it."

"You're not the kind of person who'd admit anything,

so save your breath because I won't believe a word."

"Don't go down this path, Thor, I'm warning you."

"It's too late for warnings. If anything happens to Teresa my life is over."

"What do you take me for, an ignoramus? You want me to believe that Teresa means that much to you? We've been on too many gambling jaunts together. It was always you who went looking for the broads."

"Teresa has enough on me to put me away for life. But let me tell you something—if I go down, I'm taking you with me, you and your money laundering, your leg breakers, your Dorianna Gray Cosmetics."

There was stone silence on the other end of the line. Finally, Louie's voice came clear, crisp but strained, over the phone. "You'd do this to a friend?"

"We're not friends, Louie. You don't have any friends."

More silence, then finally, "In that case, it's best we dissolve our business arrangement. You will understand if I call in your IOUs. I'm sorry if that will force you to liquidate a few of your clinics. Also, consider the Dorianna Gray Cosmetics account terminated."

"I don't care if I lose half my clinics. I should've done this years ago. Maybe I'd still have Teresa. But I'm doing it now. I'm calling an end to it. I know it'll cost, but at least I'll be free."

"Free? No, my friend. All the days of your life a part of you will forever be looking over your shoulder. Just like the rest of us."

"You better hope nothing happens to me, because if it does, the police will be getting a nice fat dossier on you."

"You heap insult upon insult, to your harm, Thor. To your harm."

"It doesn't matter now. It only matters that Teresa is released. Will you give me your word that she'll be let go unharmed?"

Louie chuckled softly. "In your bluster and fury, you have totally overlooked the obvious. And that is that I had nothing to do with this. You've been very foolish tonight, Thor. You've made an enemy for no reason."


Becky lounged on her bed, her schoolbooks scattered all around her. It was after eleven and she still hadn't started her homework. She just couldn't get her mind to work. She pushed some of the books out of the way and rolled over on her back. The ceiling needed painting. Maybe she'd paint it over the summer. Maybe she'd try blue or gray...or black. If she painted stars over the black then it would look like a night sky. She liked nighttimes the best. The day was too glaring, too bright. She closed her eyes to visualize what it would look like and heard a knock on the door.

"I'm busy," she yelled, but the door opened anyway. Becky let out an exasperated sigh when she saw her mother. "Why do I have a private room when nobody in this house respects my privacy? Didn't you hear me say I was busy?"

Nancy Taylor moved across the room as though she were negotiating a minefield.

"Mo-om! How am I supposed to get my homework

done when everyone keeps barging in?"

"I'm not everyone, Becky, and as far as I know, this is the first time someone in this house has come to your room tonight."

Becky pulled herself up into a sitting position, fluffed her pillows a little too forcefully, then propped herself against them. She wrapped her arms tightly around her chest and tried to indicate by her posture and her eyes—which scanned the books on her bed—that there was no room for anyone else to sit.

Nancy sat anyway.

Becky let out a big sigh and tried to look both bored and annoyed.

"Becky, I don't know all of what you're going through right now. I can only guess. I do know it's terrible and that you're in a lot of pain. Your father and I…we are as sorry as sorry can be, but sorry doesn't help, does it?"

Becky sat on the bed glaring at her mother.

"Parents don't know all the answers, Becky. We're human, we make mistakes. We try, we fail, then we try again. And we always hope that when we do make a mistake, it's not a whopper. Your father and I…we failed you in this, and I know you hate us for it. And we know…we know it was a whopper. The only thing is, we don't know what to do about it. If we're going to make it through this, all of us, if we're going to survive as a family, we're going to need time and we're going to need healing. I don't know how that's all going to happen, but I do know that truth is the key. Without it, we're never going to get out of this mess. You need to understand why we made this mistake,

Becky, why we suggested…why we forced you into an abortion—or rather why your dad did—and why I let him."

Becky turned away, her chin jutting out, her body rigid. A single shimmering tear dotted the corner of her eye.

"I was pregnant when your father married me. He always believed he ruined my life. I had very much wanted to go to college, and he…well, naturally he blamed himself for how things turned out. Of course it wasn't your father's fault. It takes two. Your father just didn't want the same thing to happen to you. That's all, Becky. He thought he was doing the right thing by trying to give you a future. It all seems so…so wrong now. But please, file this away, and later, when you think about it, maybe you can try to understand and maybe…maybe you can find it in your heart to forgive us."

Out of the corner of her eye, Becky could see her mother slowly rise from the bed. She could sense, more than see, her mother hesitate as though waiting for Becky to say something, but Becky just sat there, with her face to the wall, not moving a muscle, not even when that single tear ran down her cheek. It wasn't until her mother got to the door that Becky spoke.

"I'll think about it, Mom. I'll think about what you said."

She could hear her mother swallow a sob, then heard the door close.

For a long time after her mother left, Becky lay on her back, motionless, hardly breathing. Finally, she rose and went to her dresser and pulled out her diary. It had been ages since she had written anything. She returned to the bed, propped herself against the pillows, and opened her diary. She closed her eyes for a moment, trying to gather her thoughts, then began writing:

*Dear Diary,*

*My mom dropped a bombshell today. I found out that she was already pregnant with me when she got married. All these years she's been lying to me about her anniversary date. Shows you how untrustworthy parents can be. She must have been about my age. So, I guess she knows how scared I've been. Maybe she understands some of what I've been going through. But not all. Not nearly all. At least she got to have her baby. I'll never know what mine looks like, what color hair or eyes...*

*So, if she thinks this changes anything, she's wrong. Dead wrong. I still hate her and my father. I hate them a lot...no...not a lot...some. I guess they have their own heartaches. I never understood that before. I guess they've had their problems. Still...they loved each other and me enough to go ahead and get married. I suppose that's something. But it doesn't change anything.*

*My mom looked so sad when she told me. I thought she was going to cry. I'm sick of crying. I'm sick of seeing my mom cry. Dad cries too. I hear him in his bedroom at night. I guess they need as much help as I do. I guess. Maybe I should call and ask Maggie if Mom can come next time, to the meeting. What's one more chair around the table? Still, this doesn't change anything. I'm still so angry at my parents…still hate…still dislike them so much.*

Thor scraped the last of the menthol lather off his face with his razor, then splashed himself with water before towel drying. All night he had paced the floor, thinking about what he should do. He had run every possible scenario through his mind. Finally, just before dawn, he made the decision to go to the Brockston clinic, try his best to get through his routine, and wait for the call from Tooley. He couldn't overplay his hand. If he acted too concerned people would start wondering, just as Louie had. *But I am concerned.* And not just about the dossier.

It wasn't until his third hour of pacing that he realized how concerned he was. You couldn't be married to someone for fourteen years and not feel something. He had also realized something else last night—he realized he believed, had always believed, that he would win Teresa back.

When he had finished thinking about Teresa, he started thinking about his former associate. What if he put all he knew on paper and sent this information, anonymously, to the three local papers? There were always young, hungry reporters willing to take risks and dig for a headline story. And if that happened, then Louie would be in the spotlight, in the hot seat. And Louie's associates wouldn't like that, would maybe be unhappy enough to give Louie trouble, make him scramble to defend himself. Thor pictured a series of fish swimming in a line of descending size—gobbling each other up.

But would that be enough to keep Louie off his back? Or would Thor have to look over his shoulder for the rest of his life as Louie had said? Thor had decided he had no other options, then sat down at his computer and composed a five-page expose on the wheelings and dealings of one Louie Pardino. Then he put all three copies in stamped envelopes.

After he had viewed everything, run it back and forth in his mind, and looked at it from every angle, only then had he been able to sleep, and then only for an hour.

He looked in the mirror at his bloodshot eyes and grabbed the Visine. He got only one drop in when the phone rang. He snatched it off the bathroom vanity where he had placed it for easy access.

"Thor?"

"Teresa! Thank God. Where are you?" He heard noise like the phone was being handled, then heard it drop. "Teresa, come on! Talk to me!"

"Teresa's fine. I ain't plannin' on hurtin' her. She'll be okay as long as you do exactly what I say. I got to finish the job. It ain't finished, you know. I got to."

"Who is this?" But Thor had recognized the voice and was holding onto the bathroom wall in shock. "What do you want?"

"You. Nobody's got to get hurt. I wanna swap. Theresa for you. Your life for hers."

"How do I know you'll keep your word? How do I know that if I come you'll let Teresa go?"

"Because I ain't no liar. And because she's not the baby killer, you are."

"Baby killer? Is that what this is about?"

"You take innocent life. You know what you're doin' but you do it anyway, and then you lie about it."

"I provide a service. I don't make these women come to my clinics."

"Liar! Liar…liar. And you lie to them too, to all them women who come to you. You tell them it's safe and then you maim them and they die too."

"Listen, maybe we can work something out. Maybe—"

"You listen! This is what you gotta do. Come up 45 to Hunter Mountain. Go about half a mile past the bridge, then leave your car and start walkin' east toward the lake. I'll find you."

"When…do you want me to come?"

"You got two hours to get here. Otherwise I kill her."

"What if—" The phone went dead. Thor sat on the edge of the Jacuzzi, trying to collect his thoughts. *Think, think.* He ran to his armoire, pulled out Tooley's card, and began punching in numbers. He didn't know who he was talking to, but it wasn't Tooley. In rapid-fire succession, Thor recounted the conversation he had just had and asked to be patched through to the lieutenant.

"Tell me what you've got, Thor," came Tooley's rough voice a few minutes later. "And don't leave anything out."

Thor tried to recreate the conversation verbatim.

"Baby killer? That's what he called you?"

"Yes, that was the phrase."

"You thinking what I'm thinking?"

"Yes. Canon Edwards."

"Never figured he'd stay so close. Thought he'd be out

of state by now. On the other hand, that was smart of him. No one knows these woods like he does. He must be in one of those empty cabins around the lake. We're only about two miles from there. Been following the trail, and it's leading in that direction. I'll call for backup and then check it out."

"You've got to be careful. If he sees you...I don't know what he'll do. He said he'd kill Teresa."

"We'll be careful. Jake here's a sharpshooter, has the medals to prove it. Maybe he'll be able to get a clean shot."

"And if you can't...then what?"

"Hostage situations are risky at best. You just—"

"I'm coming. I'm leaving now and should be there around the same time as your backup. Maybe when he sees me, I can distract him and give Jake his window."

"You'd do that for Teresa?"

"She was my wife...for fourteen years."

"Sorry. Just didn't think there was that much left between you...rumors...you know. Sorry."

"Yeah, rumors. Shows you that you can't believe everything you hear," Thor said, then hung up.


Teresa sat huddled in a corner of the one-room cabin watching her abductor. Her hands and feet were bound. *Otherwise I kill her. Otherwise I kill her.* She couldn't get those words out of her mind.

She watched Canon move nervously around the cabin, fingering his gun, which he kept pulling out of his back pocket then replacing. When he turned to her she thought she was going to pass out from fright.

"I don't wanna do this. You can see that, can't you? But I ain't got no choice. I got to finish the job. They tell me I got to finish the job. My voices. They said it's gotta be done."

Teresa bit her lip, trying to fight back the tears. She didn't want to upset him by crying.

"But I won't hurt you, even if your husband doesn't come. I won't hurt you. But if he doesn't come, I gotta keep you tied up when I leave. I gotta do that, you understand?"

Teresa nodded her head and closed her eyes. She suddenly thought of church with Maggie. She could almost hear the music. She wished she knew more Scriptures. She only knew two and began to recite them in her mind. *For it is by grace you have been saved, through faith—and this not of yourselves, it is the gift of God—not by works, so that no one can boast. Come to me, all you who are weary and burdened, and I will give you rest.*

Did God love her? Maggie said He did. But Teresa didn't know Him well. She had accepted Jesus as her Savior and Maggie had called her "born again." Teresa found that a fitting expression. In her faith, she was like a newborn infant, barely able to lift her head.

"Don't worry. I won't let nothin' happen to you. You just stay back where you are and you'll be safe," Canon said, fingering his gun again and staring wide-eyed out the window.

Teresa could almost hear the praise and worship music from Maggie's church, and wondered at her vivid imagination. And it seemed to be getting louder too. Funny how she didn't feel so frightened anymore.

༄༅

Thor spotted the cabin, nestled among towering maples and lacy white birch. Intermingled were full red spruce and everywhere was a thick underbrush. It looked like something out of a travel magazine. Periodically they had lost sight of the muddy tracks and had to use the lake for direction. "Just head for the water," Lieutenant Tooley kept telling his men. But now Thor could clearly see the tracks, a mud-and-mulch mix pocking the ground. He followed closely behind Tooley and the others, and cursed under his breath whenever his feet got sucked into the mud. *Why did I wear these stupid loafers?* He hated the way the lieutenant kept looking at him, at his shoes, as if to say that someone better keep an eye on this civilian so he didn't foul things up and get them all shot.

He watched the lieutenant signal for the group to stop, then watched as he instructed his men, through gestures and a few words, to take cover by the trees as they crept closer to the cabin. There was a large woodpile not ten yards from the front of the house and that was the desig-nated convergence point. From there, Jake and his rifle would have a clear line to the front door and one window. Thor wondered what the odds were of Canon surrendering without a shot. Slim to none was his guess.

"Canon Edwards, this is the police. Come out with your hands up!" Tooley shouted after everyone was in position.

From behind the woodpile, Thor could see a man dart

to the opened window, then disappear. He felt nauseous and began sucking in air. He clamped his hands over his ears to muffle the noise of the gunshots he was sure would come. If Teresa came out of this alive, he'd make it up to her. Somehow he'd make things right. If she wanted, he'd even consider giving up his clinics. Move to another state. Go into something else. Maybe a small family practice, or maybe a small medical walk-in clinic, or maybe a string of walk-in clinics.

Canon Edwards ran to the corner where Teresa sat huddled and pulled her to her feet. "I ain't gonna hurt you. Nobody's gonna hurt you. But they gotta see that you're here. I gotta show them."

She pleaded with him to stop, but he half-dragged, half-carried her until they were standing by the window. He shoved her in front of him. "Don't shoot! I got a woman here. Don't shoot."

"Hold your fire," Tooley said.

"I don't want to hurt none of you," Canon shouted through the window. "You just back off, now. Give me some space. Let me clear out with the woman. Give me twelve hours' head start, and I'll leave her on the trail for you to find, alive. Twelve hours, that's all I'm askin'."

When he saw Teresa at the window, Thor covered his mouth to keep from crying out. Even so he heard himself screaming, "Teresa! Teresa!" He grabbed for the logs in the woodpile and began pulling himself up. Why hadn't he just surrendered to Canon? Why had he called the police? Teresa was in there, alone with a madman. Why had he left her to take his punishment? He had never been a coward. He had been many things, but never a coward. He was almost to his feet. *How did this happen? How did things get so badly out of hand?*

"Stay down!" Tooley snapped. "Don't make my job any harder!"

Thor stood up, his head and shoulders towering over the woodpile. "Don't hurt her! It's me you want. Take me as your hostage, only let my wife go."

"Is that you, Emerson?" Canon shouted. "Step out where I can see you."

Lieutenant Tooley grabbed for Thor's shoulder and pulled him down. "Are you crazy? You're going to get us all shot!"

"Come out where I can see you," Canon repeated.

"This is the police—no one's coming out except you. Lay down your weapon and surrender." Tooley positioned his rifle on the edge of the woodpile.

"I ain't got nothin' against this here woman. I don't wanna hurt her. See, I'm lettin' her go back where it's safe so we can talk, man to man."

From his crouched position, Thor watched as Canon released Teresa and pushed her behind him.

"But if that baby killer doesn't come out soon, then I'm gonna do somethin' I don't wanna. I'm gonna put a bullet in her." Canon Edwards began waving his gun. "You hear me? I'll do it too!"

"No, *please*. Don't do anything rash," Thor shouted from his hiding place. "Teresa! Don't be afraid. Just hang in there. We'll get you out."

"You try anything and you'll be taking her out feet first!" Canon said.

Thor grabbed Lieutenant Tooley's arm. "You've got to let him go. Give him the twelve hours head start he asked for. He promised he wouldn't hurt her."

"You can't bargain with a murderer."

"If you don't let him go, he'll kill her," Thor said.

"If I let him go, we'll lose him *and* Teresa."

Thor popped his head above the woodpile. "Canon, what if we give you the twelve hours' head start you asked for?"

Tooley jerked him back to the ground. "You want to get your head blown off? And who gave you the right to be making deals with the enemy?"

Thor glared at the lieutenant. "Canon, did you hear me?"

"You comin' with me, baby killer?"

Thor watched Tooley shake his head. "Yes, I'll be the hostage in place of my wife."

Tooley's fist knocked Thor to the ground. "You've caused enough trouble. You keep your mouth shut from here on in." Then Tooley turned toward the cabin. "This is Lieutenant Tooley. There'll be no twelve hours' head start, Canon. You just lay down your weapon and come out now. The place is surrounded. Just give yourself up and make it easy on everyone."

～∞～

Teresa Emerson kept perfectly still and tried to fade into the shadow of the cabin wall. She blocked out the pain of the ropes cutting into her ankles and wrists by thinking about Thor. She could hardly believe he was here, or that he had offered to take her place. Had he come to help her or himself? She closed her eyes. Maybe a miracle had happened and he had come for her, just for her.

Teresa heard Canon's footsteps, heard him curse under his breath. When she opened her eyes, she saw him coming toward her, a wild look in his eyes.

Canon grabbed her by the arm and dragged her across the room. He pulled her to her feet. Her ankles and wrists had begun to bleed. He shoved her between him and the window, then pressed the barrel of his gun against her temple.

"Look here, Emerson, I ain't gonna waste any more time. If you don't come out where I can see you by the time I count three, I'm gonna pull this trigger and then her blood will be on your hands, not mine. It'll be all your fault. I ain't gonna tell you again. One…two—"


"Don't shoot her!" Thor closed his eyes, then darted from his hiding place into the clearing. "Please don't—" He heard a whistling sound and felt a terrible pain in his shoulder and the sensation that he was being pushed backward. When Thor looked down, he was surprised to see blood beginning to soak his shirt. He heard another whistling sound, then nothing.

No one was sure who fired the first shot, but after Thor went down, rifles behind the woodpile began popping off in rapid fire. Within seconds, the cabin was riddled with holes.

# 14

MAGGIE LISTENED TO THE ball thumping against the building and to the laughter of children. She smiled as she watched from her window. Gray clouds blanketed the sky, and she wondered how long before the blanket ripped open and spoiled the fun.

"Is this what you do all day?"

Maggie turned to see Lieutenant Tooley standing by her desk and scanned his face. "You don't look very friendly."

Tooley slipped alongside her. "You won't believe the day I've had." He told her of the shootout on Hunter Mountain.

Maggie sat down. *Maybe if I'd prayed harder.* "I'll try to get over to the hospital to see Teresa."

"I didn't know you knew her."

"Of course you did, Tooley. You know everything."

He chuckled and took the empty seat by the desk. "Okay, so I knew. But I didn't think you had a friendship going."

"How bad is she?"

"Flesh wound. They're discharging her even as we speak."

"And Dr. Emerson?"

"Took two bullets. One nearly got his lung, but he's okay. He'll be out in a few days."

"And Canon? Did he…did he suffer much?"

Tooley shook his head. "Jake got a clean shot. He was dead before he hit the ground."

"I never thought it would end like this."

"You should've known better, Maggie. You've been around the law long enough to know how quickly folks can go bad."

"You know Canon never got over his wife's abortion or his part in it."

"That's hardly an excuse."

"And he was unable to ask God's forgiveness or to forgive himself, for that matter. Without the Lord, Tooley, tragedy can misshape anyone's character."

"Now, don't you start preaching at me, Miss Smarty Pants. Canon was practically one of yours and he still couldn't get himself together."

"He was never one of us, Tooley. His zeal was misguided and sprang from faulty motivation."

"Well, never mind that now. The man's dead. But if you want to talk about misshapen character, I've got a good one for you."

Maggie leaned back in her chair. "Stop looking like a cat who just swallowed the canary."

"Course, what I tell you is official and not for publication. Got it?"

Maggie nodded.

"Dr. Emerson did some talking and said some pretty startling things." Tooley leaned closer. "What if I were to tell you that he *hired* Canon?"

Maggie's face went white. "Why would he do that?"

"He had a doctor he was trying to get rid of. But he swears he only asked Canon to scare this doctor, shake him up a bit so he'd leave town."

Maggie shook her head, remembering Adam Bender's accusation. It was too bizarre, all of it. What kind of a world was this that doctors could kill babies, then hire someone to hurt others? What happened to the Hippocratic oath to save life? It was like they were all marching into the concentration camps of Nazi Germany, where life was cheap, expendable, where moral absolutes had vanished and only the brute survived because he carried the gun. Was this how people wanted to live? What a distance man had come from the Garden, only to end up in a snake pit. She wanted to kneel right down on the floor and weep.

"Here's another interesting tidbit for you."

Maggie sighed. She wasn't sure she could handle any more revelations.

"One of our boys got a tip that the *Gazette* is preparing to do a piece on Louie Pardino, who, by the way, left for a European vacation this morning. Seems one of their reporters got an anonymous letter in the mail."

"That can't possibly have anything to do with the Emersons."

"You always were a quick one with the opinions. Ever hear of money laundering? Everyone's suspected for years that the doc was connected. But I'll be questioning Emerson some more, when he's feeling better. I think he'll talk. Seems to want to make a clean slate of things. I mean, he didn't have to tell us about Canon."

"What's going to happen to him?"

"This is going to cost him, big time. Those Brockstons sure know how to get into a thing hip deep. You want to hear the weird thing? His wife—ex-wife—says she'll stand by him. Told him so right in front of me! Don't that beat all? He's been chasing skirts for years, and she's willing to stick with him through something like this. Figure that out."

When Tooley rose for his chair, Maggie also rose from hers. She walked over to him and looped her arm with his. She felt that familiar tug on her heart when God called her to prayer. "It's quitting time. Walk me to my car."

The two walked without speaking until they reached Maggie's Honda. Then Tooley kissed her on the cheek and opened her door.

"I owe you an apology," he said, as Maggie slid behind the wheel.

"For what?"

"All this time I thought your crowd was behind the clinic massacre. I'm glad it wasn't them. I'm glad your hands aren't...bloody."

Maggie blew a kiss to her friend, then hesitated and stuck her head out the window. "Come to church with me Sunday?"

Tooley shook his head. "No telling what would happen if I ever walked into a church. The roof would probably fall in."

"What about my wedding? You plan on standing outside while I get married?"

"No, Miss Smarty Pants. I'll make an exception for that. I plan on walking right down that aisle, proud as a peacock. And thanks for asking me, Maggie. Thanks for asking me to walk you."

Maggie reached through the open window and squeezed Tooley's hand. "I can't think of anyone else I'd rather have take me down the aisle. I'm sure Dad would approve."

Tooley's eyes misted and he pulled his hand from Maggie's. "All I can say is that it's about time. The way you were going, I thought you'd end up an old maid."

"He's great, isn't he, Tooley? Kirt, I mean."

"Now who else would you be talking about? And yes, he's the salt of the earth. He's got my approval. You two'll be happy." Tooley tapped the car. "Okay, on your way, and don't forget on Sunday to say a prayer for me."

"I always do, Tooley. I always do."


Maggie was on her patio pruning a pot of marigolds when the phone rang.

"Good news, Maggie. *50/50's* still airing my interview tonight."

"Well, hello to you too," Maggie said, laughing.

"Sorry. I guess I'm just excited…and nervous."

"And what do you mean, still? Was there any doubt?"

"No…well, sometimes people get cold feet. You never know what a TV producer will do. Think they'll believe me?"

"Yes, Adam. Most people anyway. But there's always those who'll say it never happened, that Dr. Newly never killed that baby, or that baby parts aren't being packaged and sold like merchandise in a department store."

"But I know and you know, and maybe we can get a few more to believe and then a few more and then maybe the madness will stop."

"Well, it's a start, Adam. It's a giant step in the right direction. Thank you again for coming forward. I know it was hard…scary. By the way, anything job-wise?"

"I've had one offer, as lab technician at Brockston hospital. Doesn't pay like Second Chance, but at least it has nothing to do with abortions. My wife and I talked it over, and I think I'll be heading back to school, at night. I'm thinking of becoming a physician's assistant. I'm young enough."

Maggie smiled. "Well good, Adam. Maybe when you graduate, you'd like to come work for us. We're thinking of adding some medical staff to the Center, to have them on hand to help with postnatal and prenatal care. Perhaps even get a pediatrician for the babies."

"Maybe. I'll think about it."

"Fair enough. And I'll be watching *50/50* tonight. I think you're going to make a real impact. It hasn't been for nothing, Adam, all that you've gone through. God doesn't waste anything."

"I only hope you're right."


For fifteen minutes, Maggie let the ladies chatter excitedly without interruption. Every one of them had seen *50/50* the night before. Maggie had opened the clinic for the Project Rachael group only, since it was Sunday afternoon, but when she had entered, she had seen the red light blinking on her answering machine. Ten messages. The phone must have rung off its hook after the *50/50* airing.

She settled back in her chair and sipped her coffee. In a sense, the *50/50* segment had put a face and name to the horror and shame of abortion. Truth had prevailed, for one shining hour. Maybe others wouldn't fall into the same black pit they had. Maybe others wouldn't have to suffer what they were suffering.

Maggie opened her Bible and smiled at the nervous lady who was joining the group for the first time. She prayed silently as she watched Becky pick at her nails. She hoped her decision to let Becky bring her mother was the right one. Her mother's need for healing was obvious by the grief that lined her face. *Blessed are those who mourn, for they will be comforted.*

"Who'd like to read Isaiah 61, verses 1 to 3?" Maggie said, trying to rein in the conversation and get the ladies focused.

Evelyn raised her hand, and Maggie noted, with satisfaction, that she looked less troubled this week. She watched Evelyn flip her Bible to the appropriate place and with a low, quivering voice, begin to read: "The Spirit of the Sovereign LORD is on me, because the LORD has anointed me to preach good news to the poor. He has sent me to bind up the brokenhearted, to proclaim freedom for the captives and release from darkness for the prisoners, to proclaim the year of the LORD's favor and the day of

vengeance of our God, to comfort all who mourn, and provide for those who grieve in Zion—to bestow on them a
crown of beauty instead of ashes, the oil of gladness instead
of mourning, and a garment of praise instead of a spirit of
despair. They will be called oaks of righteousness, a planting of the LORD for the display of his splendor."

"I want to tell you today," Maggie said, looking around
the table at all the sad, eager faces, "that the Lord will fulfill
every promise of this Scripture in your lives if you let
Him."

One woman began to cry. Maggie looked over at Becky's
mother and her heart ached.

"I'm sorry," Mrs. Taylor said, fighting for control. "I'm
sorry to disrupt the meeting. I just…I just can't seem to
stop crying these silly tears."

Maggie was able to stretch across the table and take her
hand. "Your tears are anything but silly. Don't you know
that God collects all our tears in a bottle?"

The publisher and author would love to hear your
comments about this book. *Please contact us at:*
www.multnomah.net/tearsinabottle

Dearest Reader,

A story about abortion makes for a harsh tale. The word *abortion* itself sounds abrasive, and so it is. Perhaps some wounds have been reopened by this reading. If so, please know that Jesus, our healer, is there for you. There is no sin too great or hole too deep that Jesus is not greater still, nor His love deeper. We are all sinners who need to be saved by grace, who need to experience the mercy of God. How much our Savior wants to draw us to Himself, to wipe away our tears!

*Here I am! I stand at the door and knock. If anyone hears my voice and opens the door, I will come in and eat with him, and he with me.*

May we all hear His voice and open the doors of our hearts.

*Sylvia Bambola*


P.S. If you wish to contact me about this book, please e-mail me at sylvia@sylviabambola.com.

# AUTHOR'S NOTE

Never in the history of the Supreme Court has a plaintiff turned around after winning a case and attacked the fundamental foundation of the very case he won. Until now—and it's times two. Norma McCorvey, the "Jane Roe" in *Roe* v. *Wade,* and Sandra Cano-Saucedo, the "Mary Doe" in *Doe* v. *Bolton,* have both gone back to court after winning their landmark cases that legalized abortion almost three decades ago. Both women, who now staunchly oppose abortion, claim they were used and manipulated by abortion-rights advocates in their groundbreaking Supreme Court cases.

Miss McCorvey and Mrs. Cano-Saucedo are currently supporting a federal class-action lawsuit (*Donna Santa Marie* v. *Christine Todd Whitman*) and are represented by lawyers with the Texas Justice Foundation. Miss McCorvey claims she was never allowed to testify in her own case and "never invited into court." This time, Miss McCorvey is counting on the New Jersey federal court, which will try the case, to have a trial based upon facts and real evidence. Her hope is that the true nature of abortion and abortion practices will be exposed, and that the interests of the unborn child and mother will be considered.

# FOR INFORMATION AND SUPPORT

AMERICAN LIFE LEAGUE, INC.
Judie Brown
PO Box 1350
Stafford, VA 22554
Phone: 540-659-4171
202-546-5550

BETHANY CHRISTIAN SERVICES
Mary Ann Boyer
901 Eastern, NE
Grand Rapids, MI 49503
Phone: 800-Bethany or 616-459-6273

CARENET
Mike Reid, President
109 Carpenter Dr., Suite 100
Sterling, VA 20164
Phone: 703-478-5661

HEARTBEAT INTERNATIONAL
Margaret Hartshorn, Ph.D
7870 Olentangy River Road, Suite 304
Columbus, OH 43235
Phone: 614-239-9533

INTERNATIONAL LIFE SERVICES
Paula Vandergaer
26061/2 W. 8th Street
Los Angeles, CA 90057
Phone: 213-382-2156

LIFE DYNAMICS INCORPORATED
Mark Crutcher
PO Box 2226
Denton, Texas 76202
Phone 940-380-8800
Fax: 940-380-8700

NATIONAL LIFE CENTER
Denise Cociolone, Director
686 N. Broad Street
Woodbury, NJ 08096
Phone: 800-848-5683 or 609-848-1819

NATIONAL OFFICE OF POST ABORTION
RECONCILIATION AND HEALING
Vicki Thorn, Executive Director
PO Box 07477
Milwaukee, WI 53201
Phone: 414-483-4141 (For Project Rachael Programs)

NATIONAL RIGHT TO LIFE COMMITTEE, INC.
Carol Tobias, PAC Director
419 7$^{th}$ Street NW, Suite 402
Washington, DC 20004
Phone: 202-626-8800

PRIESTS FOR LIFE
Father Frank Pavone, National Director
PO Box 141172
Staten Island, NY 10314

PRO-LIFE ACTION LEAGUE
6160 N. Cicero Avenue, Suite 210
Chicago, IL 60646
Phone: 312-777-2900 or 312-777-2525

WEBA (women exploited by abortion)
PO Box 267
Schoolcrat, MI 49087

# Two brothers separated at birth.
# Two destinies in collision.

Set amidst the brutal reign of Nicolae Ceausescu in 1980s Bucharest, *Refiner's Fire* is an extraordinary story of secrets, suspense, persecution, and faith. When the threat of imprisonment and torture lurks around every corner—especially for members of the underground church—no one can be trusted. Yet two brothers on opposite sides of the Iron Curtain must learn together how to discover their destinies…and each other.

**ISBN 1-57673-694-6**

"This book is simply amazing, one of those life-changing reads that so very rarely come along."

Leann Arndt,
*Buzz Review News*